# The Scholarship Trap

## June Trevino

# Contents

# Prologue

Universities. SATs. Projects. Essays. Entrance Exams. Scholarships. "Ugh."

I listed out the most important things I had at the top of my head. I was at home, laying on my bed, as I came out of a daydream after listening to some random Taylor Swift song. I rubbed my eyes and stretched my arms out. It was Christmas break and I only had a semester left until my senior year of high school. Let the internal crises begin. I reached for the standing calendar on my nightstand and flipped over to July. The month of doom. That was when I'd have to start preparing to submit all the stuff I needed for my college applications. I groaned as I dropped back down onto my bed. I am so not going to make it to my top choice. Why even put Princeton on the list. Damn. I thought to myself.

I had just uploaded my most recent test scores up onto a scholarships website. I was hoping real bad for one too. I booted up my laptop and began to scroll down list after list of supposedly applicable scholarships. There wasn't a single ray of hope for me so far. I'd applied for every grant and scholarship I could online and not a single one replied. At this point, I didn't even care anymore if I went to an Ivy League or not, as long as I could go to university– preferably out of the country. Preferably in the US.

I sighed and opened my email for nth time. I wasn't from a bad family or anything and it wasn't like I was needy. On the contrary, I lived a pretty okay life, both of my parents were teachers and we lived for free on a small flat by the school gate, so I practically lived in my school. Which is actually a lot better than it sounds – I mean I could always run home for all the missed homework I forgot on my desk, so that was a plus.

As I scrolled through my email, I expected another list of unread spam when finally something caught my attention.

Congratulations! You have been selected...

I froze...

I think my heart stopped. I clicked on the email. Deep breaths, Darce. Deep breaths.

Dear Ms. Silva,

We are proud to announce that you have been selected as a candidate to become our company's latest sponsored international student. Carter-Pavel Inc. have been greatly impressed by your latest portfolio.

I stopped reading right about there. ^

I jumped for joy. I mean I was freaking out. I was only in my junior year. I started squealing, jumping, and rolling around my bed in joy. Before I took a breather for 5 minutes.

As a result, our company would like you to fill out the form attached. Once filled out please wait for the confirmation letter that will arrive in no less than 12 hours from when your response is received. Your responses to the form will then be reviewed and evaluated.

Thank you for your interest and cooperation.

All the best,

The Carter-Pavel Intl. Scholarship Fund – CP Inc.

I squealed into my pillow. This was it. I was celebrating. If this wasn't worth celebrating I didn't know what would be. I ran out to the living room to my parents, screaming in joy.

I filled out the form right then and there and pressed the 'submit' button proudly before their eyes.

# Chapter 1

I reviewed the website one last time. The company that provided the scholarship was called Carter-Pavel. It was one of the most influential businesses in the world. I mean I had no idea who they were at first, but damn. They're freaking awesome. I mean, they boast about how they run everything from fashion stores, bakeries, restaurants, hotels... But I never thought a company like that would ever pick me for their 'scholarship program.' I wasn't stupid, but I mean, going for a full-ride type of education wasn't exactly that achievable even for the smartest person out there - especially when you aren't from the US or Europe for that matter.

I'm Filipina. Born and raised. And I was lucky enough to be born the daughter of a teacher at an international school. My dad paid minimal school fees but sent me to a well-known institution where just about everyone I knew was born into wealth. My dad's salary wasn't big. He wasn't a big saver either. So uni had always been a tricky and difficult subject. That and, well, let's just say we didn't have a smooth-sailing family relationship. But I mean, who does?

"Good afternoon," a female voice said on speaker, "This is your head flight attendant speaking, we will be landing shortly. Please remain seated with your seatbelts secured."

My flight was booked only a few days after my 18th birthday thinking that it would be a great belated present to fly for the second time in my life to a new country.

The representative I spoke with on Skype from Carter-Pavel (CP for short) told me that the flight was free. I freaked out about it. It was going to be my first flight out of the country and it was free of charge? And a flight to the US too? The surprise business upgrade at the counter made it all the better. I had never been to the country and as far as I was concerned it was going to be on a long journey, business class made flying seem like a cake-walk... if not for the long long immigration and inspection lines before the actual flight. I didn't even know I had to pay an airport tax. But I mean I was just happy I was finally approaching New York. I was so happy to have the window seat too because I mean, who could resist the urge to Instagram a trip like this? I mean I wasn't a major social media person– but come on, it was my first flight abroad and to someone that has never been, it's pretty damn awesome.

"Think you can handle it Darce?" My history teacher, Ms. Leila, asked me.

She was my favorite teacher in high school. Ms. Leila was from Minnesota and had been my teacher since the 9th grade and she's been so awesome. My parents couldn't come with me to the US since they were having a few issues (visas and moving and so on) so Ms. Leila volunteered to help me out. She was flying out too after all and since her brother worked as a flight attendant for the airline, she got an upgrade to business as well.

"I think I can," I said with a smile.

"You are so energetic. Like I'm always so exhausted after these long flights," she said and I smiled at her.

"I'm just so excited. I mean, just think. I finally get to see the city where every single TV and book character has dreamed of going. I'll see the Statue of Liberty, explore Brooklyn, see SoHo, and Central Park," I said dreamily and she laughed.

"Oh you'll make it to all those places, I'm sure. I just wanna make sure you're all settled or your dad might kill me otherwise," Ms. Leila replied.

"He's probably crying about how I'm not home. I'm his only child after all," I said and Ms. Leila laughed as she fixed the scarf around her neck.

Ms. Leila was the only blonde in our school. She was my favorite simply because unlike a lot of my classmates, I loved writing essays and all of our exams happened to be just those. It wasn't like I always did well but I did do my best. I loved words and loved history. Hence my decision to major in Literature. I wanted to take something I knew I loved before I would go into law school. Hopefully get into law school.

Ms. Leila yawned. I felt giddy as the plane shook and shuddered. When the wheels on the plane made contact with the tarmac, I fought back a giggle. Flying was so exhilarating.

Once the plane had settled and docked, the seatbelt lights were switched off and Ms. Leila unhooked her seatbelt and we stood up, grabbing our stuff so that we could get off the plane. The flight attendants smiled as they bid us goodbye and we headed through.

"You all set?" She asked me as I picked up my bag and shoved my phone into my pocket.

"Yup!" I said happily.

"Let's go!" She said cheerfully and we made our way towards immigration.

I can't say I really remember much of what happened. Really I just gasped at the pretty view. Skyscrapers aglow, all the pretty lights... they were at a distance, but hey, what could you do? I'd be in that city in a matter of minutes anyways. I think I snapchatted that to all my friends but then again, I don't remember half the things I post. Next thing I knew, I was picking up my single luggage bag and pulling it behind me following Ms. Leila as she scanned a large group of people that held banners up.

"Do you know what it's supposed to say or how the person looks like?" Ms. Leila asked and I nodded.

"He's supposed to hold a sign that has the company's logo and our names in large lettering," I said, she nodded as we continued along the line until we spotted a man in a sleek black suit. Ms. Leila looked at me with wide eyes as she pointed at him with her thumb.

"Is that him?" She asked in a hushed voice and I looked behind her.

"I don't know. Is he holding a sign?" I asked. I have terrible eyesight. I swear- but I can't stand contact lenses and my glasses were blurry from the trip. I took them off and wiped them on my shirt.

"He's holding a pillow," Ms. Leila said as I put my glasses back on.

"Why would he be holding a pillow?" I asked and Ms. Lena bit her lip and laughed at me.

"Oh my god, the sign is sitting on a pillow in his hand," she said.

"No way."

"Look!" We made our way forward and I finally saw it.

There was literally a man with a small velvet pillow with a placard holding our names. Like what.

"Ms. Reese? Ms. Silva?" the man called, his voice was a bit monotone but somehow still lively. He looked like your stereotypical bodyguard, shades, trimmed hair, and a fine black suit. I guess he looked more like he jumped out of a spy movie than a bodyguard one but, hey no complaints here.

"That's us," I said.

"Follow me please."

Ms. Leila and I shared a look between ourselves before we followed him out of the airport- and all of a sudden we were sitting in a luxury minivan.

"This is so cool," Ms. Leila said and I nodded as the TV switched over to the news.

We started taking a series of pictures in there. I didn't even notice we were already at the hotel I was to stay in until the doors slid open and a valet boy greeted us.

"Welcome to New York Ms. Silva," he greeted and I practically fell off the reclining chair I was in.

"Thanks..." I said awkwardly. What do you say to a valet boy that knows your name? Is there a norm or something?

The bodyguard from earlier walked over to him and whispered something in his ear. The valet boy – whose name-tag revealed his name was Evan – nodded and I watched as he happily skipped to the back of the minivan.

Ms. Leila and I stood in the lobby for a brief moment, not even long enough to take photos really, and are guided by an elegantly dressed woman to our room. It was only in the elevator that I realized where we were staying. The penthouse suite.

I thought my eyes would pop out of my head. Minutes later, I found myself inside a penthouse suite that as the woman explained had three floors. She excused herself then and told us to feel free to call by using any of the phones to phone the lobby if we needed anything. Like – What. In. The. Actual–

"I'm gonna go upstairs and crash Darce. I think I'm too exhausted to even take all this in," Ms. Leila said.

"Yeah sure, I'll stay up a bit later. I wanna let all my friends know about this. This is just wild," I said. She grinned at me and kissed my cheek before she went upstairs and headed into one of the rooms.

I looked around the place and ran my hands along the polished granite countertops of the kitchen. There was an actual kitchen. What in the hotel living–

"Ms. Silva?" A female voice asked from behind me. I jumped at the sound of a voice other than Ms. Leila's.

"Yeah?" I asked, suddenly embarrassed. I mean- I was in the middle of sending a selfie to one of my friends.

"My name is Holly Carter and I will be your personal assistant," the woman said. I turned and looked at her. She was blonde with short curly bobbed hair and bright red lips. But she looked like the type of person that meant serious business.

"Uh, personal assistant? For what?" I asked, obviously confused. I was just here to go to uni. Holly smiled at me as she made her way over to the living room and motioned for me to join her on the couch.

"Um... so what was that about being my personal assistant?" I asked.

"Well, according to your contract, you'll be attending Richards University – of course you're free to transfer to a university elsewhere if you don't think it's a good fit," Holly started but I shook my head, I wanted to go elsewhere – but in truth, I didn't think I could keep my grades high enough to enter Princeton like I originally dreamed. Plus, I found out Richards was, of course, somewhat related to CP (maybe even sponsored by them) and I just thought it'd be less of a hassle.

"I'm fine at Richards. It's as good as I could hope to get," I said honestly.

"I think you're underestimating yourself. You're a brilliant woman," Holly said with a smile, I nodded gratefully for her comment before she continued, "Well, as your contract states, you are now... engaged and as your fiancé isn't actually–" What?

"What?" I asked, furrowing my brows, "did you just say engaged?" I asked and Holly nodded, looking at me just as confused.

"Yes, I did," Holly said, glancing from side to side.

"Engaged? I'm only 18, I can't be engaged. You're joking, right?"

"I'm afraid I'm not and you are," Holly said and I looked at her incredulously.

"Uh, are you sure you're talking to the right person?" I asked and Holly closed her eyes. She seemed to be in deep thought before she brought out a thin sheet of paper and handed it to me.

"Read it," she said and I stared at the paper before taking it from her hands.

Holly,

A woman has been selected into the program. You know what I'm talking about. Her name is Darcy Silva. As you're closer to her age, I ask that you assist her in adjusting to life here in New York and to the life she will soon be introduced to. I'd like it so that she knows less about it. I trust you will help her out to the best of your abilities. I hear she is quite nice.

Kindest regards.

I stared at my name. No way.

"Um. Thing is, I didn't accept anyone's proposal. As a matter of fact, I don't even have a ring or anything else," I said as I looked over at Holly who shook her head. I even took out my hands to show them to her, what hand did you even put an engagement ring on?

"What an idiot," she said before she looked at me, her eyes wide, "I didn't mean, you, I swear." She pulled out a card from her bag.

"This is yours. Unfortunately it seems you didn't read the fine print nor was it explained to you thoroughly," Holly said and I squinted my eyes at her. She looked like she was thinking about something.

"What fine print?" I asked, "I'm almost 100% sure, I signed the contract with a lawyer. He read out every part of the contract for me." Holly shook her head again.

"Was the lawyer Xavier Hartman?"

"Maybe?"

"Then you're going to talk to him tomorrow. I'm afraid, there's been a very big misunderstanding," Holly said as stood up.

"Where are you going?"

Holly looked at me and sighed.

"To talk to some people. Hopefully I can set things straight. But for now, please, rest. We'll talk in the morning. I'm really truly sorry about all this, but try to enjoy things for now. You're in New York City," she said with a halfhearted smile. I did nothing but nod as Holly walked away.

Engaged? How the heck could I be engaged? Was I really that stupid?

# Chapter 2

"You sure you don't want to come with me?" Ms. Leila asks. She was about to head out and go meet up with her brother downtown. I nodded.

"I'm... a bit jetlagged." I lied. I didn't feel a single bit of the jetlag that people talked about. Like seriously. It was morning right now and I felt like it was morning. Then again- I did have a cup of coffee with two expresso shots. I am currently buzzing like a bee.

"Okay. Just text me if you wanna meet up, okay?" She says and I nod.

"Sure. Thanks ma'am. You're awesome." I say and Ms. Leila smiles.

"I know." I laugh at her and watch as she leaves. God I wish I was related to her.

When I was all alone in the penthouse, I immediately went back to remembering everything from last night.

The engagement thing. Riiiiiight. I caught my reflection on a nearby mirror and sighed. My black-dyed-brown hair was in soft curls from the bun I had tied it from earlier. I had light bags from my eyes from lack of sleep last night and I didn't bother to cover it up.

My face was pale and my eyes were just your average deep brown. I was really just the average. I stood at 5' 3", I had a very petite frame, I didn't have flawless skin... (given the stress of senior year a few months before) and I had a very average body. I barely even wore shorts... and I have very little affection towards shorts- so like everyday, I wore a pair of loose grey jogging pants and a plain white v-neck shirt over it. I was even wearing my large äss glasses.

I immediately scrammed for my laptop and opened up my e-mail. I quickly scrolled through and found the last e-mail from Carter-Pavel and read through it quickly.

Ms. Bleu,

We will be expecting your arrival soon in New York. Please, read and review the terms of the contract you have signed below.

Carter-Pavel Inc.

I opened up the pdf file attached to it and scanned through everything. My signature was already on it, along with my parents' signatures... Halfway through reading it, I heard the door of the suite open and I turned around to find myself looking over at Holly from yesterday and a middle aged man that looked very familiar...

"You!" I exclaimed as soon as I recognized him. He was the lawyer that read the terms of the contract over for me.

"Why hello again Ms. Bleu." He greeted. "I'm sure you have probably forgotten, but my name is Xavier Hartman, your fiance's lawyer."

"He is not my fiance- and we are going to fix this situation." I snap as I sit down and place my hands on the cool glass of the dining table. Holly smiled at me, she was gorgeous, her bobbed hair was curled, she wore a nude lip today and a plain white dress.

"Well, according to the contract both you and your parents signed... you are as a matter of fact, engaged Ms. Bleu." Xavier says as he sits down across me. His expensive looking black suit slightly wrinkling as he sits down. Holly sits down beside me and pats my shoulder.

"I can't be engaged. I didn't sign a single thing that said I would be engaged and not to mention, I read that contract about a hundred times over months before you gave that to me!" I exclaimed.

"Did you read the revisions we sent you?" Xavier asked and I glowered at him.

"Yes! I read every single one!" I exclaimed.

"Including this one?" Xavier asks as he handed me a sheet of paper- it was the contract that I signed. I groaned.

"Yes, of course I did!" I argued.

"Well, if you did, you would have noticed the added lines." Xavier said. "And you would have known about the engagement you'd gotten yourself into, Ms. Bleu."

"Okay, I could freaking sue, stop treating me like an idiot. I can't be engaged." I say angrily.

"Unfortunately, you can't sue. I do recall you not having enough money to even afford university and suing Carter-Pavel over a contract you'd already signed... won't do you any favors. I expect an aspiring future lawyer like yourself to be aware of that." Xavier tells me calmly... I groan. "So let us make things clear Ms. Bleu, you are now irrevocably engaged."

"What do you mean I'm engaged?" I asked incredulously. "There's no freaking way I'm-"

"Read it again." The lawyer in front of me says and I squint my eyes at him as I pick the stupid sheet of paper up and read it as he says, but I can't find anything new. The man sighs before speaking.

"Number 9, sub-clause 7-d: I solemnly agree to a sworn promise of celibacy and to-"

"Marry the man liable for my educational and living expenses..." I finish off. "Oh you've got to be kidding me, it's in the fine print!" I exclaim and the lawyer smirks at me.

"Unfortunately Mr. A, does not wish to disclose any further information. But please enjoy your stay." The lawyer says and I squint my eyes at him.

"Mr. A?" I asked and the man grins.

"Stands for Mr. Anonymous. Has a nice ring to it, no?" The lawyer says and I fume as he packs up his suitcase.

"When was this last edited?" I asked, trying to keep as calm as this ässhole. I felt Holly patting my shoulder and I heard her sigh.

"Just a few days before you and your parents signed the document, Ms. Bleu." Xavier says and I think for a second.

"The last e-mail I received with a contract attached was two weeks before the signing." I say and Xavier smirks at me.

"Are you certain, Ms. Bleu?" Xavier asks and I nod.

"I'm 100% certain." I say firmly as I stand up.

"Listen, Ms. Bleu. It is 100% fine with Carter-Pavel if you want to leave your engagement. But do keep in mind, you accepted this scholarship on binding terms. There aren't many universities willing to take you in as of this moment, not to mention, you aren't standing on very good grounds here." Xavier says and I sigh.

"So you're saying if I quit the engagement, I bail out of the whole scholarship program?" I ask and Xavier nods.

"That is precisely what I'm saying." I groan and turn away from him and face Holly.

"Judging by the way you spoke to me last night, I'm guessing I'm engaged to your cousin." I say and Holly nods briefly.

"That's right."

"Why me?" I asked. "He could have picked from a number of girls and I'm picked and I come from practically nothing. Heck, I'm not even a US citizen." I say and Holly sighs.

"My cousin's family is a bit eccentric. Think of it as a Cinderella moment." Holly says and I place my hands on my hips.

"You guys do get that this is really hard to wrap my head around right?" I ask and I turn around. Xavier and Holly share a look between themselves and it's Holly that decides to speak.

"We understand." She says before adding. "But trust me, Darcy, if I can call you that, there isn't anything much better than the scholarship we're offering. The company's willing to pay everything for the next how many years as long as you stay engaged to my cousin." Holly says and I groan.

"Not to mention, there are many women who want to whisk Mr. A away." Xavier adds and I flash him an annoyed look.

"Can you stop talking? I'm still annoyed at how you didn't read over that part." I hiss.

"Sorry." Xavier says with an amused look on his face. "May I go?" He asks Holly and she turns to me.

"Any other questions?" She asks me and I look at Xavier and back at her.

"All he's gonna do is smack me in the face with 100 reasons why I can't back out now." I say with a sigh. "He can go." I say with a shrug and Xavier nods at me before placing the contract on the dining table and walking away.

When I'm sure he's gone, I scramble towards the contract and read clause fücking seven over and over again.

"I am such an idiot!" I shout at myself and I almost scream in frustration.

"It's not that bad." Holly says and I almost forget that she's still here. I turn to face her and sigh.

"How can it not be that bad?" I asked and she smirks at me.

"For starters, if you think this penthouse is sweet, you should see the apartment my cousin picked out for you. It's stunning... although if you don't like it, we can go looking for other places- oh and I'm almost certain my cousin gave you a budget for any shopping sprees you might be in the mood for." Holy says as she winks at me. God she's trying to win me over...

I think to myself. But Holly wasn't actually that bad... well not from what I've gotten from her so far.

"I'm going to look like a total gold digger... and I don't even know this guy!" I exclaim as I walk over to the leather couch and jump on it and bury my face in one of the throw pillows.

"Well... he's a nice guy... I call him an idiot... but he's really not. I'd never say that to his face but I think you'd like him." Holly says and I hear her heels click as she walks over to me. I feel a hand run through my hair and I turn around to see Holly behind me.

"God I wish I had money to send myself to school." I groan.

"Well, technically you can... it just wouldn't be as-"

"-Good as this one." I finish for her before sighing and sitting up to face her. "Tell me the truth. Am I marrying a young one or an old geezer? Because age makes one hell of a difference- to me."

"He's young, slightly older than you. Maybe a year apart or two." Holly says with a shrug. "And if you're wondering... he's pretty cute. I mean, it's strange to say it especially since I'm his cousin, but I know a lot of girls who would kill to be in your spot... well... that's only because they know who he is though." Holly says and I sigh.

"Well... I got that going for me then."

"You know what, if you're going to mope around, then you better mope around downtown. I am not going to let you lock yourself in here all depressed. My cousin did not give me a brand new credit card just so that you could waste it lying down here. I'm taking you out shopping." Holly says and I groan.

"Not...in... the... mood." I say but before I know it, my body's being pulled off of the couch. Holy shït!

"Are you freaking superwoman?!" I shouted, my legs were already off of the goddamn couch, if I didn't move, I would be on the hard äss marble floor in seconds. "I can move on my own! Let go!" I exclaimed and Holly dropped my legs and I watched as she straightened her skirt and I stood up.

"We're going. Now." Holly says and I stare at her.

"Uh... I haven't even showered. You might wanna wait 30 minutes." I say and Holly sighs.

"Fine. But no longer than that. I'll be your personal tour guide for the day- and shopping guide." Holly says and I nod as I make my way up the stairs to my room.

"Well... at least I get to go shopping..." I mumble to myself.

# Chapter 3

How does someone get a totally new life in one day? I mean, one day I was the type of girl who's literally at her computer all day pigging out with chocolates and popcorn and the next I was here in New York walking around some of the most expensive goddamn stores while Holly gives me her opinion.

"You really love the whole black and white thing don't you?" Holly asks me and I nod.

"What's not to like?" I ask. I mean... I was wearing black jeans with a white long sleeved blouse and a pair of black ankle boots. Not to mention- my bag was black and white too.

"Don't you wanna wear contacts?" Holly asks me, I was going through racks and racks of clothes and I shook my head.

"Never tried them. Never will." I say. Now, the reason behind that comes from Discovery Channel. That show about really creepy rare diseases made me cringe at the thought of wearing contacts. This girl almost turned out blind from using those things- and I'm one paranoid chick.

"Oh come on, you can't hide behind those glasses forever." Holly says as she picks out a black sweater.

"Who says I'm hiding? I like my glasses thank you very much." I say as I take the sweater from her, Holly sighs before sitting down on one of the black leather stools.

"Go ahead and try them on." Holly says and I nod as I make my way to the dressing rooms.

I come back later in a pair of jeans and a teal top.

"Is it okay?" I ask and Holly smiles at me.

"You look fabulous." She says and I turn around and look at myself in the mirror.

"Maybe I should just go with the black sweater and call it a day." I say to myself and I watch as Holly's face twists into a look of disgust. "I'm kidding. I'll go march off to the cashier and buy this and then we can call it a day." I say and Holly stands up and folds her arms over her chest.

"Number one rule of being my cousin's new fiancé, spend every penny he gives you." Holly says and I roll my eyes.

"No thanks. This gold digger is done for the day." I say annoyingly. "Besides, how much have I already spent on Starbucks and shoes?" I asked and Holly smirks at me.

"Correction. How much have you not spent?" Holly asks.

"Good question. If I actually knew how much my limit was, I might actually turn into a decent shopper." I say with a shrug and Holly pulls out her phone.

"That's your limit." She says as she points at her screen. I look at it and my mouth goes freaking dry.

"You're joking." I say and she shakes her head.

"Nope."

"There's like 6 digits on that thing!" I shout and every saleswoman turns to look at me and I hide my face. "Holy mother of fücks." I curse under my breath.

"Exactly. So before you complain about your budget, go spend a little." Holly says and I smile at her but my phone buzzes and I groan.

"Sorry. Skype call from Ms. Leila." I say and Holly nods as I take it.

"Hello?" I ask.

"Hey Darce, I was just thinking, maybe I should just scram for the week. Looks like you've got yourself covered here anyways. My mom just really wants to have my brother and I in time for her birthday this week and I know I promised to look over you and I know that I'm supposed to be your chaperone but-"

"Ma'am, hold on... you're panicking already." I say, a smile creeping up my face. "I think it's fine for you to go ahead. I mean, I'm sure I'll be fine here, I have a... new friend with me at the moment," I say, looking at Holly and she smiles at me, "I'll message you if I have any problems." I say and I hear Ms. Leila sigh in relief.

"Thank god. Tell your parents I really would stay if it wasn't a family thing. I swear." I laugh.

"I will. Don't worry, my dad had a back up plan going on. I'll call in case of any emergencies." I say and Ms. Leila laughs.

"Okay, I'll see you soon okay?"

"Yup, bye ma'am, safe travel!" I say happily before she hung up on me.

"So... your chaperone just ditched you." Holly says in a slightly cheerful tone.

"Uh huh." I say and I watch as Holly grins widely at me.

"Then there is absolutely nothing stopping you from living in the penthouse!" She exclaims and I suddenly remember how I thought Holly was an uptight secretary like person.

She couldn't be more differnet. Sure, she had the sophisticated look going for her. But she was definitely a lot more down to earth than I thought she was. I mean she did come into the suite saying she was my personal assistant.

"Why so excited?" I asked and Holly smirks at me.

"Oh you'll see... and you'll absolutely love the goddamn place!"

"If you say so..." I mumbled.

"I absolutely hate papayas." I say and Holly grunts as she fools around in her chair. We were stuck in the mini van I rode in yesterday with Ms. Leila.

"Hm... Anything else?" Holly asks me and I think for a second.

"I don't like pineapples... Unless they're sweet- but even then it's hard to make me eat them." I say with a shrug.

"Papayas and pineapples. Got it. I'll make sure to tell Mr. A." She says, winking at me and I groan.

"Can we please not talk about him, I don't even know him and he's the one that got me into this mess." I say and Holly shrugs.

"Are you visiting Pavelton tomorrow?" Holly asks, moving on to another subject.

"Are we really changing the subject?" I ask before rolling my eyes. "I guess so. I don't exactly have anything else on my agenda. I was told that my schedule would be sent to me." I say and Holly nods.

"Well that schedule comes in the form of Holly Carter. Me." Holly says and I smirk at her.

"My newest friend and personal assistant... What the hell does a personal assistant do anyways?" I asked and Holly thought for a moment.

"I was told I would help you adjust to life here in New York and help you out when you needed it." Holly said and I nodded.

"So you're like my babysitter?" I asked and Holly giggled.

"No... More like your new older sister."

"How old are you?" I asked.

"21." She answered and I slumped back in my chair.

"You're old." I say and she rolled her eyes.

"I'm only older by 3 years." She says before the minivan came to a stop. "We're here!"

"...Yay?" I asked and Holly rolled her eyes at me.

"Come on!!!" She exclaimed and as soon as a different valet boy opened the door, I almost tripped as Holly pushed me out and dragged me into the large building I found myself standing in front of.

# Chapter 4

"J esus." I say as Holly leads me into what she calls THE penthouse.

"Christ." She adds with a wink and I fight the urge to roll my eyes. I've been doing nothing but sighing, rolling my eyes, and groaning the whole goddamned day.

The penthouse was about three floors. The first floor held the whole veranda with an infinity pool plus a stylish and large friggin living room. It also held the kitchen and dining room and a fireplace. I gawked at the sheer size of everything and the large amount of glass walls. I felt like I was in a glass cage...

"Are these things tinted or...?" I asked and Holly grinned.

"Of course they are, silly." She says and I nod as I step towards the living room. The ground is suddenly a lot softer and I jump back. Whatever I stepped on felt expensive.

"Come on! I need to show you your room!" Holly exclaimed and I tried to match her excitement... But I was too busy gawking at all the chandeliers and fancy details. The stairs were spiral and I was happy that they were spaced out in a way that didn't make you tired.

Holly led me up all the way to the top floor and walked me down a large hall with only three doors at the end. One on the wall right beside the hall and two across. There was a piano in the large space between accompanied by a living room set and you could look over the railing down to the first floor if you wanted to.

"Am I dreaming?" I asked and Holly beamed at me.

"Nope."

"Are you sure?" And Holly rolls her eyes at me.

"Just come here!" Holly said as she dragged me by the hand towards the door closest to the railing.

When she opened it, I found myself walking in through a mini hall of grey walls and when we turned to the right, there was a sleek gray bed and large open windows. I gasped at the simple yet beautiful decorations.

"Okay... please tell me this is my room." I say as I bellyflopped onto the bed. So... soft....

"It's yours alright. So is the bathroom beside the hall and a large walk-in closet that we filled up with beforehand." Holly says as she sits on the bed, I look at her and turn so that I'm lying on my back.

"Why the hell did you take me out shopping if I had a closet full of crap?" I asked and Holly shrugged.

"Mr. A's decision. Not mine." Holly says and I hear her phone buzz. She fishes it out of her pocket and groans. "Sorry. Gotta take this." She says with a wink and I roll my eyes.

"Go ahead." I say as I pull myself off of the bed and decide to explore my new room.

I hear Holly mumbling things while I open the door in the mini hallway that led to the bathroom. It wasn't enormous and I wasn't expecting it to be, but it was pretty enough. The shower was separated by thick glass and it made up about a quarter of the room already. There was a bathtub in the corner and a simple little vanity in between. I had never had a bathtub before- therefore I also have never had a bubble bath and that was probably the most exciting thing about the tub. Bubble baths.

I walked out of the bathroom and made my way to the other door right across it. I open it up and find myself standing in a walk-in closet. I was either very lucky or in very deep crap... I mean I just can't push the thought out of my mind that I'm engaged. I have everything in here in exchange for my hand in marriage. I mean I didn't think that by all expense paid, Carter-Pavel meant a whole large friggin apartment. But... I also didn't think that I only got here because someone wanted to marry me. It really just makes me feel like I used my body to get everything I could have wanted.

And that was not a good feeling. It really kind of sucked. Not to mention, I didn't know who I was even engaged to.

I walked over to one of the glass cases that held accessories and jewelry. I didn't even want to know how much all those cost. As I kept walking, I found a white leather stool that had a white envelope on it. I picked it up and sighed, I turned it over to see who it was for. Darcy Bleu. I looked at it in wonder. I looked behind me to check if Holly was coming in, but I could still hear her mumbling. Not like this would be much of a secret. But it'd be fun to pretend it was.

I opened up the envelope and found a letter inside it.

I hope you like the closet. I wasn't sure what you would like. I read your responses to the application form just to make sure that I got your favorite colors right... Of course, I added a few things I wanted to maybe... sometime, see you wear. I know it's strange that you're engaged and that I won't show my face... But I want you to somehow trust me... I'll leave a letter everyday on the dining table for you. If you ever want to talk to me-that's probably the best way... I'll have someone bring it to me as soon as possible.

That's that, I guess. I look around at the walk in closet with the envelope and letter in my hands. He sounds... kinda sweet to me. So far. I mean what can I say? One letter doesn't tell you everything about someone's personality.

"Darcy!!!" Holly shouted and I turned around to find Darcy peeking in.

"Yeah?" I asked and Holly smiled at me.

"Mr. A's sending dinner over in a second, I'm gonna go set up the table-"

"Can I take a bath?" I asked and Holly laughed at me.

"Do you have to ask? Go ahead. It's your room, remember?" She says and I smile at her.

"Whatever bruh." I say and Holly rolls her eyes at me before running away. I walk back into the bathroom and leave the letter on the sink. There's a bathrobe hanging behind the door and a pair of fluffy bunny slippers. I suddenly miss my slippers in the penthouse.

Holly said they'd bring my stuff by tonight. But I really wanted my slippers... they were freaking Totoro. I sighed to myself before going in to turn on the shower... But the tub kept calling me... I looked at the white tub... God... I really wanna have a bubble bath... I think to myself... I closed the glass shower door and closed the bathroom door... Then I made my way to the tub and looked at the shelf beside it. There were like 50 different types of bath things on it. I smiled to myself and turned on the faucet, making sure the water was warm as it filled the tub.

I looked over at the bathrobe and giggled to myself before stripping down and putting the white fluffy thing around me. Then I shoved my feet into the bunny slippers and smiled at the comfy feeling... Deciding that I wanted to listen to music, I ran back into the bedroom and grabbed my bag- that I left on the floor- and ran straight back into the bathroom giggling like an idiot.

"Welcome to New York by Taylor Swift is so appropriate right now." I muttered to myself. I pulled my cheap little speaker from my bag as well as my phone and took my time setting up a nice little playlist covered in Taylor Swift, Ed Sheeran, and Cher Lloyd.

I placed the tiny speaker on the floor and pressed play while I poured this pink bottle that smelled of roses into the bath. The bubbles began to form and I giggled as I touched the rising water. The smell seemed so relaxing too. I walked over to the mirror and started jamming out over to "Don't". I looked over at the tub and squealed at the sight of all the bubbles, I turned off the faucet and practically jumped in. I didn't even bother to fix the robe that was already lying on the floor. I groaned as I felt the warm water touch me.

At this point, I don't even care if people think I'm bathing in my own filth. I'm surrounded by bubbles and I smell amazing. I relax in the tub and let myself think for a second. I wonder how he looks like... I think to myself. I mean, who doesn't want to know how their new secret faceless fiancé looks like? I mean I wasn't picky with looks or anything, but I wanted to know either way...

I mean this was my first ever actual relationship. If you could even call it that.

I came from a school where I didn't really take a liking to anyone. I mean... what's there to like? I had my fair shair of guy friends and all, but I really didn't get the whole relationship thing. I've heard of so many bad relationship stories in high school that I didn't really want to pursue one. Besides, I'm still young... I only graduated out of high school a few weeks ago really. I sighed to myself before letting my face sink into the water until my nose was only a centimeter away from the surface. A pile of soap bubbles tickling my nose. When I finally got bored of sitting in the bath and listening to Ed Sheeran, I pulled myself out of the bath and realized... Do you rinse after a bubble bath or...? I think to myself.

I groan as I step out, getting the fluffy white carpet of the bathroom wet as I wipe my hands on the robe I left on the floor and pick my phone up.

Do you rinse off after a bubble bath? I type in google and before I know it... I'm in the shower washing off the suds and pulling on a bathrobe. What I got on the results was a bunch of opinions... and honestly, the shower part didn't sound too bad. After I got that done, I pulled on my bathrobe and stuffed my feet into the slippers.

I smelled like a rose from top to bottom. My hair was wet and just pushed it to the side, letting it drip onto the robe as I grabbed a towel. I run the towel through my hair with one hand, while I open the door with the other. I quickly run through everything in the closet and select a pair of red loose polka dotted pajama pants, a comfy sweater and a pair of fluffy looking socks... slippers... boots... uh... what the hell do you even call those things? They're like boots. Only fluffy on the inside and outside. So like socks.

Anyways.

I pull those on and shove my now damp hair in a high messy bun. I'll dry it later... I'm starving... I think to myself before grabbing my phone and making my way downstairs.

"Uh huh... Gotcha... Yeah, I told you I got it." I hear Holly say as I finally make it to the dining room.

"Sup?" I asked as I pulled a chair and sat down, the black glass round table had two neat plates on it with spaghetti and chicken.

"Mr. A just called. He told me to make sure you opened the envelope under your plate." Holly says as she sits down too.

"Uh huh." I say before lifting my plate and taking the clean white envelope underneath it.

"On a scale of 1 to 10, how romantic do you think my cousin is?" She asks, resting her head in her hands.

"On a scale of 1 to 10, 10 being the highest?" I asked and Holly nodded excitedly. "I don't know... 6? 7?" I asked and Holly grinned.

"I'll be sure to tell him that." Holly says, winking at me. I roll my eyes and open the envelope.

I'm not sure if you would have appreciated a fancier dinner. I mean... The spaghetti and chicken combo was my mother's choice. I don't mean to make you feel like you attended a children's party, though, I promise.

"So... What'd he say?" Holly asks, batting her eyes at me.

"Something about the food was his mother's choice." I say with a shrug before placing the letter down and beginning to eat.

"It honestly feels like kids party food." Holly says. "My aunt probably wanted to cook it herself."

"Did she?" I asked and Holly shook her head.

"If she did, there would be heart shaped meatballs for her new daughter-in-law."

"Soon to be... I'm not her daughter-in-law yet." I say and Holly sighs.

"Whatevs." Holly says and we laugh the night away.

# Chapter 5

I groan as I stretch my arms out. What fûcking time did I sleep last night? I yawn before peeling the four layers of blankets off of me. Crap. Where the hell did I put my phone?! I panic and I immediately start patting the bed and lifting pillows and blankets. Mother of friggin god where the hell did I put that piece of-

"Oh." I mutter when I find it on the nightstand. I grab it and lie back on the bed, scrolling around before climbing out.

I yawn once more before dragging myself into the shower. Unfortunately when I got out, I realized I left the towel and the goddamned bathrobe in the walk-in closet. Shit.

At least there's no one else here. I pick up my clothes from yesterday and use them to pat myself somewhat dry. Then I carry them in my hands before walking carefully to the closet- my hair dripping water on the floor. I'm a foot in the closet when I realize my phone isn't with me and I left it on the sink.

"I'm such an idiot." I mutter aloud, I turned to walk back before-

"CRAP!" I yell just as my heel slips and my other foot slides in vain.

With a loud thump, I end up falling on my naked äss with my clothes at least covering me from chest down... I mean I was sorta naked- bad enough that my naked âss is on the floor. My jogging pants are covering me "there" and my hoodie is covering my chest at least. Hell. Why do I even worry? There's no one here but me-

"Are you okay?!" Someone- a male voice- suddenly shouts from right outside the door. "I'm coming in!" He shouts.

"Holy shi- Don't open the damned door!!!" I shout as I lifted my poor back off of the floor and squeezed the sweater I had in my hands against my chest.

"What?" The voice asks before the door swings open...

And behold my partially naked body... and a serious cutie at the door.

In front of me is a wide-eyed surprised guy about my age. He has black hair that's slighty long and wavy, and he's wearing a maroon long-sleeved shirt and a pair of denim jeans on, topped off with a pair of brown leather slippers. Currently... we're looking at each other awkwardly. As in REAL-LY awwkardly...

"Uh..." He begins and I groan.

"Do.... you mind turning around for a second... or actually for five minutes... or more?" I ask- quickly. I watch as he takes a large gulp and his gaze sort of... lingers.

"...Oh! Uh... y-yeah. Sorry. I uh... should probably have waited for a-a response before I-I... Uh... Y-You wanted me to turn around right? Right... Uh..." He stuttered before really rigidly turning around. I groaned as I stood up- my butt still sore -before I carefully padded my way into the closet.

To make things fast, I slam the closet door and lie my back against the door.

"Oh god..." I say and I spot my face in a mirror and groan at how red I am. Who the hell was that guy?! I thought to myself.

I shake my head at myself. I swear I'm such an idiot. I think to myself before dressing up quickly in a mint sweater, loose jeans and a pair of all white sneakers before trying my best to doll myself up. Today was open house- if I wanna make a good first impression at Pavelton then this is the day to do it... I take a good look at myself in the mirror. I probably took more than 15 minutes getting ready... I pull a rosy pink bag to me and shove my phone and the contents of my other bag into it before carefully pushing the closet open and looking at the door.

It was closed now, at least, and I sighed in relief. Who was he?! I thought to myself. I looked at the new watch on my wrist and sighed. I wonder how much this was...Or anything I'm wearing for that matter... I thought to myself. I felt like a walking block of stolen gold. I bit my bottom lip before opening the door- only to find cutie from earlier still standing there, with his back to the door. He was still standing there in a really straight up rigid position.

"Uh... You can turn around now." I say and I notice how he slowly turns around and swallows.

"Hi." He says and I tilt my head- woo, I look into his eyes and start staring. They are green as shït.

"....Hey!" I say as cheerfully as I can."Sorry about earlier... Forgot to grab the towel from the closet from yesterday... plus I forgot my phone... so I was gonna go get it and then you opened the door so I couldn't really move and then I froze because I didn't know anyone else was here so I really didn't think that-"

"It's okay." He says quickly with a small smile. "I didn't really know I'd have a flatmate either."

"Yeah.... Wait. Did you just say flatmate?" I asked.

"Uh yeah. I'm living here from today onwards." He says and I squint my eyes at him. "You know... the scholarship program thing... I'm the male selection..." He tries to explain and I bite my bottom lip in frustration.

"This just keeps getting weirder and weirder..." I mumble.

"What?" He asks and I shake my head.

"Nothing. So you said you were the male selection... So... Carter-Pavel picks two scholars?" I ask and he nods.

"Yeah. The name's Lawrence Peters." He says. "Sorry for the... awkward first encounter... I can't really handle embarrassing situations well..."

"I can sorta tell by the stuttering earlier." I say with a shrug. "Don't worry about it. At least I wasn't totally butt naked." I say... although I was technically freaking naked.

"Yeah... good thing... Your name is...?" He asks, changing the subject. Yeah... probably not a good idea to talk about your naked ass moron... I scold myself.

"Darcy Bleu. Nice to meet you." I say as I hold my hand out and Lawrence shakes it. "So... what are the terms of your scholarship?" I ask. Please tell me he got engaged. I quietly pray as I start walking, he follows me down the stairs.

"Hm... keep your grades up... intern at the company... all expense paid." He says with a smile. I pause and look at him- ugh... those eyes tho.

"Uh... anything else? You know... something sorta... weird or extraordinary, special?" I ask and he shakes his head.

"What do you mean? The only thing special about this place is how awesome the house is." Lawrence says as we land on the bottom floor where breakfast is served.

"Really? Nothing weird... no relationships involved?" I ask and Lawrence looks at me funny.

"No... If you're asking about relationships... I have a girlfriend- but she's going to a different university." He says with a shrug.

"Oh." Of course he's friggin taken. All the cute ones are taken. I think to myself and I mentally roll my eyes. "What's her name?" I ask and he smiles.

"...Daisy." He says and I grin.

"When did you guys get together?" I asked as we sat down at the dining table. Blueberry pancakes topped with whipped cream and maple syrup are on our plates and my mouth practically drools.

"A few weeks ago." He says with a shrug.

"And she's... comfortable... with you being here? With me?" I asked and he pauses.

"I think she's fine... I mean, she trusts me."

"After a few weeks of being together?" I ask. "Sorry. That sounded mean and insensitive... and rude." I say with a shrug he chuckles and I eat a mouthful of pancakes to shut me up.

"Not at all... Daisy's okay with everything and anything. She's pretty easy-going." He says with a smile.

"So you're... not gonna complain about this... arrangement." I say after swallowing.

"Nope. We're grown ups, right? I mean... I think we're responsible enough." Lawrence says, taking a bite and I nod.

"True... I'll make sure to keep my boundaries." I say with a smile.

It's not like I wasn't used to the whole stay away from the boyfriend thing. I came from a place where 99% of my girl friends had boyfriends that were all sorta friends with me... and the boundary thing was pretty much normal for me. Make jokes, talk together, but don't ever ever do something as stupid as playful flirting. Not that anyone really bothered fighting me about relationships. I'm pretty good at the whole don't overstep your boundaries... I'm also pretty good at dodging every attempt my friends had at going out when it wasn't a school day... so... I'd say it's impossible to even date me let alone get me to flirt.

"...Darcy? You listening?" Lawrence asks and I notice that my plate is empty and I've downed a cup of coffee, a glass of orange juice and a glass of water.

"Huh? Sorry... spacing out." I say with a smile and Lawrence nods.

"I can see that. Do you want more pancakes?" He asks and I shake my head.

"Nope. You'll make me fat." I say before getting up and picking up my plate.

"What are you doing?" Lawrence asks me and I squint my eyes at him.

"Cleaning up?" I answer and he blinks for a second.

"Right. Sorry. I thought you were gonna..." He trails off and I arch my brow at him.

"Gonna...?" I ask and he shakes his head.

"Nevermind, leave the dishes to me..." He says with a smile and as if on cue, a beep at the door makes a sound before a voice speaks.

"Hey Darce! It's Holly! Here to pick you up and send you off to Pavelton!" Holly's voice says cheerfully. "By the way... what the hell did you pack for New York? It's almost as heavy as two people. Make that two obese people." She adds and I roll my eyes. I hear Lawrence chuckle as he stands and looks at the door.

"Who's that?" He asks, obviously amused, and I smile.

"That is my friend Holly." I say. "Can I trust you with the dishes?" I ask and he nods.

"Don't worry about it." He says and I nod as I make my way to the door and open it up.

"Thank god you're here." I say and Holly grins at me before I notice the two bodyguards carrying two of my bags. "Okay... you have no right to complain about the weight of my bags if you're not carrying them, idiot." I say as I roll my eyes and Holly rolls her eyes at me too.

"Whatever. Come on in guys, bring that stuff up to the third floor and leave it in the first room on the left." She says and the two men walk past me while Holly reaches for my hand and drags me into the house.

"Dude. Dude. Dude." I say- stopping her but she doesn't stop dragging me and I have to pull back so that we look like we're playing tug of war.

Holly today is wearing casual. Which looks pretty good on her. She's wearing a neon green blouse over a pair of white skinny jeans with a pair of neon green shoes and a white bag. Her cropped blondehair is slightly curled to frame her face and she's wearing red lipstick.

"Whattttt" She whines.

"There's a dude!!!" I whisper and she rolls her eyes.

"I just brought two dudes over." She says and I pull her back.

"No I mean there's a friggin dude in the kitchen!!!" I whisper and Holly pauses.

"Wait. What?" She asks. "How the hell did you hook up with someone, it's only 9 in the morning... we didn't finish until what? 3?" I groan and watch as Holly tip toes and peeks from the wall into the kitchen.

"What the hell are you doing?!" I whisper and Holly looks at me.

"Holy shït... How did you get him here?" She asks and I arch my brow.

"Uh... hello? I didn't. The scholarship did." I say and Holly looks at me weird.

"I'm pretty sure there's only one scholarship available." She says, crossing her arms over her chest.

"Alright. Then why the hell is that guy here and why were there two plates on the table!" I whisper and Holly rolls her eyes.

"Maybe the other plate was for me. Speaking of which, here's the letter of the day from Mr. A.... haha. See that? It rhymed." Holly says shoving a letter into my chest. I groan as I take it and shove it into my back pocket.

"Who's this?" Lawrence's voice asks and I slightly jump at the sound of it.

"Lawrence, this is Holly. Holly, Lawrence." I say gesturing to each one of them.

"Nice to meet you." Lawrence says as he holds his hand out and Holly glances at me with a smile in her face before shaking his hand.

"You too. You're on scholarship too?" She asks and Lawrence nods.

"Yeah. I have a letter that says I have to hand a letter to a Ms. Carter?" He asks and I watch as Holly rolls her eyes.

"That'd be me." She says and Lawrence gives her a look of confusion before laughing.

"Right. You're a lot younger than I thought you would be..." Lawrence says and Holly glares at him. "Well... uh... here ya go." Lawrence says as he takes a folded piece of paper from his back pocket and hands it to Holly. Holly sashays towards one of the large plush couches and jumps on while Lawrence squints his eyes at me.

"Did I say something?" He whispered, asking innocently, I giggle to myself before shaking my head and walking towards Holly.

"So?" I asked and I heard Holly groan.

"Well, apparently there are two of you. But he's got no strings attached to anyone- as in no engagements. That part somehow fell to you." She said and I nodded. What am I supposed to say to that?

"Well, he does have a girlfriend." I say with a shrug and Holly raises her eyebrows at me.

"What? What's her name?" She asked and I think for a second.

"I think it was Daisy." I say and Holly scoffs.

"Daisy? Like the duck?" She says- sarcastically, I think.

"Shut up Holly." I say as I roll my eyes.

"Hey guys, are you heading out?" Lawrence asks, wiping his hands on a towel.

"Yeah- actually Darcy here needs to take a look at her new campus and I have to go out and prepare something for Mr. A." Holly says and I smack her in the back of the head. "What?!" Holly snaps and I mouth the words Mr. A to her.

"You guys mind if I tag along? I need to go buy my textbooks." Lawrence says and I nod.

"Yeah, I'll just grab my stuff and we can scram." I say as I get up and mouth the word behave to Holly. She rolls her eyes at me and I make a run up the stairs.

"What else did you need?" I asked Lawrence as we walked through the aisles of textbooks.

"Econ 101?" He asks.

"Uh... which one?" I ask and he groans.

"Can I just give the list to a salesclerk and make her look for it?" He asks and I roll my eyes.

"Don't be lazy. I've got every single textbook I need on my laptop so... I'm good to go. You're the one who decided to get hardbounds." I say, motioning to the pile of books in his hands.

"You bought your textbooks for your laptop?" He asks and I nod. "What if you have to annotate?" He asks.

"I'll print the pages out. Or I'll annotate a pdf. Geez." I say with a sigh. "I'm tired. I'm gonna go chill by the cafe- want anything?" I ask and Lawrence groans.

"Can I place these books on a chair there?" He asks and I shrug.

"I guess so, I mean the cafe's literally right there." I say as I point with my thumb to the area behind us. True enough, there was a Starbucks right there.

"Okay. Let's go." Lawrence says and I nod as we make our way over to the cafe and he places about ten textbooks down onto the stool.

"You wait here for a second and I'll get both of us a caramel machiatto." I say and Lawrence shakes his head.

"I'll do it. You tagged along for this book shopping thing- my treat." He says and I roll my eyes.

"Uh, you tagged along for my campus tour so I should treat you." I say but before I can do anything, Lawrence just smirks and walks over to the counter.

Now I'm the type of person who doesn't like to leave things on the table. And... Lawrence just so happened to have left his heavy looking black backpack on the stool in front of me while he was all the way at the counter. So I just sat still and took about four dollars from my pocket and shoved it into his backpack. There. I think to myself. I watch as Lawrence makes conversation with the girl at the counter and I sigh as I pull out the letter that I shoved into my back pocket. My name was written at the back of the envelope in neat cursive and I gently opened envelope, pulling out a thin sheet of paper.

I opened it up and realized that there was something else in the envelope- a tiny and thin gold bracelet with a little golden flat heart with my name engraved in it. I opened the letter and read it to myself.

Darcy

I hope you slept well last night. I wanted to know how you felt about everything so far and so I wrote you a letter. I know it's a hassle to write something like this all the time, so I'm giving you an e-mail for you to respond with. I got you this bracelet, hoping you would wear it. I'm still working on a ring... I hope you don't mind that I give you a... temporary one. When we meet, I'll surely give you a real ring with me on bended knee.

Yours truly,

Mr. A.

I took the bracelet and sighed as I tried to place it around my wrist. Failing miserably- considering the stupid little hook on it, I sigh and take my phone out typing in the e-mail and writing out a letter to my new fiancé.

Mr. A (if that's what you really want me to call you)

I did sleep very well last night, thanks for asking. Breakfast this morning was pretty fine and I enjoyed dinner too. I happen to really love Holly- thanks for assigning her to me, if that was your choice. I love her and I hear a lot of interesting things about you from her so... I'll take what I can get. Anyways, if you want my advice on the ring or anything- you know... since it's temporary... a small ring with a gem in it is fine. Don't get me anything fancy. It's hard enough to decide what I have to wear everyday. So a simple ring works best. Sorry if I sound demanding- just how I am... :) Anyways. Why didn't you tell me I have a roommate? Sort of a big deal you know... considering he's a dude. By the way, I had my most embarrassing moment today- which I can talk about later. Hope you have a nice day- and thanks for the thoughtful letters. I don't think I mind e-mailing you every once in a while.

-Darcy.

"Your iced caramel macchiato and my wonderful latte is served." Lawrence's voice says, bringing me out of my thoughts.

"Oh uh, thanks." I say as I press send on my phone.

"So... what'd you think of the school?" Lawrence asked and I shrugged.

"Nice I guess. I mean I didn't really know what to expect. I looked online and stuff but that's about it. I just wanna start some work." I say with a shrug.

"Work already? Do you ever calm down?" He asks and I smile.

"Of course I do, but I got hit by senioritis and I've also had a pret- ty long two week break from school so... I'm sort of used to the whole I-have-to-work thing." I say. "And you? Are you excited for school?" I ask.

"School huh? I think I am, I mean look at these textbooks. They look so exciting." He says sarcastically and I roll my eyes and smack his arm. "Ow!" He says playfully.

I smirk as I sip my drink and open up my e-mail. Guess I shouldn't count on instant responses... I think to myself.

"Boyfriend texting?" Lawrence asks.

"Hm... you could somewhat say that." I say with a shrug. "I'm fiancé texting." I whisper with a smile and Lawrence chuckles.

"Ha ha... Nice try. What's your boyfriend's name?" He asks and I roll my eyes.

"That... is a total secret." I say before laughing. "Anyways, change the subject, not in the mood for talking about my relationship- let's talk plans for these evening- I say movie night plus video games."

"Movie slash game night?" He asks and I nod.

"Hello? There's a PS4 in the living room and four consoles. We can totally play one v one. Supposing we have good two player games... I've never actually had a PS4 before- but whatever, I can play anything as long as there's an instruction manual." I say. "Or as long as there's a sniper. Because having a sniper rifle in a player vs. player game is awesome." I say quickly.

"I prefer open combat. We could choose a city map- and no snipers." He says and I roll my eyes.

"We can decide later. Just go grab your Econ 101 book and let's go buy some snacks for tonight!" I exclaim and Lawrence laughs before standing.

"Fine. I'll be back in a minute." He says and I nod as he takes his leave.

# Chapter 6

I groan and yawn as I open my eyes up to the furry carpet of a pretty swanky looking living room. Where the hell am I? I wonder to myself. It takes a few moments for everything to register before I realize the junk food and plates scattered all over the living room- and the warm console in my hand- and the open TV with a pause screen.

"Oh." I mutter to myself. Right. New York. New apartment. I think to myself just as I realize something heavy on my shoulder.

Behold.

Lawrence asleep.

I roll my eyes at the sight of him. He's leaning on my shoulder and has the heaviest body ever. I groan as I try to gently nudge him off of me. But he doesn't budge. I look at the clock by the wall-

"Oh snap!" I gasp before totally standing up- leaving Lawrence falling down onto the carpet, I hear a slight groan and sigh. Thank god the carpet's soft... I think to myself before I mumble apologies and sprint up to my room for a quick shower.

I make sure to lock the door this time and have my towel with me.

When I finish bathing and all that, I got dressed as fast as I could and shoved everything I needed into an expensive looking leather messenger bag. I felt comfy in the comfy cotton maroon high-waisted pants, loose grey top and black blazer- just to make things a little classy. I put the bracelet on as best as I could and I sighed in relief when I finally got it onto my wrist. Then I put on some earrings and shoved my feet into a pair of pretty black boots with gold chains on the side. Looking at my appearance in approval, I put minimal makeup on.

Today was the first day of class and I wanted to look nice but not too overdone. I mean, I'll be practically walking all over campus, no point in pulling on a pair of stilettos. I sighed as braided my hair quickly into a nice long and thick braid.

I need a haircut... I think to myself. And maybe a slight change in color... I think to myself before spritzing on my favorite perfume- that I finally retrieved from my luggage. Then I made my way downstairs where I found everything absolutely spotless, Lawrence gone, and a chubby middle-aged woman was sweeping the floor.

"Um..." I mutter and the woman looks up at me. She smiles kindly, and her face reminds me of my grandmother.

"Oh! Ms. Bleu! Good morning! Forgive me if I entered without telling you, I just thought since the door was locked, you would be busy." She says and I grin.

"No worries. You are?" I asked, the woman was dressed in a black polo shirt and a pair of black slacks.

"Mrs. Janet Jones, the maid of the house. I came yesterday- but I found the place absolutely spotless!" Janet exclaimed in a very happy tone.

"We didn't really get to do much here. Tell Lawrence I'll be going on ahead. I'll just grab breakfast on campus- oh... and tell him that he totally sucks at video game hide and seek." I say, winking at her.

"Sir Lawrence should be upstairs ma'am. He should be down any minute now." She says and I nod.

"So... am I expected to wait?" I asked and she shook her head.

"Just thought you would like to know." She said with a smile and I smiled back at her.

"Alright, thanks Janet." I say before hopping off to the door.

"Do you want me to call the driver?" I heard Janet ask.

"Nope! I think I'm up for a little exploring before class!" I shouted in response before quickly getting out of the apartment.

I got to the campus fairly early. I mean, I didn't have a lecture until 9 which was 2 hours away so I spent most of my time entering the large old libraries on campus and hanging out at the small rustic restaurants and cafes they had. There were only a small amount of people and they all looked pretty busy so I didn't bother making friends.

Right now I was sitting in one of the small rustic cafes and sipping on a latte whilst opening up my e-mail to check on Mr. A. True enough, he left an e-mail.

I heard from Janet that you went to school early. I'm sorry I didn't have any breakfast planned. I didn't think you would get up so early. I'll be sure to have breakfast ready for you early tomorrow morning.

If you're worried about your flatmate, I can change the arrangements. I believe that both of you are responsible so I don't think there's room to worry. I have eyes and ears all over the place (not to sound creepy or anything)... Anyways, I hope you don't mind if I give you a number to text me with. Although I can't guarantee an immediate response or a call, I hope you make use of it. I think you would find it more convenient. Try it :)

I smiled at the thoughtful idea and typed in the number into my phone. Then I quickly sent him a message.

Hi.

I texted and I tapped my fingers impatiently on the wooden table. I was seated by a large glass window with soft violet curtains draping the sides. The cafe had a very cabin-like feeling to it and there were only two workers around that quietly hummed along to the jazz songs playing in the background. It was fairly small and I felt like I jumped into a tiny cafe from the Victorian era. When I heard my phone vibrate I stilled for a second before looking at the response.

Hey :) Enjoying your day so far?

He asked and I grinned.

Pretty much, played video games all night, woke up early, explored... You?I sent.

Just got up actually, I'll be off to work soon. He responded.

Oh. Okay. What time can I text you? I asked.

Anytime. I'll have a surprise waiting for you when you get home.

Now you can call me a romantic fool or whatever, but I couldn't help but smile. Whoever my fiancé was, he definitely knew how to be sweet.

I'm wearing the bracelet you gave me. Thanks for it by the way, I absolutely adore it. I text and the response to this one took a while.

I'm glad you liked it. :) He responded simply and I'd be lying if I said I didn't expect a bit 'more' of a reaction.

I sighed before checking the time and getting up. My first lecture was in half an hour and I didn't think there was much point sitting around. I quickly grabbed my stuff and walked out and plugged my earphones in and blasted Maroon 5 into my ears. As I quickly made my way through buildings, hallways, and a flight of stairs, I finally found myself in front of a modern door that was still locked. I leaned against the cold wall beside the door and pulled out my phone. I hadn't snapchatted anyone since Lawrence and I met- but that wasn't a problem- I wasn't that sociable anyways. So I just tapped through my friends' stories.

I see a movement to my right and notice that someone has unlocked the door to the lecture room so I make my way inside. The lecture hall looks like a high class one, there's your usual style of round arrangements, stair cases, etc. But all the desks are pure white marble that has been shaped to the round edges of the stairs. The chairs are all black leather and there's a white podium in front, a glass desk, and a smartboard.

"Woo." I mutter silently to myself before walking over to a seat beside the largest glass window I have ever seen. Seriously. It's like two stories tall.

I look outside and sigh as I sit down. The chair makes that "ssshhh" sound that it makes when you deflate something and I turn up the volume in my ears. As I wait for people to come in, I bring out my iPad and open up a book I'd been longing to read. I get in to about 10 pages before I hear some mumbling beside me and I pull out one of my earphones and turn to my side.

"... the book you're reading?" A guy's voice with a slight "twang" says and I look at my iPad and then at him.

He had blonde hair that was slicked back and he wore a white polo shirt with pineapples printed on it.

"Huh?" I asked and the guy smiled.

"Can I see the book you're reading?" He asks- in that same "twang" again... Not to be judgmental or anything but yeah... I nod as I hand him my iPad and he smiles.

"The Selection? Isn't that a young adult choice?" He asks and I nod.

"I am a young adult." I say with a shrug. "Besides, who doesn't like a story about a prince and his princesses?" I asked and the guy laughed.

"True. I myself would love a prince." He said and I nodded. Yup. Assumption was right. "The name's Martin. My girl friend, Clara is taking this class too. You'll meet her in a second." I nod and just as if on queu, a girl about my age, with black hair that's been dip-dyed purple walks in.

She's dressed in a black maxi dress and from what I can tell, she's pretty short but she's wearing big heels so that the dress doesn't touch the floor. I watch as she looks over at Martin and grins as she rushes over in front of us. It's only then that almost the entire lecture hall is full. I'm either deaf or blind... or both... I think to myself.

"Martin, your sister told me to tell you that the slots are filled up for the book signing on Thursday. So she signed you up for Saturday." The girl... Clara (I think) said and then she glanced over at me and smiled widely. "Who's this?"

"Darcy." I say as I hold my hand out. Clara shakes it energetically.

"Looks like we've found ourselves a new member!" Clara says with so much enthusiasm, a smile tugs on my lips.

"I guess so." Martin says and I smile at them.

"We're all freshmen right?" I asked and they both nodded.

"We shall be named 'The Freshies.'" Clara says excitedly and I hear Martin scoff.

Just then, the professor, who's a man that looks to be in his mid-forties, enters. He scans the room and grins before walking over to podium and setting his brown leather bag down on the floor. As he brings out a piece of paper from inside his pocket the door at the side opens again. The prof looks over and in walks another guy. He looks really tall from where I'm sitting, his black hair is short and styled... and he's wearing a long sleeved white button down shirt with a pair of black... are those slacks? Swanky much? I think to myself. I fold my arms over my chest.

The guy made all the girls that could see him practically swoon. I mean, I could hear all the girl's (and a few guys) whisper. Including Martin- who was, by the way, whispering to me.

"Who is that?" Martin asked me in a hushed tone. I shrug because if anyone knew him, it certainly wouldn't be me.

"Mr. Carter. You're late." The prof says and the guy nods. I don't even know when it started- but I noticed something strange.

Maybe it's because I'm not wearing my glasses... but... is he staring right at me? I look behind me. But there's no one seated there yet. It was the only empty seat left. The only people in front of me are Clara and some guy that I don't know. Maybe he's just eyeing the seat behind me. So I do look behind me and find a pretty young blonde, I nod in approval at my train of thought before reaching into my bag and grabbing my glasses. I place them on and notice that the guy is now talking to the prof. I almost sigh out loud. I was sort of disappointed because hey, guy looks at you that is that cute, you'd probably freak. But I wasn't one to dwell on things like this...

"He's pretty cute." Martin tells me and I grin.

"Yeah, I can see that." I say and Clara turns around with a suggestive smile.

"He's a total 9/10" She says and Martin and I send her a disapproving look.

"What? How isn't he a freaking 100?" Martin asks and I nod in agreement.

"The outfit- way too uptight for my tastes." Clara says with a dismissive shrug.

"Uh, no. The outfit just screams 'I have good and fine freaking tastes'." Martin defends and I silently laugh to myself.

Soon enough, Mr. Fine and Freaking Tastes sits down somewhere that I don't remember. I ended up texting Mr. A half-way through class- he wasn't too happy about me not listening to the prof- but I sort of did. I mean... introductions didn't make me very interested. I really wanted the list of books I needed and what assignments I had.

When the lecture finally ends, I almost groan. I was only thankful that my next class was history- something I at least thought I was personally good at. Well... I had yet to decide which specific history class I wanted...

But luckily today actually had an introduction to the different classes- otherwise I would probably get stuck in a large class for Modern European history- which I personally disliked. I always went for the smallest classes I could and it wasn't going to change now.

I took another look at the little map I drew out for myself. Left down the hall... then take the third door to your-

"Ohmyholycrap" I say in a quick string of words just as I crashed into a hard chest. "For fück's sake." I mutter under my breath.

"Excuse me?" Someone says from above my head and whaddaya know, it's Mr. Fine and Freaking I-have-no-idea-what-I-called-him. Oh crud...

"Sorry about that." I say as I step away from him.

He was even more gorgeous up close. His amber eyes stunned me in my place and I forced myself to look down. Did people like this actually exist? I think to myself. Not that I'm one to compare- but he's pretty comparable to my handsome (but let's not forget) taken flatmate.

"Where are you headed?" He asks, ignoring the apology.

"I'm headed to... Introduction to History." I said, reading the map in my hands with a sigh.

"I'm headed there too. I'll walk you." He says and I squint my eyes at him. He stops and does the same to me.

"Uh... not to be weird or anything. But who are you again?" I asked. I see a hint of confusiom flash on his face before he chuckles- cute little dimples forming near his eyes. Dear Lord help me.... I think to myself.

"Keaton. Keaton Carter." He says and I nod.

"Keaton. Right." I say and he looks at me expectantly. "Oh! Right! Darcy. Darcy Bleu!" I say as I hold my hand out for him to shake. He looks at my hand as if he wasn't expecting me to do that- but he shakes it after a few moments.

"We'll be late if we don't start moving." He says dismissively and I nod as I follow his lead. Not that I don't know where my class is, bro.

"For those interested in Modern European history, our main focus will be on the events between the years 19..." I zone out. The professor meant to teach that class looked a little plain to me.

I had already listed out the course I wanted to take- which meant an entire period of studying the beginnings of the World War 2 - in depth of course.

"Which are you planning to take?" I hear a deep voice ask beside me and I feel tingly feeling run down my back from how close this person was to my ear.

"Whoa, cowboy, stay away from my ears." I say in a hushed tone. "Gives me the freaking chill." I say in a surprisingly normal voice.

Mr. Fine- I mean, Keaton, grins at me from ear to ear and I roll my eyes.

"I'll be taking the in-depth study of World War 2 class. I know about it from high school history and I seriously wanna get into all those pre-war Hitler things." I say with a smile.

"Hm. Won't it bore you too much?" He asks.

"Uh, no. Number one, there's an in depth study towards the Japanese side and number two, the whole pre-war section on Africa is something I haven't studied."

"You're very history obsessed." Keaton says- as if it's an insult. As in, his tone did not sound like he was making a joke.

"Yup. I am- and let me guess, you're taking the Modern European History thing." I say and he nods. "Why?" I asked and he smirks at me.

"Easy way out. My parents know the prof and he'd be dead if I didn't pass." Keaton says with a shrug. Uh... what happened to the 'nice' guy from the hallway? I wondered.

"Uh huh. Cool." I muttered as I brought out my agenda and started scribbling down the things I needed to do.

"Are you free after class?" Keaton asks and I shake my head.

"I'm going straight home." I say quickly. "Why?"

"There's a party being held at a club called Hollace. You should come." Keaton tells me and I shake my head.

"I have plans tonight and I'm not the type to go party."

"Cancel your plans and see if you like to party then." He says with a smirk.

"Can't cancel and I know for a fact that I don't like to party." I say with a sigh.

"Suit yourself party pooper." Keaton says and I roll my eyes. I'm thankful when I hear the prof dismiss us and I immediately stand up to leave.

"Off somewhere?" Keaton asks.

"Didn't I just tell you that I was going straight home?" I asked and Keaton shrugs- I watch as he flicks a piece of paper at me... "What's that?" I asked.

Keaton shrugs and nudges the piece of paper towards me. I watch as other people leave the lecture hall and I groan as I take the paper from him- only to find a scribbled down phone number on it.

"Thanks but no thanks?" I mutter as I hold the piece of paper in between my index and middle fingers.

"Trust me, you'll want to have me on your friend list sweetheart." Keaton says and he gives me a wink before standing up. "See you later." He says confidently before walking off.

Uh... What the hell just happened?

# Chapter 7

I did go straight home after class. Martin and Clara traded their numbers with me and they told me they had to unpack their things at the dorms. Which, by the way, I had no idea even existed. I would have loved to experience dorm life... Then again, considering the whole engagement fiasco, it was probably better for me to stay here.

When I got home, Lawrence was already working on something at the dining table. He was wearing a plain white shirt over a pair of black denims and he had a pair of glasses sitting on his nose. I watched as his brow furrowed slightly and I grinned. Lawrence was seriously good looking- Sure Keaton today was fine and all... But Lawrence just carried the 'handsome-not-a-douchebag' thing really well. His girlfriend... Daisy, I think, was really lucky. Judging by the way his face looked, whatever it was he was doing looked pretty serious and he had a pair of earphones plugged in, so I took the liberty of quietly creeping into the slightly blocked off kitchen.

I didn't want to disturb him with any sort of smell from frying food so I went for something simple for snacks. Finger sandwiches and a bowl of fruit. I seriously love the stock of food in this place. Hell, I love everything about this place- aside from the surprise engagement. Once I was done with what I made, I walked over to the kitchen and noticed Lawrence rubbing his temples before he noticed me and grinned.

"Hey!" He greeted happily, pulling the earphones out of his ears.

"Hi!" I mirrored in a sarcastic way, he smirks and I giggle as I place the tray of sandwiches and fruits down on the table.

"What's all this?" He asks me- in what seems to be genuine confusion.

"Snacks. You look really stressed out- and I'm trying to be nice by giving you brain food." I say as I pick up a strawberry and pop it into my mouth. Lawrence chuckles as he picks up a sandwich and eats it.

"Finger food. Neat, easy, simple." He says and I nod.

"If I ever make a restaurant- that would be my slogan." I say with a wink and Lawrence laughs.

"Credits to me when you establish it?" He asks and we both laugh.

"What are you working on anyways?" I asked.

"Advanced Business Readings. I wanna get ahead, not to mention my friends are trying to get me to go out tonight- not a good idea by the way." Lawrence says with a sigh.

"Bro, you seriously just got here. Live the New York life for one night and then work for the rest of it." I say with a shrug. I'm such a damned hypocrite. I think to myself- then again- Lawrence had friends already and I had an annoying flea named Keaton that wanted me to go out.

"If I get drunk, will you by any chance come and get me?" Lawrence asks in a joking tone and I grin.

"I'll get you with an aspirin and Holly to carry you home." Lawrence grins.

"Let's trade numbers then, that way I can contact you." He says and I nod. We exchange numbers quickly before he decides to get ready, we both walk upstairs and enter our rooms.

I change into a comfy pair of plain white pajama pants and a black tank top. I slip my feet into a pair of white flip flops, braid my long brown hair into two, strip the makeup on my face and walk back downstairs. What game do I play...? I think to myself as I search up games on my phone. I decide on a horror game to play on my own and I plop down onto the long couch and boot up the TV and console. As I bought the game off of the network, someone speaks.

"Whaddaya think?" Lawrence asks, I jump not knowing that he was even there already.

I gawked at the sight of him. He was dressed in a black v-neck, a pair of dark denim jeans, and he had a sleek black blazer to top it off. I look down at his feet and see that he's wearing a pair of all black Nikes and I nod in approval.

"Looking very casual chic tonight Mr. Peters." I say and Lawrence chuckles.

"Swanky clubs require a certain amount of class don't you think?" He asks and I smirk.

"Don't get too drunk." I warn and he nods with a smile.

"If I'm not back by 2, call me. That way I won't get too hammered."

"2 o'clock alarm to call my flatmate- done." I say and he smiles.

"See ya."

I decide not to reply before he disappears behind the front doors. As I boot up the game, I decide on texting my fiancé.

Hey :)

I wait for a response.

Good Evening :)

I smile at receiving a fast response.

What are you up to tonight? I ask.

Nothing exciting. I'll be stuck doing paperwork all night... You?

I chuckle at his response as I press start on the controller.

Playing horror games alone. Am I distracting you? I text.

Not at all. I like talking to you. I giggle in amusement, paying no mind to the horror game on screen anymore.

I like talking to you too, Mr. A :P

How's the horror game going? He asks and I look at the screen. It's all black and I press through about 20 dialogue boxes.

Not well. All dialogues so far... :( Disappointed. I message and I picture a smile.

I wonder what my fiancé even looks like. I picture him as someone cute... For some reason I picture him with hazel hair and green eyes... That's cute enough for me.

Why not watch a movie? He texts- bringing me out of my daydream.

Good idea. I say and I come up with an idea. I'll flip to a channel with a good movie and you flip to it as well, that way we can both watch a movie together. Deal? I ask.

Sounds like a plan. He replies. I turn off the console, set aside my controller and use the remote to find a good channel.

I flip to a channel showing 'The Woman in Black'.

Switch over to HBO, The Woman in Black is showing. I text.

Got it. He messages.

The ending sucks. I text.

Yeah, well at least it was a happy ending :P Mr. A texts and I grin.

For Harry Potter yeah. I say.

Yes, for Harry Potter. Wish he had his wand in the movie.

Me too, anyways, I'm feeling drowsy and I'm sure I've distracted you long enough :) Thanks for watching a movie with me~ Night. I text and the response is a bit slower.

You're welcome. I'll be free tomorrow too so feel free to text me :) Night Darcy... I smile before tucking my phone into my pocket and racing up the stairs to my room.

There is an annoying goddamn noise playing.

I swear. Is that the chorus of 'She Looks So Perfect'?

What the hell?

I groan and shove a pillow over my head. SHUT UP PLEASE!!! I think in my head. When the noise doesn't stop, I sit up on my bed. I look over at my night stand and realize that it's my phone. I groan, outside my windows is a glorious view of New York city, still alive even at...

It's 2 in the morning already?! Ah crap. I look at my phone and realize that it's Lawrence caling. I slide my finger across the screena and place it to my ear, sitting up in my bed.

"Hello?" I ask.

"Daaaarcyyyyy" Lawrence's voice slurs.

"Dude. Are you drunk?" I asked and I hear him chuckle and someone speak beside him.

There's loud house music in the background and a lot of giggling and laughing- from both boys and girls.

"I'm hammered so badddd." Lawrence says with a chuckle.

"Dude who the hell are you calling?" I hear a familiar voice ask.

"It's this chick, man... Could you go the hell away?" I hear Lawrence hiss. "...Man quit eavesdropping!" Lawrence shouts.

"Lawrence? You still there?" I ask, the music gets louder and I hear a slam of a door.

"Huh? Oh yeah... I'm still here dude..." He says the slur making his voice funny.

"Do you need a ride home? I can come get you." I say and I hear Lawrence curse under his breath.

"...huh? Yeah. Sounds good." Lawrence says and I groan.

"Where are you? You moron." I say in frustration.

"Hollace... They won't let you in without good clothes though." Lawrence manages to say with a little less slurring. "Oh ycah... how was the-"

"Lawrence where the hell are you?!" I hear an angry guy shout in the background.

"Oh bug off will you!" Lawrence shouts back.

"I'll be there asap." I say before hanging up. I get up and rush into my closet.

I pull on a pair of skinny jeans and a black leather jacket. I shove my feet into a pair of expensive looking pointed flats with gold sequins adorning it and I run a hand through my hair before grabbing my phone and wallet. I check the time quickly and rush out the door. When I get to the lobby, I see a bald man in a black suit that's somehow still awake and he walks over to me. I realize then that it was the same guy who fetched me at the airport.

"Ms. Bleu?" He asks and I tilt my head.

"Yeah, and you are?" I ask.

"Wesley, at your service ma'am." He says and I nod.

"Can you take me to Hollace? I need to fetch the idiot I live with." I say with a sigh. Wesley gives me a small smile before gesturing outside.

Turns out, Hollace is still jam-packed with a long line at 2:30 in the morning. I yawn before Wesley opens the car door for me.

"I'll be back in 10 minutes." I say and Wesley nods curtly as I march off towards the damned bouncer.

"Is Lawrence Peters in there?" I asked and the bouncer- who's got a light beard going on, takes a quick look at the list in his hand. It's only then that I realized that Keaton was here too... What was his name again...?

"Is Keaton Carter there?" I ask and this time the bouncer nods at some-one inside the club and I hear a few girls groan as the bouncer detaches the velvet rope in front of me and lets me cut the line.

Music.

Loud äss freaking music is blasting in my ears. I can feel my entire body vibrate with how loud it is. There's neon lights everywhere, a large floor filled with people, and there are two levels. Someone walks to me in a neat-looking waiter outfit.

"Ms. Bleu? Keaton Carter's VIP booth is upstairs. Follow me." He says and I do as he says.

I'm led up about two flights of stairs where the music is still on but somewhat less on the vibrating. I spot two familiar heads- Lawrence's and Keaton's. I roll my eyes and march towards them with my arms folded over my chest.

"Well, well, look who decided to show up." Keaton says, a girl's leg over his knee while she caresses his face. Lawrence is laughing like a fool but he's thankfully alone. At least someone's loyal... I think to myself.

"I came to pick my flattie up." I say and Lawrence turns to look at me- a drunk smile gracing his face.

"Hey Darcyyy" Lawrence slurs and I roll my eyes.

"Hey, no one is bringing anyone anywhere unless they're both wasted. Ain't that right guys?" Keaton shouts and the entire freaking floor we're standing on erupts with some sort of hurrah.

"Well, technically, you're not wasted so you shouldn't bring anyone in here at all." I say with a sigh.

"Don't be such a downer, Darcy, just have a drink." Keaton says and I roll my eyes.

"I'm not having a damned drink Keaton, I just wanna bring my drunk flattie home." I say with a sigh. "Do you not understand freaking English?" I hiss. Keaton smirks at me and I roll my eyes. Note to self: Never trust Keaton. Ever.

"Time to go home Lawrence. The driver's waiting outside." I say in a pissed voice.

"And I thought I was the rich bastard. Look at little miss prissy pants bringing a driver over." Keaton says as he dunks the last of his glass' contents into his numbed brain.

"How do you even know this guy?" I ask Lawrence and he grins at me cheekily- the cute dimples forming on his drunk face.

"We... went to high school... togettthhher."

"Right." I say with a sigh. "Lawrence, get up."

Lawrence nods before sluggishly getting up, thankful that I chose to wear flats, I wrap his arm around my head and use whatever strength I have to lift him. Which, frankly, isn't a lot of strength. I could only stop him from stumbling to the floor- but he mostly held his weight as he dragged his feet across the floor. I hear Keaton start to make jokes and I think he stands up- I can't hear clearly with the music that's been getting louder since I arrived. But I did hear him taunt Lawrence.

"That is the funniest crap I've seen all night! Lawrence, I swear you're such a puss-" Before Keaton could even finish that syllable, I feel Lawrence's weight lift off of mine and I hear a large thump behind me.

I look, and I find Keaton on the floor. He's groaning in pain and I move against Lawrence and grab his arm.

"Keaton you need to learn to shut up." Lawrence snaps- somehow forming clear sentences between slurs.

"And you need to learn to grow a pair!" Keaton shouts back as a girl comes and helps him. Keaton pushes the girl away but ends up using her to stand up straight.

"If you wanted a fight, all you had to do was ask." Lawrence says but I step in between them. "Get out of my way, Darcy." He warns

"No." I say harshly. "You're drunk, he's an ass, and we both need to go home." I say, hoping that I can get some sense into this Lawrence.

"Listen to the girl Lars. She's at least thinking before she acts!" Keaton taunts and I roll my eyes. Lars? Is that his nickname? I think to myself before switching back to reality and speaking up.

"Will you shut the fück up?!" I snap as I flash Keaton a glare. I watch as he looks away from my gaze.

I sigh before turning back to Lawrence, who's eyes are still set on Keaton.

"Let's go." I say in a serious tone. Lawrence's eyes are dark and pissed, but he looks into mine and I see a certain calm in them.

I sigh in relief when he nods and I continue to help him out. We stumble down the stairs, but when I finally get out, Wesley is at the ready and immediately lifts Lawrence off of me. I smile my thanks to him and he nods at me before driving both Lawrence and I back home.

"Is he alright, Ms. Bleu?" Wesley asks as we drive past building after building.

"He should be fine, just astoundingly drunk." I say as I roll my eyes. Lawrence was already lightly snoring beside me. "I hope you don't mind me asking Wesley, but I could use a hand lifting him up to the apartment."

"Not a problem, miss." Wesley says, amusement clear in the tone of his voice.

It doesn't take us long to get back to the apartment. Wesley lifted Lawrence as if he was nothing but a large pillow. We left him on the couch and I covered him in the blanket I had in my room. I didn't want to intrude into his room after all. After giving him my blanket, I sat down on the armchair beside him and I dozed off there.

"My head feels like crap." Lawrence says as he holds his head in his hands on the dining table. "And whatever you cooked smells amazing." He compliments.

I walk over to the dining table with two plates holding an omelette, two sausages, and soft toasted bread. I set it down and grab the two cups of coffee I made earlier.

"Did you drink the aspirin Janet left for you?" I asked and Lawrence nods.

"Yup. Can you explain to me why my right hand hurts and has a bruise by the way?" Lawrence asks and I smirk.

"You mean you don't remember punching Keaton Carter?" I ask and his eyes widen.

"I did what now?"

"You punched Keaton because he was taunting you. I'm glad you were sober enough to walk out without throwing another punch, but Keaton sounded like a dick. So... he deserved it." I say with a shrug.

"I remember arguing with him about something...," Lawrence trails off as he takes a bite of toast. I sip my coffee and watch as his eyes flicker to mine and I raise a brow.

"What?" I asked.

"Nothing. We were probably arguing about something stupid." He says and I nod.

"Well whatever it was, I really wish I had a video of that incident. Keaton just so happens to be in my Lit class." I say with a shrug, Lawrence laughs.

"Maybe someone took a vid at the party. God knows how many people Keaton invited."

"I got invited- I had no idea you were, too."

"Well, it's a good thing you didn't go. It was a pretty crap party." Lawrence says and I roll my eyes as I finsh off my plate.

"I'm not really party-girl material." I say, I feel my phone buzz in my pocket and I fish it out.

Hey Darcy! It's Martin! Clara's asking if you wanted to hang out today. We know this awesome café downtown. 'Course we're thinking on going shopping for some things but you have gotta come with

I smirk and type a quick reply.

Where do we meet???

Well, we can pick you up in half an hour. Just tell us where ya at. Martin texts.

I'm at home- I'll get dressed quick. Pick me up at before I finish the text I call out to Lawrence.

"Lawrence, what's the name of this building again?" I asked.

"It's called NY Carter's." He says as he eats his food.

"Thanks." I mutter. I feel like everything I'm involved with revolves around Carters or Pavels... I think to myself.

I finish off my text to Martin.

"I'll be heading out to meet up with some friends. Want anything?" I ask Lawrence and he grins.

"Nope, I'll be fine. I still have to attend a lecture later... somehow." Lawrence says with an encouraging smile.

"Great. I'll see you later then." I say quickly before running up the stairs.

I take a quick shower before pulling on a pair of boyfriend jeans, a pink top, some white sandals, and a scarf. I grabbed a pair of shades and shoved my phone and wallet into a white bag before placing the bracelet, that Mr. A gave me, back onto my wrist. I'm walking down the stairs when I hear Lawrence talking.

"Sounds good. I think it'll be better if we have her go to... Yeah. I know. Thanks." Lawrence says and when he turns around, there's a slight jump in his step. "Darcy... I have an important announcement." I arch a brow.

"What?" I asked.

"My girlfriend's coming over tomorrow... She wants to meet you." Lawrence says and smile.

"Sounds good to me. Can we... discuss later? I have seriously gotta go. Martin's probably waiting for me." I say and this time, Lawrence raises a brow.

"Martin?" I smirk.

"Martin and Clara. My two new besties in the whole wide world." I say with a smile. "Martin's gay if you're wondering." I say and is it just me? Or does his shoulders relax?

"Great. Thought you might be making friends with the wrong people." Lawrence says.

"Who said I was making friends with the right ones?" I asked, Lawrence's face darkens and I wink at him. "Relax Lars, you're acting like I'm going to go on a suicide mission."

"Lars?" Lawrence asks and I roll my eyes.

"That's what you pick up on?" I ask and he chuckles.

"Whatever, Darce. Just have fun." He says and I grin.

"Not as much fun as you had last night." I say with a wink before finally making my way to the door. "Tell your girlfriend I said hi!!!" I exclaimed before rushing out the door.

I wonder how she looks like?

# Chapter 8

"**S**weetheart, do you mind explaining how the hell you live here?" Martin asks as I get into his white SUV.

Martin is seated at the driver's seat and Clara's riding shotgun- which leaves the back all to me.

"What?" I ask.

"Uh, it is almost impossible to even get a flat there. It's practically full 24/7— even if the people there don't actually live there." Clara says with a sigh.

"We should totally have a sleepover at your house!" Martin says as he pulls onto the main road and I shrug.

"Next week Saturday sounds good to me." I say and the two of them squeal. "I have a flatmate though- his name's Lawrence."

"HE?!" The two of them shout at the same goddamn time.

"Ouch, much?" I say holding my hands to my ears.

"Gay or straight?" Martin asks.

"Straight." I mutter.

"Damn." Martin curses and I hear Clara giggle.

"He's taken, though. His girlfriend's visiting tomorrow."

"Is he hot though?" Martin asks and I grin.

"Do you think I'd be able to live with someone if he wasn't?" I asked and the two of them laugh.

It takes us about 15 minutes to get to the café they were going on about. It was found at the 20th floor of a hotel.

"You know... I was expecting your usual quiet small cafe on the corner of a street. This. This is high freaking class." I say and Clara giggles.

"Well, it's a lot quieter in here than it is down there. Gives us time to relax and talk- get to know each other." Martin says.

The café made up a corner of the hotel's 20th floor. You had a perfect view of the New York City skyline, the bay area, and the bright sun didn't even touch the inside. It was modernistic, the black and white theme (that I really loved) surrounded it. We were seated at the very corner and the view was breathtaking. The black leather couches and black furry carpets felt divine. I sat by myself on one side while Clara and Martin sit together on the opposite couch. The place was silent, fairly empty, and very high-class. It was something I would have always dreamt of experiencing.

"I love you guys already." I say as I peeked out at the view.

I bring out my phone and take a picture of the view sending it on snapchat.

"Dude, add me." Martin says and I grin as I hand my phone over.

"Me too!" Clara exclaims as she grabs the phone.

"Hey!" Martin shouts and they both sound like bickering children.

Clara's short frame is wearing a pair of black high waisted shorts, a floral crop-top, and a pair of black vans. Meanwhile Martin's rocking a classic red flannel button down over a black v-neck and a pair of torn denim jeans. You almost wouldn't think he was gay at the moment. Someone clears his throat beside me and I look to the side to find a finely dressed waiter waiting for us.

"Oh. Guys?" I asked and they stop bickering.

"Oh, hi. One classic angel latté for me, a dark espresso for this one, and your best-seller for the girl in front of us- oh! And the sampler's plate... uh-" Clara pauses and looks at Martin. "Large or regular?"

"Large." Martin says with a nod.

"Alright. Large it is then. Thanks." Clara says with a grin. The waiter places his hands at his back.

"One classic angel latté, a dark espresso, our best-seller and a large sampler." The waiter says and we all nod with a smile. "Our baker just made a few petite fours, would you care for some?" He asks and Martin is the first to answer.

"Sounds good to me." He says as he winks at the waiter. The waiter grins and Clara and I exchange suggestive looks at each other.

"Great. By the way, my name is Eric and I will be your waiter for the day." He pauses, and brings out a big smile. "I'll be back with your drinks in 5 minutes." The waiter says before he walks off. Martin looks between me and Clara.

"What?" He asks and Clara rolls her eyes.

"You two might as well ask for each other's numbers." I say and Clara giggles.

"He is hot for a waiter bro." Clara comments and Martin chuckles.

"Not every guy who smiles at me is gay. You guys are so immature." Martin says. Clara and I, exchange looks and then stare at Martin with creepy smiles plastered on our faces.

"Seriously?" Martin asks but we don't say a word- we just continue smiling.

"Guys... this is getting weird." Martin says.

"I don't know what you're talking about Martin." Clara says and I nod.

My phone buzzes in my bag and I sigh.

"When Eric comes back, let's get his number." I say just as I looked through my bag and fished out my phone. I smile at the message.

Morning Darcy :)

Morning Mr. A ;) I message back.

"And who exactly are you getting distracted by?" Clara asks, I smirk at her before looking at my phone again.

Did you have breakfast yet?

Yup, did you? I text. Clara gets up and moves over to the empty space beside me and she peeks at my phone. I fold it quickly on my lap and give her a suggestive smile.

"Oh come on Darce!" Clara whines.

"...Fine. But don't judge me okay?" I ask and they both raise their hands.

"We solemnly swear not to judge you." Martin says and Clara nods in excitement. I bite my bottom lip and sigh.

"Okay." I mutter, Martin makes his way beside me too and they both look over my shoulder as I lift up the screen- Mr. A had already replied.

I had breakfast- funny thing- my sister just talked to me about watching The Woman in Black 2. We should have another one of those little 'sessions' again. :)

"Mr. A?" Martin asks.

"Who's Mr. A?" Clara asks as she looks at me and I shrug.

"You could say... he's my anonymous online boyfriend." I say with a smile.

"And what 'sessions' is he talking about?" Martin asks, wiggling his eyebrows at me. Clara laughs and I giggle along.

"Last night, I watched a movei and we were able to talk to each other on the phone about it. He won't let me know who he is so... yeah." I say with a shrug and Martin squints his eyes at me.

"What if he's a dirty old perv?" He asks and I roll my eyes.

"I know his cousin and she says that he's just about her age- which is probably about 2 years older than I am, I suppose."

"What if she's lying?" Clara asks and I sigh.

"Then I can end it. But for now, it's pretty fun to play boyfriend-girl-friend over the phone." I say with a smile. A message pops up on the phone and Clara and Martin curiously peek again.

You still there? I smile.

Of course I am. The second movie sounds great. Sorry if I seem distract-ed, I'm out with friends at the moment. I message and his reply is faster than I expected.

Oh, am I disturbing you? He messages and Clara makes high pitched noises.

"He sounds genuinely nice!" Clara says and Martin nods.

Not really, in fact, they're finding our conversation quite interesting. ;) I text back. The three of us patiently wait for a reply.

Oh. :D Hi there! This time, Martin and Clara both smile at me.

"Okay, he gets an A for friendliness." Martin says.

As we giggle about my conversation with Mr. A, Eric, our waiter, comes back with all of our drinks and even our excessively large plate of pastries, cakes, and other sweets.Eric then places a small plate with a tiny fancy looking chocolate cake, that has a fancy written decoration, down in front of Martin. Clara and I look at the cake and read the written chocolate syrup decoration. It was a phone number. Oh. My. God.

"Enjoy." Eric says and he winks at Martin before leaving. Clara and I look at each other, and then at Martin.

"Don't you guys-" Martin begins but we start giggling and squealing like children.

"OMG OMG OMG OMG!" Clara squeals in joy. I flip onto snapchat and take a picture of the adorable little cake.

"What did we tell you?" I said with a wink. Martin rolls his eyes as he picks up the plate and moves to the other couch across.

"I swear, I love how in sync I am with this one." Clara says motioning to me. I laugh before reaching out to a pink macaron and taking a bite. The sweet taste of strawberry makes me practically drool.

"Okay, these are freaking awesome." I say with a smile.

"I know right?" Martin says as he uses a dainty looking silver fork to take a bite off of his cake. He brings out his phone and we watch as he takes his time tapping his fingers on the screen.

"Did he just...?" I asked and Clara nods.

"Looks like Marty's got a date." Clara says, winking suggestively at him. I grin before looking down at my phone again.

I'm glad you're comfortable telling other people about us, I have a surprise for you. I smile and bite my bottom lip.

Can't wait to see what it is, then. I send.

"Now I feel like I'm the only single one here." Clara says with a sigh. "Why can't I get a hot guy hitting on me too?"

"Trust me, I felt like that for years." I say with a nod.

"Is Mr. A hot?" Martin asks and I shrug.

"I'd like to think he is." I say with a wink.

We laugh and talk in that cafe for at least 2 hours before the three of us decided it was time to enter the shopping zone. I couldn't wait. My butt was practically begging me to stand up. Martin and Eric exchanged flirty looks at each other before we left- which Clara and I made puking noises at. I spent the rest of the entire day at the mall with them until it hit 7 and I felt my legs feeling like jelly. They drove me home and we were still laughing like morons. I definitely knew who my new best friends were.

When I entered the apartment with at least four shopping bags, I heard two girls giggling. Uh...?

I walked through the apartment and practically tiptoed in before seeing an unfamiliar girl with shoulder-length curly brown hair. To say she was beautiful was an understatement. She looked like she was 5'10" and she wore big tan knitted sweater over a pair of denim capri pants. I guessed she was Daisy so I decided to just try to tiptoe away from the scene. But... of course. Having the worst luck ever. She saw me.

"Hey! You must be Darcy!" She greeted happily as she made her way towards me. I flash her my kindest smile.

"Yup, and you're most definitely Daisy." I say and she grins.

"Our names totally rhyme!" She says with a smile. I return the smile with what I hope is as much intensity.

"So... It must be really awkward huh. I mean you live together with him and he's a total annoying freak." Daisy says with a giggle.

"Lawrence?" I asked, slightly, weirded out, and Daisy nods. Someone's not what I expected... I think to myself.

"Who else could I be talking about? Has he told you about that one time where he-"

"Daisy." Lawrence calls out and I turn to find him walking down the stairs. I almost gawk.

He's freshly showered, his hair is still damp and he's wearing a plain white v-neck that really accentuates his chest, a pair of loose pale denims, and a pair of... are those boots? I watch as he pulls on a big black polo shirt to wear over the shirt and I swallow. Jesus... eye candy right there. I think to myself before Lawrence grins at me.

"Hey Darce." He greets and I smirk.

"Your girlfriend is perf." I mouth and he looks to Daisy with a smile.

"Lawrence, I swear you're such a killjoy." Daisy says and Lawrence chuckles before walking over to her and ruffling her hair.

"Darcy, you up for dinner? We're heading to this small downtown restaurant by the bay." He says with a smile.

"Sorry, I just ate out with Clara and Martin after a full day of walking and talking... But thanks for the invite- and besides, I don't wanna third-wheel." I say with a shrug. Daisy pouts at me and Lawrence puts a hand on her shoulder.

"That sucks. I really wanted to get to know you!" Daisy exclaimed and I grinned.

"Well, we can always hang tomorrow, I'd love to get to know you too. It'd be awkward living with that thing otherwise." I say and Daisy giggles.

"Thing? Really?" Lawrence asks and I smirk.

"You two seriously need to go have your date, I can barely hold all of these bags." I say with a sigh.

The two of them chuckle before smiling at each other. A knowing look passes between them that I raise an eyebrow at but they quickly dismiss it.

"Alright, love birds, I'll see you tomorrow- and it was lovely to meet you." I say, winking at Daisy.

As they walk past the door, Lawrence gives me a questioning look. I grin and mouth the words 'I like her already' and Lawrence grins before leaving. Once the two of them are gone, I make my way upstairs with my lone shopping bag. As I approach my door, I see a tiny pink note on the floor. I put my shopping bag down and pick it up.

Surprise, surprise ;) -Mr. A

I grin at it and slowly open my door. The lights are set to a dim yellow and I can smell the scent of roses... I slowly make my way inside and when I get to the bedroom, I smile. There's a fresh bouquet of red roses on the bed, I lift the bouquet and find a dvd of the movie 'Love, Rosie' there. I grin and read the pink sticky note attached to the dvd.

Sorry- didn't have time to get you better note cards... Shall we watch another movie? -Mr. A

I grin at the note and fish out my phone before plopping down onto the bed.

Movie? :) I message.

Leggo He responds and I giggle.

Leggo? Really? I reply.

Too lame? I grin at his response.

Nooooo ;) Anyways- gimme 5 minutes to get comfy and we can watch it 'together'. I text.

Okay, see you in 5 then

I grin before practically hopping into my bathroom. I wipe off all of my makeup before grabbing my shopping bag and shoving my body into a fluffy all white onesie. Ha! Best. Purchase. Ever.

I quickly pull my hair up into a pony tail before walking back to the room. I place the dvd into the dvd player stuck into the wall and I plop onto the bed as I wait for it to load.

You ready? I message.

Game on.

The credits begin rolling and I relax on the bed. I had already snuggled in and rested my head on the pillow. The only thing that was keeping me awake now was his messages. Although I believed my relationship with this guy was weird and atrocious, this whole texting thing made the engagement fiasco more like an online relationship than a serious weird stranger thing. If that makes any sense at all. From what I can gather from his messages, he was a sweet guy and he made sure all my needs were satisfied. I was treated like a princess from what it seems.

I can't believe it took them that long. I message, we had been talking about the movie this entire time.

Yeah... Imagine being stuck in the friendzone like that. He responds.

Good thing I've never had to deal with 'that' before.

Never been in the friendzone? He asks.

Yeah. Never been in a relationship either- this would technically be my first. ;) I send.

And last? ;) He messages back. I grin.

Hmm... what makes you think you'll spend the rest of your life with me? I message, and then realizing that it sounded mean, I added: I mean, what if I'm a total bïtch and you end up hating me forever...? :(

His reply took a while.

:) I sincerely doubt that you're a total B. I know what you're like from what Holly tells me- and I know what you're like based on the past how many responses you've given me. And I'm more worried about whether or not you'd hate me. I know you're worried over who I am. It's a strange situation to be in... and I'm a thousand times worried that once you figure out who I am... you'll make a run for the hills.

I think for a while. Whatever he said was true. I did worry. There's no way you can't worry about who you're messaging when you have no idea who he is. I'm only thankful that he's such a sweetheart... but I still knew nothing about him.

Then what's stopping you from showing yourself? I messaged... but even I was scared of his answer.

Pressure? I guess it's because I'm someone people think will always make the right decisions... and I really don't want to push you into this sort of harsh world where all anyone thinks of is how much is someone worth, who do I impress, and all that. I want you to be comfortable... not pushed into this pressure place with me... I smile again at his reply.

I get it. I really do. But we WILL meet some day right? There's only so much a girl can take... I message.

We will. I promise. :) He sends and I giggle a bit before a yawn takes over me.

Mr. A... I'm sleepy.

:) Call me Klein... It's... my second name. He messaged and I feel a smile tug at my lips.

Good night Klein :* I send.

Good night Darcy :) And with that, I drifted off to sleep.

I don't remember half of the things I talked about with Mr. A... I think I ended up doing that thing where I just start talking for ages... that and I had a Red Bull- and that crap makes me talk for an eternity.

"You were still up when I got back gome." Lawrence greets me just as I walk down the stairs- still in my adorably comfy white onesie.

"Yeah, I just couldn't shut up after my Red Bull. One of those at 2 in the morning is very very bad." I mutter.

"Who were you talking to?" Lawrence asks.

"A friend." I say with a wink. "Anyways, where's Daisy?" I asked and Lawrence sighs.

"She went out to buy my room a scented candle- apparently it stinks there." He says with a groan. "Why are girls so picky?"

"Maybe she just wants to redecorate." I say and Lawrence rolls his eyes at me.

"If she wanted to do that she'd-"

"GOOD MORNING LOVELIES!" I hear a familiar voice shout from the door- it's Holly.

Lawrence gives me a smirk and I grin at him before swiveling the bar stool so that I face the door. We were both seated at the sleek black breakfast bar and Lawrence had been sipping at his coffee while I ate from the bowl of oatmeal that was covered in berries.

"You're in a good mood." I say with a smile and Holly beams at me.

"Of course I am. Loverboy hasn't stopped talking about you my dear." She says.

"You mean her mysterious boyfriend that she won't talk to me about?" Lawrence asks and Holly grins.

"Yup." Holly says and I roll my eyes. "By the way, I feel terrible for not showing up yesterday. But Loverboy told me that you went out."

"I did, I had a fun day out with two friends from Pavelton. Anyways, youre obviously here for a reason." I say with a smile. Holly grins at me.

"My lovely cousin has decided on bringing the two of us out to a wonderful spa/salon treatment day. That is- if you don't have any lectures, plans, etcetera." She says and I grin.

"I don't. Thankfully my next lecture happens to go four straight times tomorrow." I say with a sigh. "Pavelton is seriously lenient on the whole lecture thing."

"Yup. But thank god for that, at least we can hang out today and you can tell me about your romantic views on yanno-who." She says with a wink and I grin.

"Guess you and Daisy have the whole day together." I say, turning to Lawrence. He grins before sipping his coffee.

"Yep. I have a lecture to attend to tonight though, so don't wait up for me my sister." He greets and I smirk at him, I turn back to Holly with a grin.

"I'll be back in 10 minutes." I say, she nods before plopping down onto the sofa before I disappear upstairs to change.

# Chapter 9

"You have seriously been using that closet haven't you?" Holly says with a big smile on her face.

We had just spent about 8 hours stuck in the spa. I have experienced both pain and relaxation... Klein- Mr. A- really knows how to make a girl happy. Either that or Holly has seriously been giving him some amazing advice. We had both gotten the full body treatment and Holly had finally convinced me to get a slight haircut with a bit of a new color into my hair... which ultimately landed in a hairstylist happily styling my entire look. Not that I minded, though, it was a pamper day.

"I have no idea what you're talking about." I say, winking at Holly.

We were already on our way out of the large luxury spa that had peach marble floors and creamy walls covered in golden furniture and accessories. I was wearing a silky white cardigan over a pink dress that I found extremely soft and comfy. I had also grabbed a few accessories that looked like a little fun to wear for a bit more color. I was, after all, more of a black and white girl.

"Okay, so what have you done to my cousin. He is legit non-stop thinking about you." Holly says with a grin.

"We've been trying to 'hang out' through our little movie marathons... that, and I text him as much as I can." I say with a shrug as we find ourselves at the exit of the spa, where Carl, the driver, pulls up with a white Rolls-Royce and opens the car door for us.

"He is smitten with you already- and- you have got to tell me what you think about him." Holly urges as we get into the car. Carl shuts the door behind me and I sigh as I feel my body unwind against the soft leather seats.

"What I think about him, huh... I think he's... well... I think he's amazingly sweet. It's my first ever relationship and he's making it work, despite the fact that I know nothing other than his middle name." I admit and Holly smiles at me.

"I can not wait until you meet him in person. God. I can just imagine the romantic scenario. He'll walk in, you'll gawk, he'll sweep you up in your arms, and then it's happily ever after." Holly says with a sigh.

"Whatever, Holly." I say with a sigh.

"Oh, yeah, I heard Lawrence's girlfriend was over at the penthouse yesterday."

"Yup. Her name's Daisy and she's absolutely adorable. They're almost like brother and sister when they talk though, which seems like an easy going relationship." I say. Just as Holly is about to speak, my phone buzzes.

"Loverboy?" Holly asks and I roll my eyes before grabbing my phone out of my bag. I felt a pang of disappointment when Klein wasn't on the screen- but I still grinned when I realized who had sent me the message.

"Nope. It's my mom." I say with a smile. "I totally forgot to contact her all this time!" I suddenly panic.

"Then what the hell are you waiting for?" Holly asks with a smile, I return it with my own before typing a message for my mom.

Hey mom. I'm sorry that I haven't been in touch so much. I've been really busy at school. How's Gavin treating you? I hope you're both having fun in Mexico right now, give me a call sometime. Promise I'll pick up a.s.a.p. :) -Darcy

I messaged my mom quickly. I had been so absorbed in New York and the strange situation I was in, that I had completely forgotten about her.

My mom and dad were both divorced... Mom right now is getting married to Gavin Weiland, he's a nice guy. I've met him before and he's always been around for us. Dad, on the other hand... he was left with his new boyfriend Paul, who I really disliked... Let's just say my family wasn't very family-like at all.

Mom and dad slept in separate rooms ever since I hit 6th grade. Things worsened, money disappeared, fights happened almost every day... There was just a really long spiral that led downhill for me.

That's why when I received the scholarship... I had said yes immediately without realizing what I had gotten myself into.

I needed to get out of that damned house. Dad never stopped fighting my mom no matter what we did to 'appease' him. He never gave her money despite wanting her to be a housewife. While he never stopped trying to turn me against her. I hated him for that. It was during junior year that our family totally shattered. There was no more breakfast together with daddy. No more family meals, family days, talking all together... That was all replaced by silence. Dad locked himself in his room away from the two of us and he never stopped throwing whatever insults he could.

Leaving for New York was one of the best things that had ever happened to me... and despite being engaged... I honestly didn't mind. I had a life that was content here. A good flatmate, funny friends, and even a fiancé that didn't seem bad at all.

"...Hello? Earth to Darcy. Mayday, mayday." Holly says and I'm pulled out of my thoughts.

"Sorry." I say. "Lost myself in my thoughts there."

"I could tell." Holly says, rolling her eyes at me. I smirk at her and bump my shoulders with hers.

"I was thinking of my family. Don't worry about it." I say, trying to sound as happy as I could. Holly gives me a weird look before sighing to herself.

"Fine. I won't press you on it."

"Thanks." I say with a smile.

Holly dropped me off at the mall closest to the apartment building, because I told her I wanted to go get a few things for myself before I went home. She said that she had to go sort out a few things from her work- which I had yet to ask about. So I was left alone, strolling around the mall. While I was there, I bought a few snacks and about 3 new novels that I wanted to read before I had decided to walk home.

Worst.

Idea.

Ever.

You'd think in a bustling city like New York, you wouldn't get someone to notice you in the street- even if you walked on the edge of the sidewalk.

Nope.

Two words.

Keaton.

Carter.

I was seriously just walking down the side of the street when some silver Jaguar pulls up beside me and rolls down his window and starts following me. Of course, I just tried to walk away- but then there was the voice. The voice of a total jerk.

"Nice dress you got there." He says... and I make the mistake of turning my head.

There he is. Wearing a plain white shirt and pulling a pair of expensive looking shades away from his eyes. If he wasn't so good looking, I probably wouldn't have even dared to look back.

"I'd say nice car, but you already know that." I say with a sigh. He smirks at me before driving up so that he's directly in front of me.

"Where you off to?" He asks and I, out of seriously ridiculous habit, bite the corner of my bottom lip and release it as soon as I realize what I'm doing.

"Home." I say before turning on my heel. I wasn't in an empty or secluded area- I was near the main road... and you'd normally expect the sidewalk to have cars parked by it- but for some reason, there wasn't any. Which Keaton used to his advantage to follow me.

"Listen, I'm sorry about being a dick at the party that night." He says, still following me in his car.

"Gotcha." I say dismissively before continuing to walk. I could see the wide entrance with the fountain in front coming into view.

"Are you going to stop walking?" He asks and I mentally groan.

"Nope."

"You live there, don't you?" Keaton says and I glance at him noticing that he's now pointing at the apartment building I lived in. Noticing that I probably shouldn't answer that in any way, I stopped walking and turned to him- which takes him by surprise.

"What the hell do you want Keaton?" I asked... and maybe it's the lighting... but... is that a bruise? Just at the slight hollow of his cheekbone?

"Finally. A full faced view." He says with an arrogant smile. I actually groan this time.

"Whatever." I mutter before walking again. This time, I don't hear the car pull up... I hear the goddamn door close and the sound of the lock going off. Goddamn it! I curse mentally.

I hear the sound of footsteps quickly coming and I try to hasten my pace. But alas, his legs are too freaking long. He's beside me in no time.

"Why did you pick up Lars that night?" Keaton asks and I stare at him before giving him the silent treatment and continuing to walk.

"Didn't I tell you?" I asked and Keaton looks at me blankly. I sigh. "He's my flatmate. He called me up and I promised I'd bring him home if he got drunk." I explain.

"A defenseless girl living with a man? How long have you known him? He's never mentioned you before." Keaton says.

"And he's never mentioned you. Lawrence has been a good flatmate. We chill out together sometimes but nothing more than that- we have space." A whole three full floors of it. I add in my head.

"So you're just friends?" Keaton asks and I roll my eyes.

"He has a girlfriend." I point out and I realize that I'll be in front of the buildidng within 50 steps.

"Yeah right, and I have two dicks." He says with a smirk. "The closest woman Lars has ever been close to is his sister."

"Why the hell are you even telling me this?" I ask and Keaton grins mischievously.

"Daisy's in town isn't she?" He asks.

"You know her?" I asked and he smirks at me.

"You should stop being gullible sweetheart." Keaton grins at me and I narrow my eyes at him.

"What the hell is that supposed to mean?" I asked and Keaton smirks.

"You're smart, right? Figure it out." He says with a wink.

I hear a phone buzz and know it's not mine- Keaton fishes out his phone and answers quickly- his voice turning stern.

"Alright. Fine, I'll be there in a second." He mutters before hanging up and shooting me an annoying smile. "Laters babe." He says before turning around and jogging back to his car.

"...Fücker." I curse before walking towards the building.

When I enter the apartment and the delicious smell of some sort of food starts coming towards me, I practically melt. I make my way to the kitchen and peek. I found Lawrence there, humming a soft song... Is he humming 'Thinking Out Loud'?

"People fall in love in mysterious ways... Maybe just the touch of a hand... Well me I fall in love with you every single day and I just wanna tell you I am..." Lawrence sings and I gawk. This man can sing- woo.

"Someone is a good singer." I say and Lawrence jumps slightly and I watch him tense as he smiles at me.

"Holy- Jesus." Lawrence says and I giggle.

"Indeed." I say, wiggling my eyebrows. "What 'cha cooking?" I asked.

"Dinner for two? Daisy took off with her two friends from her college. Said she had some sort of NYC travel list thing." Lawrence says just as he stirred something in the pan. I looked and saw two steaks slowly boiled around some sort of really good sauce.

I almost drooled.

"You seriously know how to make food porn." I say and Lawrence chuckles.

"Thanks." He says and I grin.

"Need any help with anything? I was planning on having a game night with both you and Daisy, but I guess that ain't happening... I even bought snacks." I say, putting on my best pouty face. Lawrence laughs before moving the pan away to a closed stove.

"We can do that. Daisy will join in when she comes back anyways." He says with a shrug and I grin.

"Great. I'm gonna go run up and change into a pair of comfy clothes... ooh and can we please play that anime arena game...? Just for the funsies?" I asked and Lawrence grinned.

"You're in a good mood." He says and I smirk.

"I said that to Holly this morning." I whined. "And maybe I'm in a good mood cause of food- and I really need to run upstairs and get into house clothes." I say and Lawrence laughs.

"Nice hair." He says with a wink, I twirl around happily.

"I know right?!" I say in the fakest most girliest accent I could manage. Lawrence laughs again and I join him. "Anyways, I'm starving and I really need to change. Be right back."

"Alright. I'll set the table then." He says and I grin before speeding up the stairs.

I didn't really try to get fancy. I just washed everything off of my face- which was a pity- but I already took my fair share of selfies and snapchats. I also pulled my hair into a messy looking bun, then I shoved on a loose animal onesie- a pink monkey with a big red butt and I laughed at my reflection. I walked into my room to find a charger for my phone when I see something else on my bed. I take it immediately and open it in excitement.

Roses are red, violets are blue, I'm pretty corny, how are you? -Klein.

I chuckle and pull out my phone... Then I remembered Keaton.

"Yeah right, and I have two dicks." He says with a smirk. "The closest woman Lars has ever been close to is his sister."

I shook my head at myself. But as I pulled out my phone, I suddenly came up with a plan.

"Daisy's in town isn't she?" He asks.

That's what Keaton said... so... is he trying to say that Lawrence and...

I groan. I have to figure this out.

I pulled on a pair of my fluffiest socks so that I don't make a noise and I carefully made my way outside of my room. I silently crept my way down to the second floor. From there, I could make out the slight hums Lawrence made... and I could see a bit of his arm as he moved to put the plates on the table.

I took a deep breath. I can't just not trust him. He's been awesome and kind to me. But it's bugging me too... I think to myself... How else can these notes get here...? And Lawrence has so far said nothing about these things... I pulled my phone out, sat down with my knees pulled to my chest, and I sent 'Klein' a message.

Nice note bro. :) I messaged- trying to sound casual. I silently look down to see if Lawrence is doing anything- but he's disappeared to the kitchen where I can't see him. I mentally groan.

Glad you liked it... Klein messaged and I bit my bottom lip.

How do you get these things into the apartment? I messaged.

Janet. Duh. The reply was almost instantaneous. I decided that there was only one way to find out if Lawrence was who I thought he was.

Really? I messaged back as I started to quietly walk down the stairs. My heart raced against my chest as I swallowed and felt my dry throat.

Yeah... Sneaking in there would be rude- and I respect your privacy. He messaged and I was already at the part where I had to make a turn around the stairs to see what Lawrence was doing.

I see... So what if I wanted you to invade my privacy? Would you do that? I message, adding a flirtatious winky face to see what reaction I'd get.

I took a deep breath and practically jumped down the last five steps...

Bad bad bad idea...

Note to self.

Don't jump five steps no matter how shallow.

Especially freshly polished steps.

With fluffy socks on.

I.

hate.

myself.

It felt like day 1 of meeting Lawrence all over again.

Except this time, I was actually fully clothed.

My foot just happened to land wrong. For the second time in this house.

I heard a few things clatter before I fell. Probably Lawrence- from shock. I braced myself for my terrible landing.

3.........

2.........

1........

There it is. The thwack of my arse hitting the marble floor... I groaned in pain. But I didn't even have time to react before I felt something else hit me. I thought for a moment that it was some sort of vase I knocked over somehow- but it felt like a freaking pig fell on top of me...

And... there's only one other person in this place that'll be as heavy as that...

Freaking.

Lawrence.

"Jesus... movies make it seem so easy..." Lawrence mutters and I notice he's right beside my right cheek. I freeze at the proximity.

He's taken... He's taken. Taken. T-A-K-E-N. Don't do it Darce... Don 't... I can't. I catch a whiff of his scent. I feel like such a perv. But he smells of mint... Ugh... I breathe softly and realize he's still on me. Like... I am stuck to the floor on my back and he's lying down on my body with his own large and heavy frame.

"Darcy?" Lawrence asks and for a second... I have an idea... I decided to pretend that I fainted. Not exactly best actress material... but hey? I need some sort of plan to get me out of this...

"Hey? Are you okay?" Lawrence asks and I feel his weight lift off of mine. The warmth from his body disappears and I fight the urge to take a peek. "Oh god... What do I do? " Lawrence says in a panicked voice.

I feel his arms in the crook of my knees and at the back of my neck... And then I'm being lifted up into the air and I'm close to what I'm sure is his chest. I mentally sigh. Boundaries Darce... Just cause Keaton tried to say something doesn't mean it's true... I think to myself.

"Are you... are you really?" Lawrence asks but I don't stir. I try to remain limp as possible.

I hear something clatter to the floor.

Shït! That was my phone! I mentally shout. Damn it. I hope it's fine... I bought a thick enough case... Just hope the marble floor doesn't... dent it... I feel myself being lowered down and I feel Lawrence's arm under my knees, move. Then I feel myself being lifted up again as I'm gently cradled and placed down on what seems to be the couch. Lawrence props my head up on a pillow before I feel the couch dip... He's probably sitting down right now.

"Darcy...?" Lawrence asks. I don't respond, I try to act... Try being the keyword here. "Can you hear me?" I hear him ask.

Suddenly, I can feel a slight movement of air right at the tip of my nose. Then I feel warm skin touch my forehead.

"Good... you aren't sick. God... I hope you didn't hit the stairs." He mutters. But... he lingers.

Lawrence...? I think to myself. Keaton couldn't be... Hell how would Keaton even know anything? I suddenly feel something trail along my bottom lip... Something slightly callussed. His thumb. I feel it trail there for a bit, and I fight the urge to open my eyes. It should feel creepy... but it doesn't... it feels... like he's thinking about what I think he's-

"Bad idea." Lawrence mumbles. "Daisy." He says, like reminding himself that I shouldn't be touched....

Wait.

What?

Even if Lawrence isn't Klein... then...

No way.

Could he possibly...?

Oh God... Darcy... He's taken. His girlfriend is perfect. He's hot. There's no way he is what you're thinking he is. I think to myself. You're engaged. ENGAGED. YOU'RE BOTH TAKEN! I reason out in my head.

"I can't do this." I hear Lawrence whisper. I mentally sigh in relief, at least he was loya-

And then I felt it. Soft... Almost like a breeze...

A light and breathy kiss...

I almost melt and have a heart attack at the same time.

# Chapter 10

I had never had a kiss before.

Never.

In my 18 years of existence, this would be my first... I had to really hold back on this kiss. I was playing fake sleeping. So I let him... and I know... This event has totally ruined the whole back-away-he-has-a-girlfriend thi ng... But...

I don't know...

It just felt... like it meant something. Or maybe that's just me trying to make my first kiss actually be something.

I didn't even know if Lawrence and Mr.A/Klein were the same person... But the soft whisper of a kiss he gave me made my heart almost lurch straight up out of my chest... and even though I knew he was taken, I didn't feel the urge to push him away. I let him stay there for the few seconds that he rested his lips on mine.

God, I've only known him for a week... I thought to myself.

I felt Lawrence pull away and sigh, and a sad and lonely feeling, already, blooms in my chest.

"I'm such an idiot..." I heard him mutter- it was almost inaudible.

I'm reeling.

I feel an uncomfortable pang in my chest and a maelstrom of emotions hit me hard. So many thoughts gathered in my brain. My mind was going all over the place. Was Lawrence actually Klein? Was Daisy his sister like

Keaton tried to tell me? How does Keaton know? I thought to myself. My eyes were still shut, and Lawrence was still seated beside me. I fought the urge to ask the questions out loud... But the effort in trying to fake this 'black out' was already making my brain tired... and without even noticing...

I fainted for real.

How do I know that?

I somehow magically poofed into my own bedroom with my own blankets over me. It was already morning and when I checked my phone, I had to practically make a run for the bathroom. I hardly felt like getting ready. So I pulled on a bright teal sweater, a pair of jeans, some type of fancy white sneakers with a silver-tipped design, my plain glasses, and what I know to be a Louis Vuitton backpack- but it was the fastest thing I could grab.

Hair? Okay. Clothes? Check. Bag? Uh... I frantically shoved my things into my bag. The book I needed for my English lecture, my iPad, a notebook, a few pens, etc... I had tried to dress as modest as possible today. I took a quick look at myself in the mirror. I put on a bit of mascara and pulled my hair into a really quick braid before I made a run for the kitchen. Lawrence was already there, but I had no time to really react to his presence- despite the fact that that happened last night.

"Morning." Lawrence greeted, nonchalantly if I may add, he was sipping on a mug of what I think is coffee.

"Morning." I said fast as I walked and grabbed a piece of bread off of the table and put it to my mouth. I opened one of the cupboards and placed a tablet into the coffee machine.

I put the tumbler underneath it and pressed the button for my coffee.

"Whoa, slow down." Lawrence says with a smirk, I look at him and grin as I took the bread out of my mouth to chew and swallow.

"If I slow down, I will inevitably be late." I point out before grabbing my tumbler of coffee, sealing it, and then finishing off the bread in my mouth. "I gotta go." I say with a smile.

"Really don't want breakfast?" He asks. "You didn't even eat dinner last night."

"I'll be fine. We can talk about my wonderful fall later. I've seriously gotta run." I say and Lawrence chuckles before I run off and catch him winking at me. Uh...?

I thank the freaking heavens for the chauffeur service, Wesley was already there waiting by the car door. He nodded at me and I smiled.

"Morning Wesley!" I greeted happily. "I'm running late so if you wanna drive faster than usual... I would really appreciate it." I say and he smiles before opening the car door for me and letting me inside the big black Range Rover.

"Alright miss." He says with a kind smile before closing the door and going in as well.

Wesley is an amazing driver.

Yep.

I got on campus 10 minutes less than the usual- pretty amazing considering all the stop lights that were on the way.

"Thanks Wesley. I'll text if need a ride home." I say and Wesley gives me a curt nod. "Could I have a smile please?" I asked and he chuckles.

"Yes ma'am." He says, flashing me a bright smile, before I return it and close the door and run off on campus.

Turn left... right... stairs... and then... There it is. The lecture hall for my first lesson of the day. I entered and found two large wooden double doors with golden handles. I sighed as I opened one door and walked in.

Phew.

There was yet to be an entire class... I think. I mean there's practically no one here. Not even a professor was to be found. Only one guy with headphones on, a girl with curled blonde hair, and one familiar face that belonged to no one other than... Keaton Carter.

He smirks at me and I roll my eyes before making my way to the middle row a few steps up. Then I turn to my right to sit by the large window seat. All the lecture halls were almost identical. But who knows? Maybe my smaller classes would have tinier halls. Hopefully, at least. I look at my phone. Class was going to start in 2 minutes... but the prof was nowhere to be found. I sigh before sitting down on the comfy reclining chair and I lay my head back on it... Lawrence kissed me last night... I thought of immediately.

I had to think about it some time and I guess now would be the time... Considering how quiet it is in this damned classroom. Even though I really didn't want to process the events of last night.

"Looks like someone's daydreaming." A voice I hated said. I groaned as I looked to my right.

Sure enough, there was Keaton Carter. Grinning ear to ear, with his amber eyes glistening from the sunlight that entered from the windows. I rolled my eyes.

"And someone's annoying me." I mutter.

"I'm sure that someone isn't me." He says and I roll my eyes. "How did the confrontation go?"

"Confrontation?" I asked and Keaton smirks.

"I didn't tell you those things yesterday for it to go to waste, now did I?" He says with an arrogant smile plastered onto his face.

"Well, too bad the confrontation didn't happen, thanks for the tip by the way. Ässhole." I say and Keaton stares... As in stares.

"Do we have a problem here?" He asks and I sigh.

"We do." I say, biting the corner of my bottom lip. "How do you know about my situation?"

"Wouldn't you like to know?" He says before turning so that he completely faces me. "Unfortunately, a magician never reveals his secrets.ad" Keaton says, flashing me a cheeky grin.

"But you're not a magician and you have a stick up your-" Before I can finish talking, we all look at a person who stumbles through the door.

It's a woman with her black hair perfectly braided to the side. She's dressed in a plain white dress and a pair of plain black flats. She walks in and I see her take a nervous sigh before she goes to her desk. She clears her throat.

"Is this all?" She asks and I look around. A few more students were here, sure, there were around 20 of us now...

When the classroom started filling up happened... I have no idea. I just know that Keaton just kept sneaking glances at me. I tried my best to just focus on the task at hand, which was to analyze the introduction of the novel, The Memory Keeper's Daughter. I was finally able to focus on analyzing and adding notes to the book on my iPad when Keaton decided that staring wasn't enough. He began to nudge me with his elbow, earning him a glare from me.

"Stop it." I whisper in a warning tone.

"Make me." He says with a quiet snicker.

That was practically routine and it lasted just about the entire damned lecture.

Or the whole day.

Considering he didn't stop goddamned stalking me.

I only had about three lectures today and somehow Mr. Annoying always found me or had some sort of lecture right beside me.

It was already noon when I finally stopped walking down the god-damned hall and turned around to face him. He stopped directly in front of me- as in I had no space at all because he bumped into me.

"Could you please tell me why you've been following me all day?" I asked, stepping away. I haven't even been able to text Klein cause of you. I added in my thoughts.

"Would saying that 'I'm interested in you' be a good enough answer?" He says stepping closer and closing the distance- so much that I can smell the faint hint of some sort of deep musky perfume on his clothes.

"Does it look like that would be a good answer?" I ask, folding my arms over my chest.

"I don't know. I need a good answer." He retorts with a cheeky grin. I roll my eyes and sigh before stepping away. "Don't you just think today would be a great day to go out?" Keaton asks, suddenly appearing right beside me.

"It's a great day to go out of your goddamn way." I say before pulling out my phone, but before I can even text Wesley- Keaton takes the phone out of my hands.

"Who's Wesley?" Keaton asks.

"Driver." I say, rolling my eyes.

"Hmm..." He says and then he brings out his own phone. It takes a moment for me to actually process what was going on at the moment.

That's when I started trying to grab my phone away from him. Trying being the key word here.

"If you wanted to hold my hand all you had to do was ask babe." Keaton says, an arrogant and overall irritating smile gracing his stupid face.

"I want my phone back." I hiss before reaching for his left hand. He only holds it up higher and I'm stuck to his chest as I use my left hand to boost me up.

"Really wished you wore a different top sweetheart, it would have made the view so much better." Keaton says with a smirk. At that point I give up and sigh.

"What do you want from me, Keaton?"

"Your number." He says as he brings my phone down to my level. I groan and try to snatch it from him, failing again when he raises his hands up.

"Fine. Give me your phone then." I say with a sigh. Keaton grins victoriously and brings his phone to me.

He unlocks it and hands the large black iPhone over. I take it and quickly type in my number before handing it back to him. He takes a look at it and calls the number. My phone plays my usual default ringtone, the chorus of "Sugar" booms and Keaton grins.

"Glad to see you're a reasonable person." He says with a smirk. "Now then, before I give you back your phone-"

Of course there was an ulti-freaking-matum.

"-let's go have a nice date."

...

"What?" I asked blankly. Keaton grins at me.

"A date sweetheart, never been on one before?" He asks.

"Wait." He says and I peer into his amber eyes. "You're kidding right?"

I bite the corner of my bottom lip again. Damn it.

"Is it so surprising?" I asked. I'm pretty sure I'm not the only 18 year old who hasn't been on a single date yet.

"Not surprising, just... Unexpected I guess." He says and I roll my eyes.

"There really isn't much of a difference." I say with a sigh. Keaton chuckles and I watch as he places my phone into his front pocket.

"I can't even have my phone back?" I asked.

"Nope, I think I'll keep this wonderful thing... until you earn the right to get it back from me." Keaton says, he's still too close for my own comfort and all of a sudden he uses his free hand to pull me into his chest and take a quick photo of me landing at the crook of his neck. I groan.

"Don't you look cute?" He asks as he shows me the picture.

"Yeah, sure, whatever." I mumble.

"You know most girls would be happy I pay them this much attention." Keaton says and I push myself off of him.

"Well I bet you don't steal most girls' phones or take pictures with them out of the blue." I snap and Keaton chuckles.

"I can't believe I'm going to be your first date." Keaton says, changing the subject.

"I can't believe it either." I answer in amusement.

"Then I might as well go all out on this date then huh?" Keaton asks and I shrug, but he grabs me again this time he pulls me to his side and places a hand on my hip.I try to push away from him but he firmly places me there and I sigh in frustration.

"Let go of me dïck face." I say and he just chuckles in response.

"Now that's not how you're supposed to talk to someone on a date." Keaton says and I roll my eyes.

"Please, I'm hardly date ready or date material."

"We can change that... Come on." Keaton says as he grips my hip and starts leading me to the road, where a sleek black Audi waited for us.

Keaton opens the door and motions for me to enter. I give him a I'm-really-unhappy-with-my-current-situation kind of look before I get in. The soft black leather seats are so comfortable that I sigh in contentment.

"Glad you like my car, sweetcheeks." Keaton says.

"Ruined my moment of peace. Thanks." I say, rolling my eyes.

"Where are we off to, sir?" The driver in front asks. I have no clear view of him due to this screen being there- how does even see the rear with that black thing up?

"We'll go to Harley's first." Keaton says and I hear the driver chuckle before it turns dead quiet in the car.

I swear. Luxury cars are so smooth. You just... don't feel that annoying bump on the road. It's just like gliding in air... I sigh in relief.

"Tired?" Keaton asks me and I turn my head to him.

"After a day of you stalking me? Yeah I'm tired." I say before he sighs.

"You can take a nap, we aren't going to get anywhere in at least 30 minutes." Keaton says, in a surprisingly calming voice.

"I don't think I can trust my defenseless sleeping body with you." I say just as I yawn and cover it up with my right hand.

"True. But it'd be better to sleep here than to collapse in public." Keaton says with a wink.

"Right."

"Right." He repeats and I roll my eyes before I actually zone out and fall asleep.

"Darcy..." A familiar voice called. I groaned. "Darcy, we're here." The voice said and I turned to my left, away from the voice.

"Darcy..." The voice continued to call. Damn it.

"Go away..." I muttered, using my right hand to swat the person beside me. But instead of hitting someone, someone grabbed it and laced their warm fingers in mine.

The person started pulling me and I tried to pull away.

"Leave me alone..." I murmured. I heard an annoyed sigh and the pulling stopped.

Instead, I felt someone sneaking their arms behind me and my knees. I laughed at the tickly feeling I got from being held behind my knees. Note to self: I am the most ticklish person in the entire universe.

"Stop!" I squealed with a giggle.

"Darc. Stop. Moving." The voice said but I still didn't bother to open my eyes.

That was until I felt myself being lifted up and smelt a faint scent of familiar perfume against my face. Where did I get a whiff of that before? I wondered. I snuggled closer- only to be in contact with warm skin.

Wait.

A.

Second.

I opened my eyes.

"Oh my freaking- Keaton put me the hell down!" I exclaimed.

I was being carried bridal style by Keaton Carter. In public.

No.

Way.

"Nope. I have decided that I like having you right where you are now." Keaton says, as he looks at me. My head was at the crook of his neck and I, again, did that annoying stalker-ish thing I do.

I sniffed him.

I freaking sniffedthe guy. He smelled like lavender... soft, minty, and musky. It was the type of scent that was so subtle, you just want to really go in and... well... smell the guy.

"Remind me to give you my shirt at the end of the day." Keaton says in that arrogant tone of voice.

"Nope. I'm good." I say quickly. "Just... It's a weird habit." I say, almost forgetting that Keaton had been holding me up whilst the people walking around us have been staring. Oh dear...

"Sniffing people?" He asks and I sigh.

"Sort of. Can you put me down please?" I asked, this time, kindly. Well, as kindly as I could.

"Hmm... then we're going to have to come up with some sort of com-promise."

"What?" I asked quickly. "Just put me down. This is embarrassing enough." I whine.

"Ah, I have an idea. If you won't let me carry you, then we'll hold hands. Less embarrassing right?"

"As long as you put me down." I say when I hear a few people giggling at the sight of him carrying me.

Let me just say... I am completely underdressed. Keaton was already rocking his normal outfit of a classy button down- this time in black- and a pair of clean and plain deep blue jeans. Then there was the whole issue of him holding me in front of an expensive Audi. Keaton smirked at me when I said that and he gently placed me down. Once my feet were flat on the ground, I held my right hand out and he smiled as he took it.

His hands felt extremely warm compared to mine. I felt him interlace his fingers in between my own and I felt my fingers go limp. What was I supposed to do? Clutch his hands like there was no tomorrow?

"You know, when you said hold hands, I was expecting you to willingly do the same." Keaton said as he pulled our hands up. Mine loosely lying in his tight grip.

I looked at him, planning to flash him a sarcastic smile, but I slightly gasp as I realize that his amber eyes are looking at our hands. He has his lips pressed into a line, almost as if he really wants me to do it willingly. I sigh before actually giving him a smile. I squeeze his hand with my own.

"There. Happy?" I asked, and Keaton beamed at me.

"100%. Now let's go get you date ready." Keaton says and I roll my eyes at him as he brings me down the street.

"Where are we going again?" I ask.

"My sister's studio."

"Studio?"

"She's a stylist." Keaton says with a shrug before we make our way into a large building with white marble floors.

The place is amazingly grand. There's a giant crystal chandelier hanging up at the top of a tall ceiling. Racks upon racks of clothes are everwhere as well as shelves upon shelves of shoes and jewelry. It was probably a stylist's dream room.

"No... I think it'd be better in black. Thanks, Tay." A female voice said.

"Jen!" Keaton shouted, surprising me a bit, considering I had been zoning out on how girly this place was. "Sorry 'bout that." Keaton muttered, squeezing my hand, I shook my head.

"No worries." I say with a shrug.

"Keaton!" The voice from earlier exclaimed.

Walking towards us was a slim young woman. She had the same amber eyes as Keaton, but she had a kinder look on her face. Her hair was black with one streak of platinum blonde near her face. She wore a slim fitting black dress and a pair of classic black Louboutins.

"You should have called first bro!" She said, giggling as she approached Keaton and gave him a tight squeeze. I tried to pull my hand away from his grip so that he could return the hug, but he only held onto it tighter.

"If I did, you would just keep asking me questions." Keaton says with a sigh. The girl grins at him and then brings her eyes to me- her eyes seem to almost brighten.

"And who is this pretty little thing?" She asks and I bite my bottom lip.

"Her name's Darcy. I'm taking her out for a date- but she doesn't think she's date ready." Keaton says with an annoyed sigh.

"Excuse me? I said that so that you would bug off." I retort and the girl laughs.

"Glad to know Keaton's doesn't impress someone for once in his life." The girl says before turning to me. She was really tall, granted she was wearing heels, but seriously. I felt tiny compared to her.

"My name's Jenny Carter. I'm Keaton's older sister." She greets me with a bright smile.

"Nice to meet you." I say. "This place is amazing" I compliment.

"I agree. When I finally got to establish this place, I wanted everything to be perfect. And this is as close as I can get to perfection." She says and I grin.

"If you two are done, can we please move on? We have places to be, Jen." Keaton says, an annoyed tone in his voice. Jenny rolls her eyes.

"Right. Well then, let's get Mr. Grumpy off of you and have you scurry into the dressing room down the hall-" Jenny said before looking around. I follow her gaze and see a girl with a red pixie cut wearing a plain black halter top over a pair of white jeans.

"Quinn!" Jenny called out. The girl immediately turned around and I saw her happy-go-lucky smile. Is everyone here nice or what? I thought to myself.

"Yeah?" The girl, Quinn, asked as she walked over to us.

"Quinn, this is Darcy and my brother wants her to be styled for a date. Do you mind taking her to the dressing room down by the jewelry section?" Jenny asks and Quinn shared an excited look between Jenny and her.

"Sure thing." She says and I notice Jenny wink at her and Quinn returns it with her own.

"Now then, brother, you can come back in 15 minutes and leave your cutiepie to Quinn and I's wonderfully professional hands." Jenny says and I watch as Keaton looks over at me and sighs to himself.

"Fine. 15 minutes tops and I'll be back." He says, Jenny nods with a smile plastered on her face before Keaton decides to bring my hand up to his lips and kiss the back of my hand. "I'll be back for you soon sweetheart." He says winking at me.

I bite my bottom lip in embarrassment. I was in front of his sister.

Jenny scoffs before Keaton lets go of my hand and walks out of the swiveling glass doors. I watch him as he makes his way to the Audi we had arrived in and he gets inside. He flashes me a reassuring smile before closing the door and I feel an absence in my hands. We'd been holding hands for who knows how long. It was one of those moments were your body got used to feeling something on it so the feeling just sort of... lingers. I sighed to myself. First date and I'm already setting expectations. I think to myself.

"Well then, he's gone." Quinn, whose presence I'd almost forgotten says. Jenny giggles before she presses a quick kiss on Quinn's cheek.

"So then, Miss Darcy... what kind of look do you want to pull off in front of my brother?" Jenny asks me as she holds Quinn's hands.

"This is going to be so much fun." Quinn mutters and I give them a smile.

"Black and white sounds good to me... Although... I want to keep my jeans on... if that's okay..." I say shyly. And I want to pay for it... Sort of. I add in my brain.

But I guess I could do that later.

# Chapter 11

"I think it looks chic." Jenny says as I look at my reflection in the large mirrors in front of me.

Jenny and Quinn had placed me into a large dressing room that looked like it was made for princesses. The ceilings were high, a tall crystal chandelier hung above, I was surrounded by golden tipped mirrors, and there was a round white marble platform where I stood. The entrance was covered in large decorative and heavy looking pale pink curtains. I thought I was in a palace.

"I think it's way too much." I say with a sigh. "I told you guys that I wanted to keep my jeans..." I whined.

"Oh please." Quinn says as she rolls her eyes at me. "Stop talking." She says and I sigh as Quinn applies a thin layer of tinted lipbalm onto my lips.

"Was the whole makeover thing really necessary?" I asked, as soon as the lipbalm was lifted from my lips. Quinn grins at me before slipping the tiny lipbalm into the pocket of the tan leather jacket i had on.

"It wasn't. But if Keaton brings his date here, then I just know he's into you." Jenny says with a sigh before walking over to me.

Quinn backs away to get something and Jenny adjusts the jacket while fixing the golden collared necklace they placed for that extra "bling" or whatever.

"I feel way too fancy." I say with a sigh.

The two of them had gone all out- you'd think 15 minutes was too little time for a makeover... but Jenny made me look like I had gotten ready for hours when it only took 10 minutes. Of course... there were two of them working on me at the same time. Quinn got me dressed as fast as she could while Jenny fixed my hair and makeup. I felt like I was going to some fancy party rather than a spontaneous date.

"Are the earrings there?" Jenny asks Quinn, who's behind her and is fetching something.

"Yup." Quinn responds, walking over to me. My hair was up in a tight ponytail that somehow has going up to the ponytail section.

Quinn quickly slipped on a pair of large chandelier-like gold earrings on me. So far, the two of them wanted me in a fairly simple golden accessory themed outfit. They let me wear the bracelet Klein gave me as well as a ring, the earrings Quinn just put on me, and the collared statement necklace. They put me in a cropped white tank top, a black leather skater skrit, and a pair of tall white and gold stiletto heels that I could possibly fall in.

I'm not bad at wearing heels. But considering that these are the first time I'm wearing these gorgeous ones... I might just stumble in the streets of New York. I just hoped Keaton would bring me to leveled land and hopefully not anywhere with jagged stone floors. That would be hell in my current situation.

"If I fall today... I blame you two." I mutter and Jenny giggles before stepping back.

I look at my reflection and I can't help the smile that tugs at my lips. Damn. I look amazing.

NOT to be vain or anything.

Okay.

Yeah, I'm totally being vain right now. But so what? I can have my moments too.

"You guys have outdone yourselves." I mutter.

"Not really. Just imagine what would happen if Keaton asked us to dress you up for a company ball. That would totally outdo both of us." Quinn says and I giggle as the two of them share a high five.

"Okay. We need a pic before my brother takes you away." Jenny says before she brings out her phone. "Say 'gorgeous'!" Jenny says before we all huddle together for a pic.

"She's going to take 10 million pics. So prepare your poses." Quinn says and I laugh as the first picture is taken.

After about 2 minutes, I hear Keaton shouting from outside the large dressing room.

"Someone's impatient." Jenny says, rolling her eyes. "You mind telling him to wait a bit, Quinny?" Jenny asks and Quinn sighs.

"You owe me sweetie." Quinn says before kissing Jenny on the cheek and going out to talk to Keaton. Jenny then turns to me and sighs.

"Hey, I just wanna give you a head's up. We dressed you all up because if I know Keaton, he'll bring you out and you'll crash into one of his friends. They aren't a terrible group- well, actually yeah they are, but don't let it get to you." Jenny says with a sigh. "They're known to make girls like you cry."

"Girls like me? What is that supposed to mean?" I asked.

"It means, girls like you who like her jeans because she sometimes wears her insecurities on her sleeves. If you wanna kick his friends' ässes, be my guest. I do it all the time." Jenny mutters.

"Got it. Keaton's friends are total douchebags." I say and Jenny chuckles.

"Exactly. Now let's go get you to my ugly brother." I laugh at that one, before Jenny and I make our way outside the dressing room.

The heels click on the floor as I walk and I'm conscious about how much the skirt flows around me. A series of what-if situations play into my head, but I shake the thoughts off. I was dressed and going on a date with Keaton.

There was no way I could chicken out when Jenny took the time to really "set me up"...

"I approve." Keaton says with a smirk on his face as he judges me from head to toe.

"And I don't need your approval. But thanks." I say with a dismissive shrug.

"I like her a lot, Keaton. If she comes home crying, I will personally kick your äss." Jenny says before handing me my backpack, I take it from her and give her a grateful smile.

Quinn comes in with a smile and a large shopping bag of what I think if full of my clothes.

"Here's her things with additional goodies from us both. We trust you'll love them." Quinn says with a wink.

"I'm sure I will." I say. And that I really don't need you guys to add more things. I add in my head.

Before I can even reach out to take the bag, Keaton takes it for me and also grabs my backpack from me too.

"I'll tell Greg to bring them over to your apartment." Keaton mutters. I nod before he uses his free hand to clasp one of mine. "Let's go before my sister decides to keep you." Keaton says, winking at me.

I roll my eyes at him and look over at Jenny and Quinn, who are both holding each other's hand and grinning at me. Quinn mouths the words 'Good Luck' to me while Jenny gives me an encouraging smile.

"Bye!" I said quickly before Keaton dragged me out of the place.

"Who's Greg?" I asked as soon as we were in the pavement. I tried my best to walk nicely in the heels, I was only thankful that the pavement was nice and flat.

"The driver." Keaton answers before stopping in front of his black Audi.

The driver from earlier comes out and opens the door for us. Keaton silently passes the bags to "Greg" and I give the driver a smile before I get into the car. Keaton follows behind me and I sigh in contentment at the wonderful softness of the seats here. Now I remember why I took a nap in here... I thought to myself.

"If you fall asleep again, you can forget about having a phone for the whole week." Keaton says and I pout.

"If I fall asleep on your shoulder, can I have my phone back when I wake up?" I asked, batting my lashes.

Keaton smirks at me.

"Maybe."

"Hmm..." I mumble before nudging closer and resting my head on his shoulder.

"...Are you serious right now?" Keaton asks me. I look up at him.

"Uh? Yeah? It's a lean on the shoulder, not a makeout session." I say, rolling my eyes. "Besides, I hate staying up in traffic." I mutter.

"What would you do if I kidnapped you?" Keaton asks.

"I'd be kidnapped. Geez. I have very low issues with touching people. So if you want me to back away, tell me now." I say, but Keaton shakes his head and instead, he rests his left hand on my shoulder, pulling me closer to him.

"We'll be there in 30 minutes. So... do whatever you want." I sigh contently before resting my head. "How are you okay with this but not holding hands?" Keaton asks suddenly.

"Because I'm tired and I used to do this with my mom all the time." I answer lazily. "And I'm not picky when I'm tired." I answer.

"I can see that."

"How's the bruise on your face by the way?" I asked, in amusement.

"It's healing well, thanks for asking." Keaton says, unamused. I chuckle before falling back against him.

"Wake me up when we get there please." I say and before Keaton could even respond.

I passed out.

Again.

I have got stop doing that when I'm with strange handsome rich bastards. I swear.

"...Wake up sleepyhead." Keaton said and my eyes fluttered open.

"I'm up! I'm up! Don't carry me please." I exclaim, my eyes really wide and awake now. Keaton chuckles at my reaction.

"I won't. Let's go." Keaton says as he opens the door and exits. I reach for the door next to me, but Keaton takes my hand and pulls me out his way.

"Gee. It's not like I couldn't exit the other way." I mutter.

"I like having you follow me. I also get to have a close eye on you." Keaton says and I watch as his gaze travels down my body. "You should wear skirts and heels more often."

"And you should wear jeans more often. But hey, that's just my opinion." I say as I nudge him playfully with my elbow.

"Have you even noticed where we are yet?" Keaton asks me and I realize then that I've only been talking.

I immediately take a look around and I smile. The bright lights, kids laughing, the distant screams... I immediately felt giddy.

"Amusement park." I say in a hushed tone. "God, I haven't been to a legit amusement park in 10 years."

"Really?" Keaton asks and I nod my head in excitement.

"Please tell me we're riding all the roller coasters." I say as I look at Keaton in excitement.

"Of course. Why else would we be here?" Keaton says and I smirk as I look at the large roller coaster.

Keaton offers his hand and I take it without bothering to make a fight out of it. Hey? I'm a sucker for thrill rides. Keaton walks us over to the line for the biggest roller coaster and I feel my stomach lurch in excitement.

"I'll be back, I'll just go buy a package deal for us." Keaton says with a wink. I nod impatiently and he chuckles before walking off.

I listen to the screams of the people who were already on the roller-coaster. I was feeling so giddy. It was hard to get me excited on rides since they went by too fast. This was the first time I'd actually ride a full-sized rollercoaster. Damn. Why couldn't I snapchat this?

Oh.

Right.

"Hey miss, I couldn't help but notice you standing here by yourself." Some guy behind me says, I whirl around and tilt my head. "Mind if I join you?" He asks.

"And cut the line? I don't think so." I say with a sigh, he chuckles in response. The guy was fairly tall, he had a strong build, and he seemed to have that "stiff" appearance that comes with people who like to work out.

"Just wanna keep you company. Can't have a pretty thing like you standing around here all by herself." He says.

"I'll be fine. Thanks for the kind gesture, stranger. But I'm with some-one." I say.

"Rob's the name." He says, ignoring what I just said, and I sigh. I fight the urge to roll my eyes, I'm an anxious person and talking to guys is annoying and very nerve-wracking. "So... you're the type that's into rollercoasters huh?"

"Yeah." I answer. That's right. Keep those answer short and clipped. I think to myself.

"I guess you come from a fairly well off family."

"Maybe."

"There's a nice club close by, mind hitting it up with this stranger after the ride?"

"I just got here." I state, hoping that the icy tone in my voice wasn't too harsh.

"Have you ever-"

"No, she hasn't." Keaton's voice says and I practically sigh in relief.

"Whoa, calm down. I was just trying to keep the nice girl some company." The guy says and I roll my eyes.

"Sounds like you were trying to pick her up, that's my job by the way, not yours." Keaton says and I roll my eyes again. Really? Cheesy much?

Stranger smirks at me and then at Keaton.

"Well, can't say I didn't try. Hope I see you around, cutie." The guy says before walking off. I watch as he makes his way to a group of guys who laugh at him.

"Didn't think there'd be a downside to getting you dressed up." Keaton mutters.

"Huh?"

"Nothing. Let's go." Keaton says and he clasps my hand again and I follow him as the line finally moves.

"Am I even allowed to wear heels to a rollercoaster ride?" I asked.

"Why not?" Keaton asks, a mischievous grin on his face.

"Please tell me you put my phone somewhere safe." I say with a sigh. "I do not wanna break that thing."

"Greg has both our phones. Wouldn't want our attention to go any-where other than the two of us and this date, right?" Keaton says and I bite my bottom lip as Keaton and I make our way to the front.

Surprisingly. The front was empty. I felt that giddy feeling lurch up into my throat. I couldn't help it. I let out an excited squeal as I excitedly took a seat. Keaton looks over at me and I can't help but shake my legs in excitement.

"I don't know if you're excited or really scared." Keaton says and I smirk at him.

"Both." I answer and Keaton holds out his hand just as the large seatbelt thingies- I have no idea what you call them- go down.

"Let's enjoy this together." Keaton says and I look at his hand before rolling my eyes and taking it in mine.

"If your hand falls off. Don't blame me." I say and Keaton chuckles just as the ride slowly begins to move. "Ohgodohgodohgodohgod!" I begin to mumble.

I look over to the side and wait in excitement as the rollercoaster begins and it doesn't start slow at all. It's at a medium speed as it approaches what doesn't even look like a tall slope. I'm squealing and my stomach waits in anticipation. It climbs up and we're at the tip and a speaker on the coaster somewhere decides to yell out an "ARE YOU READY?".

Which you don't have the time to react to.

The coaster all of a sudden speeds down the rails and I squeal in joy and laugh at the bursting feeling of elation cooursing through me.

"Ohmygodohmygodohmygod!" I mutter and I hear Keaton laugh as I squeeze his hand.

I giggle to myself as the coaster turns and twists around and the wind whips at my face.

"Best first date ever!" I shouted and Keaton looks over at me with a wide and proud smile on his face.

"Glad to hear it!" He shouts back just as the coaster decides to go down again and I scream in excitement. Keaton's hand grips mine tightly when we go down another steep hill and I grip it back as I laugh uncontrollably.

The coaster then slows and decides to go up an even higher slope. I look at the view and gawk. The bay is spread right out in front of us and the setting sun is making all the buildings glitter. I can see the Statue of Liberty off in the distance and I giggle when the rollercoaster stops again to signal another drop.

"Woohoo!" I scream just as we fall down and go in a series of rough twists in turns that make my voice jump up and down. Keaton shouts in joy as well and he lets go of my hand as he holds his hands up, he looks at me with a face that says do it. And I do.

I raise my arms as high as I can and scream until the ride finally slows down and I'm a jumble of giggles.

"Fun right?" Keaton asks and I still giggle, tears prick at my eyes and wipe them away gently with my fingers.

"No shït!" I answer excitedly. Keaton laughs at my enthusiasm. "How many more of these do we have?" I asked as the seatbelt thingies lifted.

"Four. Including one of those things." Keaton says as he points to a tall structure where people are raised up to the top, dangling their feet, and all of a sudden are dropped at different points, brought up again and repeated. I grin and the exciting feeling climbs back into my stomach again.

"Sounds like an amazing plan. Let's go." I say with a wide smile as Keaton gets off and I follow his lead.

Keaton and I are a giggling mess by the end of it. We had gotten into all four rides and somehow our stomachs were still able to handle it.

"I can't believe we're still standing." Keaton says as we sit down on a park bench.

"I can't believe we're not puking all over the place." I say with a laugh. "If you wanna bring me out on another one of these dates, I'll go, no questions asked."

"You've got a strong stomach, you know that?"

"I do now." I say with a giggle as I pick at the popcorn we'd gotten. Keaton looks up at the purple sky, the rides don't take too long, so it wasn't surprising when the sun still had a few rays out.

But I'm pretty sure it'd get dark any second now. Keaton totally zones out on me and I take a piece of popcorn and throw it at his face.

"Hello?" I asked and Keaton looks over at me. "Where are we off to next?" I asked.

"You mean you're expecting more?" Keaton asks and I flush in embarrassment.

"Oh."

"I'm kidding, we have dinner at a small place and then I'm bringing you over to a party." Keaton says.

Oh.

"Who's party?" I asked.

"A friend of mine's. Don't worry, he's a cool guy."

That's what Jenny meant. I thought to myself. I take a deep breath and let it out while I move my feet around in the air. I look at my shoes and smirk, I have a certain obsession with pretty shoes. And I haven't tripped once. Miracle. I know.

"Do you wanna go, now?" Keaton asks and I nod.

"Yup." I say with a smile. He offers his hand and I'm used to it by now.

*

"You know, when you said dinner at a small place I pictured tiny rustic restaurant in the corner." I said. "Not fancy pants dinner with French names I can't even pronounce." Keaton laughs in amusement and I bite my bottom lip in frustration.

"It is small, Darcy."

"Yeah, maybe because of the price on these things. Isn't that just mushroom soup? How is that 15 bucks? I could buy a full meal down the street with that." I say as I fold my arms over my chest.

"You could pay for a trip to Europe with what you're wearing sweetie." Keaton says. I was used to his endearments by now.

"Yeah, I know." I say. My whole wardrobe is worth more than what my dad used to earn a year.

I sipped from the fancy champagne glass that Keaton had ordered for us. It was filled with sweet and not overbearing champagne- to be honest, it tasted like fancy alcoholic soda.

Don't ask me what it's even called. I don't think I'll ever be able to pronounce or even spell that right. The moment Keaton came into the restaurant, a waiter had immediately come to bring us to a window seat table, given us drinks, and walked off. I only knew what I was eating based off of a small piece of fancy paper that held a list of French food. There was a menu placed beside me and I skimmed through what I was having and gawked at the prices.

"If you're uncomfortable with the place, say so, we can move if you want." Keaton says. I look up at him and see that he's trying to figure out what I'm thinking.

I shake my head and sigh.

"The food's already cooking and I know this menu didn't make itself." I say, giving him a smile. "But we could seriously just eat at IHOP and I would be totally be good with that. Or Chili's. Chili's is a win-win for me."

"I'll keep that in mind for our next date." I arch a brow at that.

"What makes you think there's a next date?" I asked, amused.

"I don't know, I know." Keaton says as he picks up his glass and drinks from it.

The waiter from earlier comes back and brings us two bowls of soup. I feel my stomach grumble and my mouth waters at the smell.

"What are you waiting for?" Keaton asks and I roll my eyes.

"What are you waiting for?" I repeat and Keaton smirks before lifting his spoon and I do the same.

The rest of our dinner was spent on snarky comments and little conversations about the rides earlier. There really wasn't much of a variety in our topics but hey, I didn't mind. Keaton didn't make anything feel awkward at all. Except for that one time he decided to just stare at me as I devoured dessert. That was pretty freaking awkward. Keaton was actually pretty funny company. Especially since we both wouldn't stop answering each other with sarcasm.

"Are you still good to go?" Keaton asks, his voice actually having some tone of concern. I giggle at him.

"Yeah." I say. Keaton had already brought us into his car and we were on the way to his friend's house party.

"Can you handle alcohol well?" Keaton asks and I nod.

"I'll have you know I was the only one still standing sober- and yes, I did drink as much as my classmates... well not as much as this one guy- but let's face it, there's always that one douchebag that shows off how much he can or really can't drink." I say. Said guy actually puked outside and I had to pat him, give him water, and make him stay outside so that he wouldn't die of dehydration.

"You'll meet a lot of those guys later. So stay close." He says and I roll my eyes.

"How am I supposed to have fun if I have to stay close to you?" I asked, jokingly, but Keaton's face doesn't turn up with a smile.

"Maybe I should just bring you home." Keaton says and I sigh.

"Up to you. I'm just tagging along so that I can have my phone back."

"Whatever." Keaton says, probably finalizing his decision. "We're here." I nod as Keaton opens the door and I step out as well.

There's a large party going on in this mansion. And I mean mansion. It had a big fountain at the center, party streamers and cups lay everywhere, and the whole place was vibrating with the loud songs playing from the inside. I swallowed a dry lump in my throat. Can't back out now... My subconscious warns.

"You okay?" Keaton asks as he noticed me gawking.

"Y-yeah. Sure. Not intimidated or anything by the giant house in front of me." I say, sweet sarcasm coating my voice.

"Come on, then." Keaton says, this time, he doesn't offer his hand.

Not that I wanted to hold it or anything. But... there was a look in his eyes that made him seem a lot guarded. Like he really didn't want to look like he was involved with me- or anyone for that matter. It made him look... cold. He starts walking off to the large front door, and I hear the car door open behind me. The driver, Greg, comes out and hands me my phone. I look at him questioningly.

"Please. Call when you require a ride home. I will wait for you both right here." Greg says and he flashes me a kind smile.

"Thanks. Did Keaton...?" I asked.

"Yes. My phone number and his are on your phone. It should be the last call you received." Greg says and I nod.

"Alright. Wish me luck, then." I say and Greg nods as I dismiss myself.

Keaton was already nowhere to be found as I made my way through the doors. That probably marked the end of this 'date'. Let's get straight to the point then.

This place was as trashed as it could be. There were people making out in every corner, drinks spilt on the floor, music banging the entire place which made, what would have looked like pretty chandeliers, into precarious death wishes that could fall on your face and kill you. Okay, I'm exaggerating. But the amount of people in here suffocated me. I had to push past couples making out by the walls, walk through dancers, and eventually I reached an open area where the cold air cooled me down. The outside was no better though.

The music blasted loudly through giant speakers, steam rose from the big heated pool, shirtless men and women were walking about, drinks were served in every corner. I spotted Keaton sitting down by a group of people that looked to be the same age as him. I groaned when I saw how skanky the girl sitting with them looked. I bit my bottom lip and grabbed a shot glass from a waiter walking by. Daddy always said not to drink if you didn't see it come out from the bottle. I thought to myself. Then again, daddy lost his daughter when he made mommy cry. I dunked the contents of that glass down my throat, loving and hating that burning sensation that travels down my body.

With whatever courage I somehow mustered, I walked up to Keaton's little group.

"Oh look, it's the princess from that other night." A girl, the skank, says. She was wearing what could have been a red bathing suit, if it didn't look so... fragile.

"Yup. Tch. That's me." I answer with a smile.

"You've got serious guts coming up here." One guy says, he has a cap on covering his blonde hair and he's wearing a white tank over a pair of shorts.

"And you have a stick up your ass." I say, rolling my eyes. I look over at Keaton, who's only looking at me in amusement. "Do you have a staring problem?" I asked him, sharply.

"Nope. Just enjoying the sass." He says. "Considering I took her out on her first date a few minutes ago." The group chuckles.

"She's a sucker, isn't she?" The same douchebag says and I roll my eyes.

"Yeah, yeah. Thanks for the newsflash." I say with a sigh, I turn back to Keaton and groan. "Let me guess, ultimate deal of 'Hey, let's take the new girl out and make her miserable', right?" I asked.

Keaton rolls his eyes.

"I was just having fun, weren't you?" Keaton mutters.

"Yeah, sure. Go have fun ässhole." I snap before turning on my heels and walking away. "So much for a great first date..." I mumble before pushing past through the packed amount of people again.

I soon find myself back at the entrance and I groan as I push the doors open to the cool night air. This time, the sounds were muted, and I could actually hear myself breathe. I wasn't one to chase or pine after some guy after a first date. Hell, after my dad? I didn't really want to pine after anyone. Screw that. I'm not chasing some guy who thinks he has me in his pocket because of a date. I'm not chasing anyone for anything ever again.

I open up my phone and see a few messages from Klein.

Hey! Good morning :D

How was your day???

I guess you're probably really busy, huh? I'll bother you later. ~Klein.

I sighed to myself, I had yet to even face Lawrence after what happened. I barely had time to process that that happened. I took a deep breath and sighed. I seemed to sigh a lot more often lately. I groaned before deciding that I might as well have some fun while I'm here. I didn't have to go to where Keaton and his dickface friends were.

"Let's have some fun." I mutter to myself before quickly making my way inside.

I may not usually be one to party. But hey, no one knew me here. What could possibly go wrong?

I grabbed another drink that was being served around and sipped at it as I made my way through the vibrating rooms. I soon found one that almost looked like a mini rave party. The music blasted the loudest in here and I laughed as the alcohol began traveling through my body. I jumped about and danced in probably what looked like the crappiest dance ever. But whatever, the neon lights and the fog machine should be covering that up anyways.

I think I'd had about 10 drinks. Not counting shots. And.. I was somehow still standing- you see, I wasn't lying when I said that my tolerance was high. I had danced with just about everyone in the room by then. I even made a few "drunk" friends. If they even remembered me in the morning. When I finally had enough dancing all over the place, I decided to make my way out again. That room was way too hot for comfort- that, and people also started making out everywhere.

"Hey." Someone greeted behind me, I was in the foyer and the large empty space was really peaceful. I turned and found a fairly cute guy smiling at me.

He had brown hair that was a bit shaggy, amber eyes, and cute dimpled cheeks as he grinned at me. In his hands were two plain shots.

"Hi." I greeted simply, he raises the shot glasses and I roll my eyes as I take one from him.

"Not a party person?" He asks and I roll my eyes.

"I was legit in the rave room for a few minutes." I say with a smile. "If I'm not covered in sweat, I'd freak out." I mutter, he laughs and throws me a cute smile.

"The name's Hunter." He says.

"Darcy." I reply with a smirk. We stand around awkwardly for a few seconds before he breaks the silence.

"So... are we just gonna stand around with these drinks in our hands or are we gonna drink them?" He asks and I roll my eyes. Rule number 1 of drinking: never take any drinks from strangers.

"Bad idea, Darcy." Keaton says as he comes into view behind Hunter.

"Yeah, yeah. I've heard the lecture before, Keaton." I say with a sigh as I place the shot glass on a fancy looking decorative table. Keaton doesn't smile and Hunter smirks at me before turning his head.

"Look who finally found his date. Tell me, Keaton, how many girls did you make out with before you even got back to her?" Hunter says and I look at Keaton. "Can't even count huh." Hunter adds with a snicker.

"Get away from him, Darcy." Keaton says, a dark look on his face. I look to the side in confusion.

"Sure thing, bossy-pants." I mutter before walking off, but Hunter grabs my wrist, and pulls me so that I'm in his arms. "Uh..."

"You don't have to listen to him." Hunter says.

"Uh... I won't listen if you let me go." I say with a sigh. Hunter blinks his eyes at me, which are actually pretty close up. "Are you expecting a kiss or something? Let go, bruh." I say, pushing away from him until he loosens his grip.

"Jesus, what is up with you people and touching me?" I hiss before getting away and sighing. The two of them look at me and I groan. "Whatever. I'm not going to get in the middle of a stupid testosterone fight, you two can sort your shit out."

"Darcy-" Keaton calls but I hold hand up.

"I get it. You wanted a date, a fun one, a little play, fine. Whatever, you got it. I'm going home." I say with a sigh before I pulled out my phone and began walking off.

Whatever he had to say, could go right back up his stuck up äss.

"Darcy, come on." Keaton said, chasing after me.

"Keaton, I don't do this. This? This party, that date, whatever. I don't need these things. I just wanna graduate in peace, go to school in peace. I won't chase after you thinking that date meant anything, okay? Just, I don't know, leave me alone." I say and he decides not to talk as I walk away and call his driver.

Greg picks up in no time and I sigh as I make my way outside and take one last look back at the party mansion. Keaton's at the door, looking over at me. Not having my glasses makes it hard for me to see his expression. So when Greg comes up with the car, I shoot him one last smile before getting inside.

"Take me home, please." I say and Greg asks no questions as we pull away.

# Chapter 12

U known POV

"You're a real son of a bïtch you know that?" Lawrence shouts at Keaton.

"Excuse me? I'm just trying to get gold here." Keaton says, the smirk hinting at his eyes.

"Will both of you shut up?!" I shout.

"Oh please, as if you aren't trying to get her too. Mr. A? Really?" Keaton says.

"I'm trying to be nice to an innocent girl we brought into this mess." I say.

"We didn't do anything. Blame the old man for this mess."

"Yeah, well try not to screw with her head. We have our ways and you all know she has to take a pick."

"She won't pick the stranger. There's no chance she would ever pick the stranger one her phone."

"And she definitely won't pick you, you son of a-"

"Could the two of you calm down?! If I could take her away from the two of you, my life would be so much easier."

"Whoa, whoa. Are you actually falling for her?"

"I didn't say that. She's just a girl and we're all pursuing her whether we like it or not, because of a stupid bounty set on her head."

"That bounty is the entire company. No offense, brother, but I could care less about using her."

"He's insane." Lawrence says and I roll my eyes at the two of them quarreling. My phone buzzes in my hand and I look at the dimmed screen.

Sorry about not answering yesterday. Got suckered into a date with an annoying person. Pls. tell me that Keaton Carter isn't you, if you don't mind. If you are... I might just commit suicide. -Darcy

I smirk at her message.

"She'd adore me if she met me." I said. "And I would take care of her."

"Yeah, right." My brother scoffs. "If she met you, she'd probably use you."

"Don't be such a pessimist brother." I say before typing up a reply. "I think she'd love me."

"Yeah, for your face value." Keaton butts in and I roll my eyes.

"I'm leaving. You two can sort your shït out together." I say before smiling down at the fast response on my phone, and walking out on the two of them.

Darcy's POV

The day I become Keaton Carter is the day I die. :) Klein messages me. I giggle as I suck eat a forkful of cheesecake. Martin, Clara, and I had spent the entire day at Pavelton and we wanted a break from all the lectures. So we went to the same cafe where Martin met Erik.

"So... let me get this damn straight..." Martin says, bringing me out of my wonderful conversation with Klein. "Keaton Carter, hot douchebag wonder, took you out on a date only to ditch you because of a party?" I nod my head and Clara sips her coffee silently.

"Yes. That is indeed what happened." I say before picking up my coffee. "He's a serious douche."

"No kidding." Clara says with a sigh. "Ugh, but you at least had a date with one of the hottest dudes on campus."

"And you got invited into one of the biggest parties." Martin adds and I roll my eyes.

We were back in the same café and unfortunately, Martin's boywonder wasn't there.

"So... how was your day yesterday guys?" I asked, trying to completely change the subject.

"I spent the day with Erik." Martin says with a smirk on his face.

"No. Way." I blurt and Martin laughs as both Clara and I give each other shocked looks.

"He's hooked like a fish." Clara points out.

"Uh huh." I say in agreement. My phone buzzes again and I look at the screen.

Are you hanging out with friends today? I reply with a quick 'yeah'.

"But for real, how is he?" Clara asks with a smile.

"He is... sweet. We like most of the same stuff, except for his movies, I mean I like horror, but not 'Texas Chainsaw' horror... Sucks that he can't be here today, he said he had a group project to do..." Martin explains and I giggle.

"Our Martin is growing up so fast." Clara says and I laugh at her as I sip my coffee.

"I swear, soon we'll be having mini-Martins." I say and Clara laughs with me as we share a high-five. Martin rolls his eyes at us.

"What's so funny?" A familiar voice asks from beside us.

We all look and stare at the source blankly.

"Whoa. Did it just get colder in here or what?" Keaton asks.

"It just got ice cold." Clara says and I mentally groan.

"What do you want, Keaton?" Martin asks.

"Just wanted to see if Darcy's okay. I mean she had so many drinks last night- I was surprised how she could still stand." Keaton says with a smug grin.

"What part of 'Leave me alone', did you not understand?" I ask harshly.

"Ouch, after that date yesterday? You break my heart." He says.

"Sucks for you then." I answer. "Do you guys mind if we switch locations now? We can chill at the house. I know you guys wanted to come over." I suggest.

"Yeah, sure." Martin and Clara say, almost simultaneously. We all stand up and Keaton makes 'tsk'-ing noises.

"You forget, I know where you live."

"And you forget, I don't give a single shït." I hiss before we all walk out of the place.

"Ugh! He's so annoying!" I say as we enter the apartment.

"No kidding. He's a persistent little shït, isn't he?" Martin says as he closes the door behind him.

"At least he's pleasing to the eyes, you know?" Clara says, always the optimistic one.

I giggle as Martin nudges her with his shoulder. Clara scrunches up her nose and we make our way to the couches.

"This place is freaking awesome." Clara exclaims as she looks around.

No sooner did she sit down on the couch did she get up and walk over to the windows.

"Ugh... the view..." Clara says with a sigh. I smile as Martin takes pictures of the view outside of our window.

"Penthouse. Sweet." Martin says with a smirk. I roll my eyes at him before we all sit down.

We spend almost the entire afternoon together before Martin and Clara decided to head home.

I walked over to the fridge and brought out a tiny carton of Almond milk. I pop the cap and drink it down with a sigh. I loved ranting and talking about everything with my friends and all, but now that I was alone, I felt super bored. I just feel like I spent all of my time and energy on talking. I was only happy that I was dressed so plainly. A comfy sweater, a pair of black leggings, comfy espadrilles, my usual bonnet with cute bear ears on top, and I wore some cute Beats headphones that I found in the closet too. Klein has good tastes- well- expensive tastes...

"You okay?" Lawrence's voice says from directly behind me and I jump at the sound of it.

"Holymotheroffreaking- please don't do that." I say with a sigh as I turned around. Lawrence laughs, he was wearing a loose navy blue sweater over a pair of khaki shorts.

"You spaced out in front of the fridge, what else was I supposed to do?"

"Tap me on the shoulder?" I suggest and he smirks at me.

"Whatever. How was your day?" He asks, as I make my way to the dining table.

"Good. I brought Martin and Clara over. Seeing as someone who irritates the absolute hell out of me showed up at our hangout." I say as I lean over the table.

"Keaton Carter?" Lawrence asks with a chuckle.

"Uh huh. The usual. Anyways, how was your day, Mr. Lawrence?" I ask.

"Good." Lawrence says as he sits in front of me with a bag of chips in his hands. My phone makes a tweeting sound before I look down. Huh. First time it isn't on plain old vibrate huh.

Are you in the mood for a party? I smile...

Wait.

What.

I look over at Lawrence and find him sighing as he flips through a tiny magazine. I look down at my phone and type in a reply.

What kind of party? I asked and I watched Lawrence.

Not a Keaton Carter party for sure. ;)

Lawrence hasn't even budged to touch his phone.

"Crap..." I muttered and Lawrence looks up at me.

"Huh?"

"I just realized I have somewhere to go tonight. You mind eating dinner alone again?" I asked and Lawrence shakes his head.

"I have somewhere to go tonight too. Guess we're both busy, huh?"

"I guess so." I say as I look to the side.

But he freaking kissed me. What is wrong with the world?! I thought I was close to figuring out who Klein was too... Damn it.

Holly will pick you up in 5. Gotta get you dolled up for it, you know? ;) I look down at my phone and sigh.

Guess it's a fancy kinda party :P I message.

Fancy parties make for fun introductions, don't you think?

....Huh? My eyes widen at my phone and I quickly type a reply.

Will I finally get to meet you, then? I asked, my heart pounded hard against my chest as I anxiously waited for his answer.

Yes

I held my breath. Was I really going to meet him tonight? I mean yeah, he said so... But what if he's... I don't know... Some sort of creep? Well... I know that's not true. He's been so nice to me. But... someone's words on a phone is nothing compared to who they are in real life... Especially in situations like mine.

I hear a loud noise at the door. Holly.

"You know, next time you're invited to a party, tell me a day before, please? It's hard to get a hold of a good stylist that isn't a relative." Holly says with a sigh. "Hey Lawrence."

"Hi." Lawrence greets.

"Come on, chica, let's go get you glammed up." Holly says, hooking her arm in mine.

Holly looked really casual today. She only wore a white T-shirt over a pair of blue jeans and she topped it off with bright red lipstick, golden flats, and a pair of shades that rested like a headband on her head.

"I'm getting really tired of all this dress-up..." I mumble just as Holly pulls me away.

Everything moved in such a flash, that I can barely even contemplate what was going on.

Holly pushed me into a fancy looking studio with black and white decorations everywhere. I swear, three women just came up to me, all of them in this black jumpsuit kind of uniform, and they uh... stripped me bare, gave me a silky red robe, and threw a series of underwear and gowns at me before Holly stepped in wearing the same robe... Except she had a hanger with a beautiful deep violet dress with silver flowers emebellished onto the sides. Holly smirked as she looked through the hangers of clothes that were supposedly laid out for me.

"Hmm... are you in for white and gold or black and gold?" Holly asks me and I groan. "I thought they were your colors." She adds with a look of concern.

"Now white and gold. Brings terrible memories of yesterday." I say and Holly nods her head.

"Tell me all about yesterday while we pick out some gowns... Are you in for classic red or more on the colorful side?" She asks and I bite my bottom lip.

"Next to black and white, I'd love a nice blue dress." I say with a shrug. "No red. Ugh. I hate the attention it grabs." I mutter.

"Gotcha. No red. Blue." Holly says as she skims through the racks. "Considering how much time I really do want to spend on you... Let's go with a quick decision then."

Holly grabs three hangers and displays them on golden hooks in front of me. The dressing room was glorious. I mean, I loved every aspect of it. The modernesque chandelier, chill techno music, sleek black leather couches, classic white tiles, and clean racks of clothes.

"Ugh, this place is style heaven." I blurt and Holly chuckles.

"I knew you'd like this place. I went here when my cousin wanted to get gowns for a charity event. Trust me, it's the best place for gown-shopping." Holly says with a smile. "You never take that bracelet off, huh."

"Nope." I say as I look at my right wrist where the golden bracelet with the heart was. I loved it too much, it was Klein's first gift to me. "It was a sweet gift." I say.

"My cousin's gift, right?" Holly asks and I nod.

"Mhmm." I mumble.

"Which one, bro." Holly asks and I grin at her before looking at the three dresses hung in front of me.

I walked towards them and ran my hands through the fabric. I was relieved that they weren't made of chiffon... I hate the stuff. Well, I like it, when used appropriately. I looked at a sleek pale blue dress and how it had sheer cloth on top to make the jeweled embellishments look like they were on my skin. But I didn't feel comfortable with how... "tight" it looked. I looked over at the second dress, it was a sleek pale blush dress. It was your usual high-low skirt and it had a cute ribbon that went just below the chest area... But it cut short in front, the back was non-existent, and the chest area was bedazzled with gems. Not exactly something that I would wear.

But... the last dress was definitely the one.

It was a plain blue draped dress, strapless with a sweetheart neckline... or something like that. I don't really know what those are called, whatever. The back was fine and the cloth felt majestic, like it was silken and it looked so comfortable.

"This one's it." I say with a smile.

"I knew you'd like that one. I just wanted to see if you'd ever pick something with embellishments like that." Holly says and I roll my eyes.

"I would wear something with glittery stuff, if I was going to something that needed all the sparkles. But I love my plain and simple." I say with a shrug.

"Well, sucks for you, the dress may be plain, but the accessories the stylist had for that, are gorgeous."

"I'm fine with accesories." I say. "I love accessorizing."

"Well, I hope you love gold." She says with a smile.

"Whatever matches best." I answer and she smirks at me.

"Alright then, now that the dress is picked, let's get you over to hair and makeup." Holly says. "Well, let's get both of our ässes over there." Holly says with a smile.

I grin at her before we open the door of the dressing room and Holly leads me over past several rooms into an even larger studio... well, parlor.

"Oh gosh." I say as I see all the blonde, pink, aqua, hair and highlights.

"Impressive right?" Holly asks and I nod.

The mirrors were all lined with pretty large bulbs. The place was actually pretty packed, but the music was calming and there was only small soft conversations going on. The vibe of the place was soothing. The floor was a diamond black and white tiled one, the ceiling had studio lights, and the chairs looked nice and comfy. One of the workers, who was a guy with platinum blonde hair, smiled at us and made his way to us.

"Ms. Carter and Ms. Bleu?" He asks and we both nod.

"Yup." Holly says with a smile.

"My name is Gail. Please, come this way. Sir Klein told us to only give you hair and makeup, unless you both want to have any extra treatments done, he says he leaves the choice to you both." The man, Gail, says.

"Fancy." I whisper to Holly and she smirks at me.

I'll spare the boring details of Holly and I talking to each other about boring things like school and how New York is like. I will however dicuss Holly's fantabulous outfit. She wore her violet dress which hugged every slim curve of her body. It draped nicely and had soft embellishments on the side and her short hair was curled and the hairdresser made it look like it was in an elegant bun. Her lips were glossed and her eyes were darkly rimmed with eyeliner and sparkly silver eyeshadow.

"You look amazing." Holly tells me and I roll my eyes.

"If I look amazing then you look like a freaking goddess." I say and Holly squints her eyes at me.

"I am not playing compliments." She says and I smirk.

"You started it."

"I said you look amazing because you do." Holly points out and I grin.

I took a look at myself. My hair was braided in some sort of side half-up do. The bright blue dress was paired with pretty gold accessories and my heels were comfy but tall. My makeup was fairly okay, slightly smokey on the eyes matched with a nude lip. I loved it. I looked elegant in a not-so-overdone kind of way.

"Are we ready to go?" Holly asks me as she hands me a tiny golden clutch. I looked inside and saw my phone along with a few things like perfume and a spare lipstick.

"I guess so." I say with a smile before Holly linked arms with me.

The party, I have to say, is intensely fancy.

Think glamorous elegant party with fancy violin music in the backgro und... in a penthouse suite.

Yup.

I feel like I got thrown into the world of the rich and famous. Everyone looked so refined and posh... The floors were made of cream and gold stone tiles, chandeliers hung on the high ceilings and paintings of pretty little angels decorated them. Champagne was being passed around endlessly and dinner was to be served in a bit. Holly and I walked around together, she greeted a few people here and there and even managed to introduce me to people who were introduced as CEO's, or the wife of the managing partner at blah blah blah... To which I nodded and smiled and shook their hands.

I was more pre-occupied with trying to spot Klein. Not that I had any clue who he was... But I felt more nervous about meeting him than meeting these important rich guys.

"Ms. Bleu?" A deep voice called from behind us. Holly turned first and she immediately grinned.

"Uncle Gerald!" She greeted, giving him a kiss on the cheek.

The man was old, his hair was grey and slicked back, his eyes were amber and he wore a crisp black suit. The man radiated with confidence and power. His eyes even hinted at a glint of mischief... He was probably around 60 or so and he grinned at me with a kind smile.

"Holly! You've gotten taller, my dear." He greets and Holly smiles.

"It's the heels, uncle." She says and I stare at them. Holly looks at me and grins. "Oh yeah, uncle, as you know, this is Darcy Bleu." She says and he sends me a kind smile.

"Enjoying yourself?" He asks me and I nod shyly.

"Yes, sir." I say, trying to sound cheery.

"Please, Uncle will be fine." He says and I smile.

"Uncle it is, then." He grins at me and it's contagious.

"I'm sure you're well aware of the strange situation you've been put in, so far, I hope you haven't come face to face with any strange proposals from random men."

"Huh?" I gave him a confused look. Instead, he grins and gives Holly a dismissive nod, she squeezed my hand quickly before disappearing.

"Ms. Bleu, please follow me." Gerald says and I nod as he offers his arm. I take it and he walks me out of the ballroom and into a large and dimly lit office.

There was a lit fireplace, three arm chairs, and a desk with an revolving black leather chair with a large back on it. Gerald leads me to it and makes me sits down. He then turns the chair so that I face the back of the room where the fireplace was lit.

"What are we-" I begin but Gerald holds a finger up to his lips.

"Xavier told me you were unaware of the engagement. I'm sorry if I caused you any trouble." He says and I stare at him.

"It's... alright. I'm dealing with the situation somehow. It really isn't that bad. Klein's been pretty good to me." I say with a shrug and Gerald looks at me.

"Klein?" He asks.

"...Yeah? Isn't he my fiancé?" I asked and Gerald pauses before chuckling.

"Klein, as you know him, is a candidate."

"Candidate for what?" I asked, confused.

"You know what, why don't you... have some wine." Gerald says, changing the subject. Before I can even protest, considering I hate wine and I am also underage..., Gerald walks away and pours a small glass of white sparkling wine. "I know you're underage, my dear, so this is really more like a soda than wine, but it'll do right?" He asks kindly and I nod.

Gerald hands me the sleek wine glass and I take a sip. It tastes like sweet peaches and I cross my left leg over my right.

"Carter-Pavel is a strange company. We never simply pass on the company from son to son." Gerald begins and I nod my head, he gives me an encouraging smile before moving on. "Every year, there are three candidates officially selected. We mean officially because so long as any member of this incorporation- provided they're of a good enough position- tries to win, they can. But they'd have to have my approval first."

"Huh?" I asked. What's he going on about now?

"The three candidates I've selected are people, I am sure, you have met... somewhat. In Klein's case, he prefers his own method of meeting you." Gerald says and I squint my eyes at him. "...Everything will be clearer in a few minutes. I suggest you remain silent as I deal with the three. I want you present, but unknown. You understand?" He asks in a kind tone. I nodded my head.

"I met my wife this way. I didn't plan on becoming the company's CEO, but it all worked itself out. You get the choice here, my dear. There isn't a forceful way of going about it. If you really are unhappy with the situation, you may contact me through Holly." Gerald says and I nod my head, trying to wrap my head around it all.

So... what he's saying is the engagement isn't exactly limited to Klein... It's three candidates... I think to myself. Why do I get this damned feeling that I know the other two already.

"If you're going to call me over, try getting someone hotter, Holly barely makes the cut." I hear Keaton's voice say.

"She's your cousin, Keaton." Gerald says with an exasperated sigh. He glances at me and I mentally groan. Why him?

"Keaton, you really need to grow up." Another familiar voice says.

"Lawrence. Glad you could make it." Gerald says with a smile and I bite my bottom lip.

What happened to having a girlfriend?!

"How's your fake girlfriend, bro?" Keaton says and I can already sense the smirk on his face.

"Stop glaring at each other." Gerald says in an almost angry tone. I hear the two of them sigh before I hear the couches make plumped sounds.

That makes two seated candidates.

"I suspect you interrupted my business for something important." Another voice says, this one unfamiliar. I gasp and cover my mouth, hopefully keeping silent.

"Nice of you to make it douchebag." Keaton's voice says and I bite my bottom lip.

"Thanks brother." ...Klein says.

"Don't start a fight now boys." Gerald says. "Archer, I don't want to hear anything about business. I know for a fact that you invited Darcy Bleu here. Holly told me, herself."

I think I'm going to faint.

# Chapter 13

"Well, these two have already met her up close, I figured I would try to meet her, at a distance, of course." Klein says- or really- Archer says. I really wanted to take a peek but... Gerald did tell me not to and I'm sure he's trying to be the good guy here.

Archer's got a deep and soothing voice. Guess that's because I'm a bit biased. He did sweet talk me over the phone.

"Stop trying to fix your suit and sit down." Keaton says. "You look way too stiff."

"You invited her?" Lawrence asks. "Where is she then?"

"Lawrence, quit whining, she's out there somewhere." Keaton says, in an annoyed tone.

"I need all of you to keep quiet!" Gerald shouts. I stiffen at the anger in his voice and he briefly looks over at me.

I watch as Gerald walks over to my chair and places a hand on the top. I was completely hidden behind the tall back of this chair, I just had to stay still.

"I chose the three of you for a reason. Don't make me regret that decision. Remember that this isn't all fun and games. There's a real person involved- and if you don't truly cherish her, you lose everything. After all, the moment anyone of you is chosen, she immediately takes hold of more than half of the company. You will have no chance to leave her." Gerald says and I practically gawk at what he says.

What?

"We're all aware." Kle-I mean Archer, says. "I have no intention of using her to get power." I hear someone else chuckle.

"If that were true, you wouldn't be the first to pursue her." Keaton's voice says.

"I don't understand how you were chosen." Lawrence hisses and I hear Keaton snicker.

"It's because he's so good at manipulating people." Archer says.

"It's also because Keaton needs to know what it's like to work for something in order to earn it." Gerald says. "Darcy Bleu isn't one to be easily persuaded. I made sure she wasn't. Keaton, Archer, your mother was one of the most stubborn women I had ever met. Lawrence, your grandmother, I hear, was the same. No one wins over women's hearts without falling for them as well."

"Says you." Keaton mutters and I roll my eyes.

"Could you shut up?" Lawrence asks and I smirk. Lawrence has the most awkward reactions sometimes.

"Why do you keep checking the time?" Gerald asks. I hear someone go "hmph".

"I want to make sure I have enough time to steal my girl from the crowd." Archer says and I hear Gerald chuckle.

"Right, your, girl. You haven't even met her in person." Lawrence says.

"I won't meet her unless this meeting ends." Archer says and the three just end up bickering over each other.

Gerald sighs to himself.

"Am I the only that did not sign up for 'The Bachelorette'?" Keaton says with a huff and I roll my eyes. Yeah, well I didn't either dickhead. I want to say.

"Well, you can always pull out, my brother." Archer's voice says with a hint of amusement. "Lawrence would make better company anyways."

"Shut up." Keaton says and I hear a clap- probably a high five. I stare blankly at my half-full glass of fake wine and take a big sip.

"Have you guys gotten her a ring?" Lawrence's voice asks and I almost spit out my wine. What?

"We can pick one up any time." Keaton says and I hear someone chuckle, probably Archer.

"Is this meeting done, yet? I don't want her to go home." Archer says.

"Wait, do you actually have a ring for her?" Keaton asks and I freeze.

"That is for me to know and for you both to find out."

"Oh shut up, you cocky son of a-" Keaton begins but Gerald clears his throat.

"You may all leave. Considering how you all fight like cats when I put you all together in one room, you are all dismissed. I don't know why I bother." Gerald says and I hear all of them sigh.

"Excuse me, then." Archer says before I hear the door open and close.

"Bye uncle." Lawrence says and then I hear a low grunt before I hear someone else leave too- Keaton.

Which leaves me with an empty glass and Gerald sighing to himself.

"I... I'm so confused right now." I say. Well. Not really confused. Just sort of mind boggled.

I thought I was engaged to one, at least, definite, stranger. Not a "take your pick" sort of thing.

"I am sorry, for not talking to you about this prior to this entire fiasco." Gerald tells me as he walks over to the fire place.

"This is a regular occurrence, though... right?" I asked and Gerald nods his head.

"Of course it is. I met my wife this way." He says with a smile.

"So... why am I here again?" I asked. "I mean, I understand that you wanted to inform me about the whole, as Keaton says, "Bachelorette" thing, but... why do you guys do this weird, uh, ritual, thingy majiggy...?" I asked.

"It's a... humbling way to teach them things. Well, let's say you grew up in a life where you got everything you wanted. Or you grow up like that and knowing that you can gain so much more. That makes most people conceited. We like to think we're killing two birds with one stone here with this little 'ritual'. We get to offer someone a chance to go to university and the next successor, well, 'works' for his position."

"And how do you make sure it's hard 'work'?" I asked. "I mean, I could be some totally flimsy girl who'll fall for Keaton as easily as anyone." I say with a shrug. Gerald gives me a kind smile.

"A smart person knows what's at stake. You're not only choosing who you'll marry, you're choosing the type of person you leave an entire company with. We select a woman not just based on her academic record, we try to get as much history as possible. Average people are easier to investigate- forgive me if I've invaded your privacy... But... You have gone through rough times that I expect- have made you wiser than others."

"But there are others that have problems, problems that could be worse than mine." I reason.

"Perhaps. But the way you dealt with it was quite wonderful, really. You fought your way through school, got up to the top three of your class, and the entire time... no one other than close friends knew what really happened behind closed doors." Gerald says and I bite my bottom lip. I almost wince when I realize I'm scraping the lipstick off of my lips- ew.

"It's not hard to bottle up emotions." I say with a shrug. "With a bit of self-convincing, you can believe that everything is fine even when they aren't."

"And that is why I chose you. You have learned from your problems to deal with it in a way that not most can do. You didn't turn to any vices. I received no report of you doing anything quite 'teen-like'." He says. "No parties, no smoking, no drinking- the only reports I've received of you doing any of those are on the common exceptions. Prom night, farewell parties, so on and so forth."

"That doesn't make me special."

"No, but it makes you strong. Your wrists bear no scars and from every teacher report, I've read, you had no hiccups."

"I really don't want to talk about this." I say, honestly. "Can I... Can I go now?" I asked Gerald with a pleading look, he pauses to analyze me, I probably look like I'm near tears- what he was talking about happened recently. I wasn't over it... not yet, at least.

"Of course my dear. I'm sorry if I brought back any painful memories. I truly am." He says and I nod weakly. I am an emotional freaking wreck. I think to myself before I offer him a kind smile and make my way out of that office.

I hated remembering everything that happened.

Mostly because I convinced myself that it wasn't real. That what I went through wasn't real. So when Gerald told me how strong I was for it all, it cracked my tiny wall. I entered the musical ballroom and sighed to myself. My eyes were beginning to fill with tears that threatened to fall any minute now.

I had to go somewhere. I needed to get some fresh air and just think. I needed to divert my attention onto the situation at hand. That. That would stop the tears.

I slowly made my way to the exit- just so that I could get into the hall and relax. Once I made it there, I sighed to myself and continued walking around aimlessly.

Stop thinking about it Darce. You'll only end up hurting yourself. I think to myself. Ugh...Think about the engagement stuff not the past stuff.

Ugh... right. The engagement stuff. Crap.

Keaton was right, we're all practically in 'The Bachelorette'. I feel like screaming in frustration- except this place wasn't exactly the right location to do it. I groan as I take a left turn, followed by a right, and then a left.... and then uh... Where the hell am I?

"Oh no." I mumble. Fück. "I can not be lost right now." I mutter in frustration.

"Ms. Darcy Bleu?" A girl's voice says from behind me. I jump at the sound of it and whirl around to face the source.

It's a young woman dressed in an all black sort of suit. She looks slightly older than me and has a set of neatly trimmed brown bangs and she's tied her hair up in a high ponytail. She has a kind smile on her face which makes me smile as well.

"Oh gosh, you scared the crap out of me." I say with a sigh. "How do you know my name?" I asked.

"Mr. Klein informed me. I'm his secretary, Nancy." She says and I smile.

"Nice to meet you." I say, not knowing how else to react.

"Mr. Klein is waiting for you in Room 2109, I'm here to escort you there." Nancy says.

"Okay..." I say, unsure, I mean, I heard him a while ago- but I wasn't sure if I was ready to meet him just yet. She smiles at me and motions for me to follow her.

"Uh... I was just wondering- how did you even find me?" I asked as I followed behind Nancy.

"I noticed you walk out of the party a few moments ago. You seemed to be in distress. Was there anything that bothered you?" She asks formally.

"Not really... I just remembered something sad and I needed to get over it." I explain. She nods her head before stopping at the end of the hall.

"Here we are, Ms. Bleu. Do you need any help coming back?" She asks me and I nod my head shyly. "Well, I will be waiting at the corner for you then. Enjoy." Nancy says with a large smile before she opens the door for me and I make my way inside.

It's colder in here and dimly lit. I almost shiver when I feel how cold it is in comparison to the other ballroom. Geez. I hear the soft familiar song of "Lay Me Down" by Sam Smith play. As I continue walking, I spot a lone tall table that holds a black metal filigree mask that I smile at. I pick it up and place it around my head, trying to carefully tie it without ruining my hair. Once I finish tying it, I catch my reflection on a small mirror on the table where a small note lies.

If I remain a stranger, would it be okay? - Klein

I smirk at it before I hear footsteps behind me. My heart pounds against my chest- but it's not really from fear- I don't know... I somehow know who it is already. I turn around and there's a finely dressed man only a few feet away from me. His eyes are the first thing to catch my attention, they're green with a tinge of yellow near his pupils. He's wearing a black mask that covers the upper half of his face, which matches with his entirely black attire. His brown hair is slightly tousled and I find that he has a strong chiseled jaw and dimples that I can barely see. Woo.

"Ms. Bleu?" He greets with a wide smile on his face.

"Mr. A?" I asked with a grin of my own. "Or would you prefer Klein?"

"Archer sounds better." He says with a shrug and I smile at him.

There was just something about him that clicked. He had a warm and friendly feeling that radiated from him. That, or maybe his letters and sweet gestures were getting to me. But I can't say I didn't love his well, "approach". Then again he's part of the whole Bachelorette thing... A bad thought tries to creep up my brain and I immediately shake it off.

"Archer huh." I say as I fold my arms over my chest.

"Were you expecting a different name behind Mr. A?" He asks with a smirk on his face and I laugh.He offers me his hand and I willingly take it.

"Shall we dance, milady?" He asks and I giggle at the sweet gesture.

"Do I have a choice?" I asked and Klein-well Archer, now I guess, smirks at me.

"You do, but I'd be happier if you let me have a dance." Archer says and I roll my eyes before letting him take me into a soft dance.

It's only then that I realize how much space this room has. It's practically a ballroom of its own.

"How was the party?" Klein- Archer asks. Damn it. This guy needs to stop changing names!

"Good, I was getting slightly bored though." I say with a shrug. "You should've shown up sooner." I say with a smile as he chuckles and places his hands at the small of my back. I wrap my arms around his neck- thank God heels helped me reach him.

He stands a foot above me and I groan at how tall he is.

"What's wrong?" He asks.

"You're too tall." I say, pouting, and he laughs as he begins to sway us around the room.

"And you're adorably small." He says, smiling down at me and I squint my eyes at him.

"Shut up." I say with a huff.

"You're wearing the bracelet." Archer says as he glances at my wrist. I nod and he lifts his hand and takes one of mine so that we're in a real dancing position- you know- the type those princess characters do.

"I've worn it every day since you've given it to me." I say proudly. He gives me a smile and tilts my head upwards and I giggle as he attempts to lead me around.

I look down at our feet and giggle as I try to step away from his feet. Archer laughs at my attempts and we move round and around like this.

"I'm surprised we haven't stepped on each other yet." He says and I laugh.

"It'll happen." I say with a shrug. I look up and I find Archer's gaze staring deep into my eyes, I feel a warmth climb up my face before I look away and Archer separates me from him.

He twirls our hands so that I turn and he takes me against his chest. He smells of vanilla and I giggle as he rests his head slightly on top of mine as we sway.

"You're such a romantic." I comment.

"And you smell like roses." He says before he turns me so that we're facing each other again.

"Do you promise not to change your name anymore? It's starting to confuse me." I say with a pout and he laughs as he nods.

"I promise. My name is Archer Klein Carter."

"Darcy Bleu, nice to finally meet you." I say with a wink before the music ends and we bow to each other. I laugh and he follows as he offers his hand to me.

I take it and grin as he brings me to his chest. Archer trails his hand down to my waist and he leads me to a window seat that's only illuminated by moonlight. Although he has his mask on, I don't feel insecure, in fact, the masks seem more like a romantic gesture to me. When we sit by the windows, a person quickly comes in and places a tray of food and drinks in front of us, I look up at Archer and find that his eyes look like he's trying to gauge my reaction. I smirk at him and pick up a sugar covered cookie and I throw it at his face.

He scrunches his nose as crumbs fall onto his expensive looking suit.

"Health first, sweetie." He says with a cheeky grin, I giggle at the nickname before I reach out and poke his left cheek. He makes a funny frowning face at me. I stick my tongue out and he uses the opportunity to pop a strawberry into my mouth.

I roll my eyes before I eat it.

"Killjoy." I mutter and he chuckles as we both eat from the array of fruits and sweets in front of us.

"What movie do you want to go see, if we have the chance to go watch one?" Archer asks me.

"Hmm... what do you recommend?" I asked.

"We've watched horror, romance... should we go for something with a bit more action?" He asks and I nod.

"Sounds good, what film?" I asked and Archer shrugs as he throws a blueberry at me and I successfully catch it with my mouth. "Ha! I got it!" I exclaim in joy and he laughs.

I stretch my arms out and a yawn suddenly reaches my mouth.

"Ugh... what time is it?" I asked and Archer lifts his left arm and I notice a watch around his wrist.

"Way too late for us to stay up." He says with a sweet smile, I nod my head before Archer gets up and he offers me his hand.

"Since I've technically met you- does this mean I get phone call privileges?" I asked.

"You'll receive one as soon as I get up tomorrow." He says with a wink.

Archer leads me to the doorway and he pauses part way to the door.

"This is as far as I should bring you." He says, in a somewhat depressed tone. I give him in encouraging smile.

"I get the whole secrecy thing. Don't worry about it. I'm fine with this as it is." I say with a shrug.

"Glad you understand." He says and I nod my head.

"Be glad I'm not clingy yet." I say with a smirk and he chuckles.

"I'll remember that." He says just as we reach the door. But as I reach for the knob, Archer stops me by holding me by the waist. "Do you mind if I... take off the mask?" He asks, almost in a shy way.

I bite my bottom lip and nod. Archer smiles and I gaze into his eyes as his hands reach up to the back of my head to untie the mask. I hear the ribbons slip away from each other and I watch as he carefully removes the mask from my face. He stares... for quite a bit before I start to fidget around.

"This is... really awkward." I admit and Archer blinks for a few moments before he clears his throat.

"Sorry. I just want to remember how you look like- I'm not exactly free to see you all the time." He says. "...unlike the others." He adds- almost inaudibly, but I catch it nonetheless.

"How about, we take a picture together on your phone? 'course, you'll have to send it to me too- I want a copy myself." I say with a smile. Archer's eyes widen as if he wasn't expecting me to say that at all. "Is that a no?" I asked and he shakes his head furiously.

"Let's take one." He says, almost excitedly. And in all honestly, it's the cutest thing.

He immediately pats his pockets to look for his phone when he realizes that he'd placed it in his breast pocket. Archer laughs awkwardly.

"Sorry." He says and I smile at him as he takes out his phone and opens the camera.

Archer holds his phone in front of us before he wraps an arm around my waist.

"Smile." He says and I roll my eyes before smiling brightly at the camera.

# Chapter 14

"Abusio is a type of catachresis known as the mixed metaphor..." A preppy blonde girl in front of me says and I roll my eyes. Shut up, your iPad's on the dictionary. I want to say.

I groan to myself. It had been 3 days since the party and Archer had been wonderful. He left me messages all the time and called me up to talk me to sleep. Lawrence so far had been busy as well- we barely even bumped into each other. Keaton, apparently, has business somewhere and was absent for two days but for some reason has showed up today.

I groaned inwardly during class. Today was not my day.

There are two reasons I hate being a girl.

One, I carried way too much baggage in my bags- perfume, makeup, and all that stuff.

Two...

Periods.

I didn't feel much pain yet, but judging by the way a slightly familiar crappy feeling was creeping in, I knew I was in for some deep crap. I was only happy that, for some magical reason, this was my last lecture.

"You okay?" An irritating voice asks from beside me. Ugh. Ew. It's freaking Keaton.

"I'm fine." I say in a clipped tone.

"You don't look fine at all, and it's unattractive." Keaton says with a smirk. I roll my eyes.

"Sucks for you then." I say.

The lecture ends and I breathe a sigh of relief as everyone, including me, gets up and packs away.

"No, seriously, are you okay?" He asks.

"Keaton. Stop asking. I'm fine." I say coldly before I pick up my black bag and rush off.

I thought I would be able to bear the freaking pain. But no. It was just getting started.

I briskly walked through the halls and I called Wesley to pick me up asap. I was going to die in a few short moments. When Wesley finally arrives, I don't wait for him to get out of the car and let me in, I just get in and accidentally slam the door of the car shut.

"Sorry." I say with a sigh and Wesley just nods at me with a smile.

"Don't worry about it Ms. Bleu." He says. "Home?" He asks and I nod.

"Yes please." I say. "If possible, in lightning speed." I say and Wesley gives me a curt nod before driving off.

"Are you sure you don't want to take any medicine Ms. Bleu?" Janet, the maid, asks me. I nod my head.

"I'll just sleep this off. I'll survive." I say as I groan on the couch.

I was still wearing "at-home" clothes. Only because I knew that I was going to end up moping all day. So I had worn a white shirt over a pair of silky black joggers.

"Do you want anything?" Janet asks thoughtfully and I shake my head as I bury it into a pillow.

I hear her laugh before I sigh to myself. The pain was bearable but definitely not comfortable. You know, it just felt like a knife was being twisted into my abdomen. No big deal. No big fücking deal.

"I'll make you a berry smoothie and a Caesar salad." I hear Janet say and I nod.

"Thanks..." I groan. I quickly pull out my phone and smile at the message that greeted me.

Up for a date night?

I'll see :( Not feeling too well. Might just lie in bed like all day.

I type in. I really would go out. But my body might just end up feeling like it's been shoved into a blender.

"Here you go, sweetheart." Janet says as she walks over to me with a tray with a really delicious looking Caesar salad and the pretty pink smoothie.

"Thanks Janet!" I say as I get up and sip on the smoothie and immediately dig into the salad.

"I'll just clean up Mr. Peters' room and then I'll be off. Unless you want me to cook dinner." She says kindly as she stands at my side. I shake my head.

"I'm just happy you make me food every day and look after the place." I say. "I'll climb up to my room after I eat."

"Alright. Don't push your body too hard, who knows when the pain will end." Janet says, winking at me. I giggle before she tidies her skirt and makes her way upstairs.

I check my phone quickly and spot a new message.

Why? Are you sick? Archer asks, I smile at his concern.

Girly things. ;) Lucky I was in a good mood 3 days ago. I'm normally a real bïtch prior~ I message as I finish off Janet's salad and I sit there sipping on the smoothie.

Oh. Awkward. He sends and I smirk as I haul myself off of the couch and climb up the stairs.

I groan as I enter my room and fall smack against my bed before sending a message to Archer.

Sleeping off the pain. I'll text you when I wake up, kay? I message, and I don't wait for a reply before I immediately fall asleep.

I wake up feeling happier and better than before. The pain was gone-although I did make a run for the bathroom- and then I went straight onto texting Archer. I decided to take a quick shower and I changed into my favorite 'chill' outfit. A funny shirt covered in ice cream designs, a pair of silky pink pajama pants, and soft slippers.

I'm up and about :3 I text Archer as I make my way out the door.

I walk downstairs to the main floor when I smell something delicious.

"What's cooking?" I greet Lawrence happily as I go sit at the kitchen counter. Lawrence turns and his adorable grin is plastered onto his face.

"Janet told me it's a special day for you." Lawrence says with a wink. "And since I haven't been catching up with you so far, I thought why not give a girl a sweets-covered chill kind of day." He says as he walks over to me with a spoon full of whipped cream and strawberries.

He placed the spoon to my mouth and I laughed as I took it from him and licked it clean.

"Ugh. No wonder Daisy loves you." I say with a wink as I get up and stretch my arms. I give the spoon back to Lawrence who's got an amused grin on his face. "Movie night?" I asked.

"I chose a few already- they're on the coffee table. I'll be with you in a second." Lawrence says and I nod as I skip my way over to the couch and look at the DVD's that are on.

There are a few Disney films, Insurgent, and oh... my... gosh.

"We have to watch Guardians of the Galaxy!!!" I squeal in joy. "Best Marvel movie ever." I say.

"I disagree, I prefer the Avengers." Lawrence says as he walks over with popcorn and a tall chocolate whipped cream and strawberry filled short-cake.

"You're gonna make me fat." I say, as I practically drool over the food.

"That's the plan." He says with a grin as he sits down.

Lawrence was in his pajamas too, a pair of plain grey pants and a white shirt. He places the food down onto the coffee table while I snuggle up on the couch. Then he walks over to the TV and plugs in the DVD before he sits down and we begin to watch the movie.

About ten minutes in, my phone buzzes and I glance over at Lawrence who's laughing at the movie. I pull out my phone discreetly.

Special delivery for a special girl :)

I arch a brow, but before I can type up a reply, the doorbell rings. Lawrence pauses the movie and looks at me. I shrug before getting up- not forgetting to stuff my face with popcorn first.

I wipe my hands on my shirt and open one of the doors- only to find Wesley carrying a large basket filled with chocolates, ice cream, macarons, and a few other things.

"Mr. Archer requested me to send these over." Wesley says and I nod my head.

"Thanks Wesley." I say and he nods his head curtly.

"May I go in and place this on the table?" He asks and I nod as I open the doorway for him.

Wesley quickly walks in and Lawrence gives him a nod of acknowledgement before Wesley begins to leave. I give him a smile.

"See you tomorrow!" I greeted and Wesley nodded his head, before disappearing into the elevators.

I shut the door and walked back over to Lawrence and found him looking through the basket.

"Hungry, much?" I asked and Lawrence rolled his eyes.

"No. Just wondering who they're from." He says with a shrug. I bite my bottom lip before deciding on what to answer.

"That is a total secret." I say with a smile. I'm pretty sure you already know who it is, Lars. I think to myself.

Lawrence smirks before playing the movie again.

"Who's your favorite?" Lawrence asks as we watch.

"Guess." I say as I eat a piece of popcorn.

"Rocket?" He asks and I shake my head.

"Nope."

"Gamora?"

"Nuh-uh." I say with a smirk. "Isn't everyone's favorite Groot?" I asked with a grin.

"Nuh-uh." Lawrence says, copying me, and I roll my eyes. "Some people actually like Rocket." He says.

"Groot is adorable and technically- immortal." I say as I stick my tongue out at him.

"You're such a kid." Lawrence says and I roll my eyes.

"Says the guy who freaks out when I kick his äss in Halo." I say with a smirk.

"Wanna bet?"

"Oh sure. Leggo." I say with a grin as Lawrence gets up to turn the PS4 on. "Wait! We haven't even finished the movie!" I whine. Lawrence chuckles.

"We can watch it later- after I kick your äss." He says and I roll my eyes.

Before I can even speak again, the doorbell rings and I groan.

"Who is it now?" I asked and Lawrence shrugs.

"How should I know?"

"Uh, I don't know, maybe it's Daisy." I say.

"Not possible. Daisy went back home."

"What?" I asked. "But I wanted to hang out. Damn. Tell her I feel bad for not saying bye." I say and Lawrence chuckles.

"Will do. Now go open the door before whoever's there breaks that door open." Lawrence says sarcastically and I roll my eyes before walking over to the door.

I immediately regret opening it.

"'Took you long enough."

I contemplate on shutting the door on his face.

"Lawrence! Did you order an ässhole for dinner?" I shouted and I hear Lawrence drop something.

"Gee, thanks." Keaton says and I roll my eyes.

"Did the whole 'leave me alone' thing not ring a bell up your butt?" I asked.

"I came to buy you goodies and this is what I get?" Keaton asks.

"Goodies as in the pizza you can't hide behind your back and the box of chocolates in your hand?" I asked before I sighed. "Lawrence sorta beat you to it with his own stuff." I say as I begin to close the door.

"Lars! If you don't let me in there, I'm telling Sweetie-McPhee here how you once fell off a-"

"LET HIM IN." Lawrence shouts and I arch a brow.

"Seriously? Sweetie-McPhee?" I asked and Keaton chuckled. "And he fell of a what now?" I asked, Keaton smirks just as Lawrence shows up at the door and I fold my arms over my chest.

"Ugh. Do we have to let him in?" I asked.

"Yes."

"Why?" I whined.

"Because I don't like embarrassing stories."

"Oh you mean like the time that I fell in front of you-" I began to talk but then Lawrence put a hand to my mouth.

"Yeah. Like that." Lawrence says and I roll my eyes.

"You're clumsy." Keaton says to me and I groan as Lawrence releases my mouth.

"You're an äss. Good to know we all know each other." I say before rolling my eyes.

Keaton smirks before walking in and I mouth words to Lawrence.

That guy needs to go. Like now. I mouth and Lawrence sighs.

We can kick him out in a second. He mouths back and I roll my eyes before I pull out my phone.

10 messages.

I missed 10 messages.

What.

I scroll through them quickly.

7:40 PM Do you like them?

8:01 PM Darcy?

8:01 PM :( Are you ignoring me?

8:05 PM Don't like sweets then?

8:07 PM Hey.

8:08 PM Hi.

8: 09 PM Sup?

8: 10 PM Nothing, just waiting for my girl to reply.

8:11 PM Oh man, that sucks. Why isn't she replying?

8: 15 PM I don't know.

I smile at the messages. Archer was doing the "let's talk to myself" thing and it made me giggle. Lawrence arches a brow at me before I roll my eyes at him.

"Go entertain dick face, I'll just text this guy." I say with a shrug.

Lawrence nods before walking off. Before I can even text, another message pops up.

I really wish I had SOMEONE to talk to around here.

I laugh.

I wish that too ;3 I type in.

Yeah right? It'd be great to have a conversation. Archer says and I bite my lip to stop my giggling.

I wonder what we're having right now... I send.

OH... EM... GEEE. We're totally having a conversation!!! <3 Archer sends and I laugh.

"Hey, you might wanna eat the pizza before it gets cold. And close the door." Keaton says and I roll my eyes.

"Yeah, yeah. Quit bossing me around bro." I say as I close the door and make my way to the two. Halo is on and I grin as I grab a controller.

Gonna go play Halo with two morons. Wish me luck. ;) I text.

Who morons? He asks.

Keaton and Lawrence. Imma kick their butts. I'll call you some time soon, kay?

Kill 'em. Metaphorically. You can kill Keaton for real if you want. Archer sends and I giggle before making my way back to the two idiots who were arguing over what map to play.

"I leave you guys for how many minutes and you guys still haven't decided on what map to play on?" I ask as I fold my arms over my chest and I place my phone on the coffee table.

Lawrence and Keaton suddenly stop and just stare at my phone.

"Is there a problem?" I asked.

"N-no. It's nothing." Lawrence says but Keaton's glaring at my phone.

"No phones during game nights." Keaton says and I roll my eyes.

"Yeah well, this isn't your apartment so bug off." I say before I sit down and I make the decision of the map for them. "Let's play before I actually murder Keaton." I say with a sigh.

"You're still angry?" Keaton asks.

"Nooooooo." I say sarcastically as I roll my eyes. "Can we please play now?" I whine and Lawrence nods as he takes the other controller.

"And what about me?" Keaton asks and Lawrence rolls his eyes.

"Look for it over by the TV." Lawrence says.

"Right..." Keaton says.

Lawrence and I look at each other.

"Really?" I whisper and Lawrence shrugs.

"Might as well." Lawrence says to me before I roll my eyes.

I don't know how long we play for- I just remember completely zoning out and focusing on the game. Like seriously. I did not want to remember the fact that Keaton was in my apartment (not really mine but you get what I mean). From the way he acted at the night of the party- I was just someone to be won over so that he could get the benefits of the company thing.

Speaking of which. The idea of being a kind of "trophy" kind of didn't really sit in yet. I've sort of tried to busy myself. But out of all three of them, I have to say, Archer's been one of the sweetest and Lawrence has been the most confusing. Why would you even try to compete if you have a girlfriend?

Well.

Supposing Daisy is his girlfriend. But what's his strategy?

I just don't get it.

I yawned as I finished one last round with them. I'd won 9 out of 13 times. Lawrence won three times and Keaton well- we gave him a free win. The guy sucks at games.

"I'm gonna go straight to bed." I say as I get up.

"No sleepovers?" Keaton asks with a mischievous grin.

"No sleepovers. Not with you." I say as I roll my eyes.

"What, so you guys have had a slumber party?" Keaton asks and I sigh.

"We're flatmates, slumber parties are inevitable." I say as I take my phone.

"You're not seriously gonna text while we're both here are you?" Keaton asks, looking at Lawrence for support. But Lawrence was just staring at my phone.

"Why not?" I ask rhetorically. I yawn once more and check the time. Jeez. 2 in the morning already?

"It's disrespectful." Keaton answers and I roll my eyes.

"Not when you're in my apartment and definitely not when you disrespectfully took my phone from me." I say with a sigh.

"Touché." Keaton says with a wink.

"Whatever guys. I'm gonna go to bed. You guys can go do whatever the hell you want." I say as I make my way upstairs. My phone buzzes and I look at it as I go up.

Did ya kick their butts? I smile at the text message, before typing in a reply.

Totally. I'm heading to bed like right now. I'll message you tomorrow, kay?

Okay. Good night. :)

I grin just as I enter my room and practically black out on my bed.

A loud noise wakes me up and I groan. Who the hell? I wonder as I look over at my window. The sun was just about to rise. I groan as I grab my phone and answer it, not bothering to check who it was.

"Hello?" I asked.

"Darcy! Where do you live again?" A familiar female voice asks.

"Wait... Mom?!" I say, my eyes wide and awake now.

"I thought I'd give you a surprise visit- but then I forgot where you said you lived now." Mom says and I giggle before pausing.

"Where are you going to stay?" I asked.

"Hopefully with you, is that fine?" She asks.

I gulp down a lump of air in my throat. Oh dear.

"Y-yeah. Sure." I say. What about Lawrence you dumb fu-

"Okay, do you mind telling me where to go?" Mom asks.

"I-I'll pick you up in a bit." I say. "Just text me where you are. Okay?"

"Alright. Be here soon, baby girl." She says and I smile before she drops the call.

"Crap. Crap. Crap. Crap. Crap. Crap. Crap." I repeat over and over again.

Lawrence is here. Hell, what do I do if Keaton's still here?! Oh god oh god oh god.

I am so screwed.

# Chapter 15

I dress quickly, deciding that showers weren't the best idea considering mom was waiting- and I'd already taken one last night. I quickly get dressed in a pair of comfy leggings, a cream sweater, and a pair of espadrilles before I grab my favorite bear-eared bonnet to hide my mess of hair in.

I grab my phone and my wallet before slowly slipping out of my room and creeping down the apartment. I hear snores coming from the couch and I sigh to myself. Gotta wake these two idiots up then. I think to myself.

I quickly message Wesley about picking me up and he replies fast. Does that guy ever sleep? I wonder before I grab a pillow from one of the couches.

Keaton is asleep on the couch with a pillow over his head and Lawrence is passed out on the floor with his head against the couch. I bite back my laughter as I creep up to them and I smash the pillow against Lawrence's head. He shrieks and before Keaton can respond, I grab the pillow covering his head and smash it against him as well.

"OW!" Keaton says as he groans. Lawrence has his hand on his head and I roll my eyes.

"My mom's gonna be here in less than 30 minutes and if you guys don't want to piss me off, you guys gotta clean the place up and hide. Lord knows what my mom would do if she finds out there are two guys in here- Lawrence is nice enough but you," I pause, looking at Keaton. "Are going to give her a heart attack." I say with a sigh.

"...Wait... what's going on?" Keaton asks.

"My mom's coming over." I repeat. Lawrence yawns and stretches his arms up before standing.

"Got it... Keaton... go up to the guest room on the second floor..." Lawrence says sleepily.

"...Fine." Keaton says as he slowly begins to move. I sigh before quickly heading out.

"Let me just message my mom, she should be here somewhere." I say as I wait in the car. Wesley nods his head.

Where are you? I'm at the entrance waiting in the white mini-van. I text quickly.

"Would you like me to go look for her?" Wesley asks and I contemplate it for a second.

"That'd be great, Wesley. Sorry for causing you so much trouble all the time." I say and Wesley chuckles.

"Don't worry about it Miss Bleu, it's my job." He says before getting out of the car, locking it, and then making his way out.

I shift in the luxury mini van and grab a bottle of water from the side. Nope. Still not used to this. I think to myself. I mean, I have been technically using this van or another car that Wesley brings over. But jeez. The mini-van was always fully stocked with all kinds of things. Be it drinks, food- oh and did I forget to mention wi-fi? So useful.

My phone makes a dinging noise and I quickly look down.

Heard you got up nice and early Archer sent and I grin.

Mmhmm... Mommy's here I reply.

:O Can I meet her? Archer asks and I giggle a bit.

I haven't even really met you- it's not fair if she meets you before I do :(

:/ But it wouldn't be fun if you knew who I was He sends.

:/ Why not?

Cause I like having you wonder what I'm really like

I smile at that one.

And why is that? I asked.

Because it means I'm on your mind more ;) He sends and I laugh.

You're a cheeseball. :P I send.

Do you hate cheeseballs?

No...

Then I'm fine being a cheeseball for you babe. See that. THAT. Was corny. I laugh at his text and he quickly follows it up with another one.

As in, I-wanna-die-right-now-for-sending-that-text corny. Archer sends and I giggle at his message.

I hear the door slide open from the side and I look over.

"Mom!" I practically scream as I run to her as best as I can and give her a big hug. I feel my mom's arms wrap around me as well and she laughs.

"For a second, I thought this guy got the wrong woman!" She exclaims.

We let go of each other and I examine her.

Mom was a short woman, even shorter than I was. She had soft brown hair that went just below her shoulders and fell flawlessly straight. Her hair was turning grey at the tops, but she dyed them every now and then. She smelled of fresh roses and flowers- her favorite perfume scent. She was wearing her usual attire of black leggings and a loosely flowing blouse. I grin at her when I realize how happy she looks.

"Mrs...?" Wesley asks and my mom turns to face him and smiles.

"Oh don't call me by my last name- it'll change soon enough either way. Call me Rose." She says with a smile and Wesley nods his head.

"Mrs. Rose, is there anything fragile in your luggage?" Wesley asks motioning to the fairly medium sized black luggage bag in his hand.

"Nope. Thank you-"

"Wesley." I say and my mom nods.

"Thanks Wesley." She says with a smile before she gets into the van.

Mom immediately closes the door and looks at me.

"Am I dreaming, or do you have a driver?" She asks and I laugh.

"I have a driver, mom. I told you this scholarship was amazing." I say and mom laughs. Wesley quietly goes in and immediately sets onto driving.

"Of course. I knew you could do it. You've always been my smart little girl." She says and I smile at her. "How's school, sweetie?" She asks me and I smile.

"It's been great. I mean, a whole lot has happened and I'm really glad you're here." I say and my mom smiles. "How's Gavin been?" I asked.

"Oh he's been such a sweetheart. I've left the wedding planning to his sister and all. I'm far too old to even think about those things." Mom says and I smile. "But enough about me, I wanna know if my baby girl got herself a guy."

I smile at her.

"I'm in a bit of a situation..." I say. I really should tell her... I think to myself. She's an open-minded person right? I ask myself.

"Boy trouble, already? I haven't even left you for a month, sweetie." Mom says and I grin.

"Pardon me, Mrs. Rose, Ms. Darcy, but would the two of you like to have breakfast at Buvette? Mr. Archer suggested it."

"If he suggests it, it's probably good." I say with a smile. "Sounds good to me then." I say and Wesley gives me a smile before continuing to drive.

"Who's Mr. Archer?" My mom asks and I giggle.

"I'll tell you everything in a bit." I sat, winking at her. My phone dings and I look at my screen.

Where you at????? Lawrence messages me and I roll my eyes.

Having breakfast with my mom somewhere. I'll be there soon. Keaton still there? I asked.

Yeah. He crashed in my bed.

Great. Tell him to leave as soon as he's up. >:) I send.

We arrive at the restaurant and I smile at how cozy it looks.

"This place is cute." Mom says and I nod. Mom was picky when it came to restaurants, so if this place was expensive, it was very open to scrutiny.

"Let's go," I pause before looking at Wesley, "Can you pick us up after an hour?" I say and he nods with a smile before going back into the van and driving off.

Mom takes no time to find us a seat and I chuckle as she skims through the menu. She squints her eyes at a few things before we both agree to order two things that we'd both taste from each other's plates. My mom loves playing food critic. Rightfully so, since her cooking is absolutely amazing- and no, I am totally not biased. Everyone, including Ms. Leila, says her food's amazing.

"So, tell me about this Mr. Archer, guy." Mom says and I sigh.

"Promise me you won't freak out." I say and mom squints her eyes at me. She was seated right across me and I bit my bottom lip.

"Darcy Bleu, are you pregnant!?" Mom almost yells- almost being the key word. and my eyes widen.

I thank God that there aren't many people here and the one's that do look decide that it's none of their business.

"MOM!" I say thwacking her arm. "I am not pregnant, god, would I look this calm if I was?!" I asked.

"Well, you made the 'I have something serious but I'm nervous about talking about it' face. And I've told you before. I'm fine with you doing what you want and all- as long as you keep studying and the guy's hot. I am not taking care of an ugly grandson- well, no, I would still take care of it- but it'd be better if-"

"Just stop talking about it mom. I'm embarrassed enough." I say with a sigh. My mom laughs at me.

"I missed you too baby girl." She says and I grin. "Now tell me about Mr. Archer before I shout out false accusations." I roll my eyes as a waitress kindly places two cups of coffee down along with glasses of water.

"Remember that contract I signed about the scholarship?" I asked.

Mom nods as she sips her coffee.

"Well... apparently... I signed into a bit of a, complicated, little thing..." I say, trying to delay things.

"I mean, I didn't mean to sign up for it but then I don't know how I even missed something as big as that and all- Not to mention, I made sure it sounded so exciting like I was worth every penny the company was giving me and then it turns out that I was just a suitable candidate for this- this... thing." I say and just as I'm about to speak my mom interrupts me.

"Oh... sweetheart, by any chance..." Mom says and I pause. "Are you talking about that engagement section on the contract, sweetheart?" She asks.

What did my mom just say?

Hold up.

What.

Did.

She.

Just.

Say?!

"Oh, sweetie, don't tell me you didn't read that section." Mom says and judging by my the blank look on my face, she sighs to herself and grins.

"Sweetheart, I was asking you the day before you'd received the final copy, if you were sure about your decision and I thought that you had read over the revisions already. They sent a copy to both me and your father.

But I'm guessing he didn't even read it- he was too busy bragging about the scholarship." Mom continues and I nod with a sigh.

After I even received the scholarship, my dad had been immediately set on bragging about it to everyone we knew. There wasn't a single conversation he had with someone that didn't mention the fact that I got in. After that he would say that it was because of him that I got in and that if he hadn't provided me money, I would have never gotten into a university abroad in the first place.

It wasn't that it wasn't true. It was that he liked to shove it in our faces that it was his money that we were living on that pissed both mom and I off.

"That being said, are you okay with such a situation?" Mom asks me and I nod my head.

"I'm fine, well, as fine as I can be. I mean, what can I do, really." I say and mom gives me an encouraging smile.

"I'm always here for you baby." She says just as our food is placed and we begin to eat.

As we eat, my mom begins to praise the food, which I'm thankful for. Mom normally criticizes every restaurant I actually bring her to, so to hear that this restaurant is an absolute A plus is amazing. I'm definitely going to talk to Archer about other restaurants in town.

"So this Archer guy... is he the fiancé?" Mom says, wiggling her eyebrows and I smirk at her.

"That's actually what I wanted to talk to you about. Apparently..." I begin.

I tell my mom all about the arrangements. I was never one to hide things from my mom either. I told my parents everything.

"Hmm... so there are three of them, huh- and from what I can gather, they're all very good looking." Mom says, winking at me as I roll my eyes and eat my dessert. "Well then, I can't really advise you to pick any of them, since I've yet to meet any of them... But I can tell you this. You're a brilliant girl, Darcy, and no matter your decision, I will fully support you. I'm sure you'll make the right choices for you my dear."

"I sure hope so." I say with a sigh. "Sometimes it just feels like it's a bit too much, though."

"When it is, just call your old mom here or even Ms. Leila. Speaking of which, I have yet to thank her."

"Bake her some brownies and we'll be good to go." I wink and mom chuckles. My phone dings and I look down at it.

Hey there Darcy-boo ;) Martin here. Erik, Clara, and I were wondering if you'd like to hit the café today- Clara wants a get-to-know session~ Martin texts and I smile.

I'm with my mom at the moment but I'll see if I can tag along I send.

What? A Mama Bleu is here? Oh hell, bring her with you! Martin sends and I laugh.

"Mom, do you wanna hang out with my friends for a bit, or do you wanna rest up?" I ask her and she yawns.

"I think I'll go rest up a bit sweetheart. Besides, I have to Skype call Gavin and make sure he's eaten breakfast. That man's been working his äss way too hard over nothing." Mom says and I burst out in laughter.

"Mom! Don't say that!" I shout but my mom just smiles at me.

"Well, if he's gonna be my husband he better deal with it."

"I'm glad you found him mom." I say and my mom smiles.

"Me too Darcy... I wish I found him sooner." She says with a smile. "But then I would've never had you."

"Mom stop it, you're gonna make me cry." I say teasingly and my mom giggles.

"We better head out if you're still gonna meet up with your friends." My mom says and I nod as I wave for a waitress.

"Yes?" The waitress, a petite woman with curled brown hair, asks.

"Can I have the bill please?" I asked and the waitress gives me a confused look.

"Mr. Archer has already paid for it. He said to give you this note when you asked for a bill, though." She says with a smile as she hands me a small note written on a fancy looking piece of paper.

"Oh, uh, thanks." I say as I take the paper from her.

"Mr. Archer has been a long time customer of ours, we hope you liked the food here." She says in a somewhat nervous manner.

"I loved it. Even my mom here enjoyed the food and she's a major food critic." I say.

"That's great to hear. Especially from Mr. Archer's girlfrie-"

"Pardon me... Darla, we need you to grab a few towels from the back room. I have to go run an order from someone, sorry." A waiter with short black hair says. The waitress that was talking to me sighs before offering my mo and I a kind smile.

"Got it. Anyways, thank you for the compliments Ms. Blue." She says before slightly bowing her head and leaving with a smile on her face.

"Girlfriend already? This Archer guy is pretty confident isn't he? Not that I don't like that in a man." Mom says and I feel a blush creep over my face.

"I sort of told my friends that he was boyfriend... And he knew that so..."

"Oh my, sweetie you sure are taking things fast over here." I frown.

"You think so?" I asked and my mom laughs.

"No sweetheart. Don't even second guess yourself, I know you have sense in you. I know for a fact that I did not raise an idiot." She says and we both laugh.

I brought my mom to the penthouse a few minutes after that.

I unlocked the door with my key card and passcode before making my way inside.

I gawked.

The place was spotless, smelled faintly like vanilla, and behold, a peaceful conversation between two hot men over at the breakfast table.

"Did the wold just end or am I actually looking at the two of you having a civilized conversation?" I asked and both Lawrence and Keaton looks up.

"Things tend to get civilized when you're dealing business." Keaton says with a shrug.

"Well then, if these two are your flat mates I'm guessing life never gets boring for you, Darcy." My mom says and I laugh as both Keaton and Lawrence's eyes widen.

The two of them suddenly stand up and run their hands down their outfits. Lawrence is wearing a red V-neck over a pair of acid wash jeans and Keaton is dressed in a crisp black polo shirt and a pair of dark wash jeans. They both look like they could be on the cove of a teen magazine together. My mom laughs as well before we both make our way towards them.

"Lawrence, Keaton, this is my mom, Rose Bleu." I introduce and my mom grins, causing her dimples to show near her eyes.

"Call me Rose. And I won't be a Bleu for long- never got to changing that name after the divorce, but what can you do." My mom says casually. Lawrence and Keaton look as stiff as sticks shoved into the ground as they both force smiles on their faces and shake hands with my mom.

"Nice to meet you Ms. Rose! Your daughter's been the best flattie I've ever had." Lawrence says with his signature cute smile.

"Suck up." I hear Keaton mumble, almost inaudibly.

"Anyways, Lars, can you bring my mom up to the guest room? I have to go somewhere." I say and Lawrence nods excitedly.

"Of course. Come this way!" Lawrence says excitedly.

Mom gives me a smile before she hugs me and kisses me on the cheek.

"Be back soon little missy." She says and I giggle.

"Yes momma." I say and she grins before turning to face Lawrence.

"Well, I don't know about you two, but I'm very sleepy right now. So lead the way Lawrence." My mom says as she yawns and Lawrence chuckles. "Oh and Keaton?"

"Huh?" Keaton asks and I bite my bottom lip, wondering what my mom was going to say.

"If my daughter says no, she means no." My mom says for me before she urged Lawrence to take her to her room.

Once the two of them were gone, I immediately texted Martin that I'd be at our usual café in a few minutes.

"What was that about?" Keaton asks me and I shrug.

"You figure it out. I'm going to go meet up with my friends, so do me a favor and don't ruin anything or, better yet, just get out of my apartment." I say with a sigh as I make my way outside. As I'm about to head out, I feel someone grab my wrist and I'm immediately pushed against Keaton's hard chest.

"I'll drive you." He says and I roll my eyes as I tug my wrist forcefully away from him.

"No thanks. I don't feel like getting forced into a date, ditched, and then treated like absolute nothing." I snap.

"It was one time." He says.

"Yeah, well, I'm not doing that again. Hell, I am never going out with you again. You're an insensitive prick with a stick so far up your äss that it practically pops out of your thick brain." I say before whirling around and making my way out the door.

I sigh angrily to myself before I make my way to the café.

"Oh man, I really wanted to meet Mama Bleu." Martin whines and we all laugh.

We, being, Erik, Clara, and I. Erik was a pretty nice guy. Although Martin and Erik had just started dating, they were absolutely open with each other. They didn't give off the 'we're too lovey dovey' vibe either, which both Clara and I appreciated.

"Can we meet her tomorrow?" Clara asks and I smile.

"My mom would love to meet you all. We can hang around the apartment and get her to cook us food." I say and they all nod.

"I still can't believe the two of you actually hooked up." Clara points out and I giggle.

"Right?!" I asked and Erik grins as he places a hand over Martin's.

Clara and I make stupid squealing sounds as Martin turns beet red.

"Guys..." Martin says shyly and we both laugh out loud.

"So cute!" Clara and I exclaim and Martin ends up looking like he wants to disappear into thin air.

"I've never seen Martin so flushed before." Erik says with a chuckle and both Clara and I giggle.

"I am so glad you're part of the group now Erik. I mean, Martin's great, but when we add you, we're just better balanced." I say with a smile and Erik smiles.

"Glad to know I pass the best friends test." He says and we nod.

"You pass with an absolute A plus!" I shout and Clara hollers and Martin looks like he wants to shrink.

"Guys..." He whines again and Erik laughs at him before placing an arm around him.

The two of us squeal at their adorable-ness.

"I can't even handle this..." I say faking a heart attack.

"Oh god... they're so cute I feel bad for our single selves." Clara says as she leans her head on my shoulder.

Erik laughs even harder and Martin finally pops a grin.

"Well, technically, Darcy-girl here's got herself a boyfriend." Martin says with a wink and Clara pushes off of me and fakes a glare.

"Traitors! Both of you!" She says in a chipmunk voice that makes all of us laugh.

Clara giggles and then sighs to herself.

"You guys make it look like dating is so easy." Clara says and I smile.

"Oh please, if you wanted a guy, Clara, you could totally get him. I mean, look at you." I say and Martin nods.

"For reals." Martin adds.

"Gee, thanks for the encouragement guys." Clara says with a smile.

"But seriously, do you have anyone you actually like?" I asked and Clara blushes.

All of our eyes widen like barrels.

"WHO?!" We all practically yell. Thank God there isn't many people in here. I think to myself.

"His name's Blaine... and he goes to my dance studio... like every freaking day..." Clara says and Martin and I share confused looks.

"What dance studio?" Martin asks.

"Yeah, what dance studio?" I asked.

"I sort of manage a dance studio for my parents downtown. It's nothing that special... But, ugh, the eye candy that is Blaine Michaelson is to die for." Clara says.

"Clara's Dance Studio, tomorrow." I announce and the two guys nod.

"Mission: Get the apparent "eye candy that is Blaine Michaelson" to notice Clara." Erik announces and Martin laughs.

"What time is he normally there baby girl?" Martin asks and Clara grins.

"5 in the afternoon."

"Is Mission Eye Candy for Clara good to go then?" I asked and we all can't help but laugh.

"Oh it is so good to go." Martin says and we all laugh.

I got to my apartment building, NY Carter's, just after the sun went down and I was looking forward to my mom's cooking. I haven't had it in weeks! I giggled to myself as I entered the elevator. My phone suddenly vibrates in my pocket and I immediately take it out and smile at the sight of the Caller ID.

I answer it fast.

"Yes?" I asked in a sickeningly sweet voice. I hear a laugh just as I get off on my floor.

"How's your mom doing?" Archer asks and I smile as I unlock the door.

"She's doing fine-" I say pausing as I smell my mom's famous curry. Ugh, to die for.

"I visited her a while ago." Archer says, proudly, if I may add, and I stop my tracks.

"You did what now?" I ask, trying to sound pissed.

"Uh... W-were you not comfortable with that?" He asks and I smirk at his nervous response, holding back a giggle.

"What did I tell you about meeting her before me?" I scold.

"...Sorry." Archer says- no- wait... he freaking whimpers. So... freaking cute...! I think to myself.

"Archer..."

"...Are you mad at me?" He asks.

"Hm, ask me that in 10 minutes." I say.

"Don't hang up on me!!!" He shouts through the phone, so loud that I almost threw the damned thing away.

My mom comes into view with a spatula in her hand and her eyebrows raised. I mouth the name Archer and my mom giggles to herself before giving me a thumbs up. Well, glad to know momma approves. I think to myself. I hear Archer clear his throat.

"I mean... Please don't hang up on me." He says.

"I'm not hanging up on you babe." I say with a smile, trying to sound really annoying when I say the word babe. I hear Archer sigh in relief and I giggle. "But seriously, Archer. Stop going around me. If anyone else meets you before I do, I might just freak out." I say.

"But-"

"No but's." I say.

"Okay. No dodging you to get to know your family better." Archer says in a sad tone. "But... am I forgiven?" Archer asks.

"Don't say it like it's a bad thing... You'll make me feel bad." I say with a pause. "But yeah, you're forgiven." I say, smiling to myself as I lean against the wall and twirl my hair around my fingers.

"Ew, the two lovebirds are talking." I hear a familiarly annoying voice say.

"Is that Keaton?" Archer asks and I bite my bottom lip in irritation.

"Seems like it. Hold on a sec." I say before looking to my side.

Sure enough, there was Keaton, his head popping out of the sofa.

"What part of leave did you not understand?" I practically hiss.

"Oh please, as if I could leave when Lawrence is here and Archer makes a magical appearance." Keaton says, rolling his eyes.

"He makes for somewhat good company. Mediocre at best." My mom says with a shrug. "I'm making oven-baked chicken with mashed potatoes, I would've made Archer stay, but he said he didn't want to risk it."

"Thanks mom." I say with a sigh. I put the phone back to my ear. "Sorry, Archer, I'm gonna have to go. I'll call you up later, okay? The annoyance that is Keaton is currently making ugly faces at me that make me want to throw up."

Archer laughs which makes a smile creep up onto my face.

"Alright. Don't forget to call me. Please." Archer says and I roll my eyes before hanging up.

All of us have dinner except for Lawrence, who was apparently out for a study project at a friend's house. Mom told me over dinner that she was only staying tonight because her friend was expecting her and they were going to go over mom's honeymoon plans. Which, by the way, is disgusting. That was not something I wanted to know about.

As it turns out, Keaton was also staying another night, because apparently he was having a fight with his sister- and yes it was Jenny from the store. Apparently Archer told her about the party incident and Jenny freaked the hell out. At that moment, I really wanted Keaton to go home then. I'd love to watch Jenny freak out over her brother. Ha.

I quickly prepared to go for bed. Mom was having her lovey-dovey chat with Gavin and again. I did not want to know what they were talking about. It's not right for my innocent ears.

I sighed as I plopped into bed dressed in a pair of white cotton joggers and a loose blue shirt- I practically fainted.

My phone buzzes. Again.

For the how many'th god damned time. How many people are going to freaking interrupt my wonderful sleep?!

I grab my phone from under my pillows and look at the screen.

Archer?

I look at the time.

It was 2 in the morning.

2. In. The. Morning!!!

I groan as I answer it and place it to my ear.

"Archer?" I asked.

"Darcy!" Archer's voice greets happily, I hear loud music playing in the background... Why am I getting this really weird feeling of déjà vu?

"Archer... where are you?" I asked, sitting up.

"Somewhere... Over the rainbow..." He says/sings giggling as his words slur. Ugh, his voice is cute even when he's drunk.

"Okay Mr. Leprechaun man, on a scale of 1 to 10 how hammered are you?" I asked.

"One.... thousandddddd." Archer slurs and I stifle a giggle. Don't. Laugh. At. Your. Drunk.... Uh... Something.

"Oh god. Are you with any friends?"

"No..."

"Archer, please, tell me where you are so I can come get you." I say, worriedly.

"I'm fine... Just wanted to call you since you forgot..." He says and all of a sudden, I hear sobbing.

Oh my god.

Is Archer a sad drunk?

Oh my golly gracious he's a sad drunk.

"Archer... babe..." I cringe at that word- which is why I always use it teasingly.

"Yeah?" Archer responds in between sobs.

"Archer tell me where you are." I say.

"Nope. No no no no no..." He says stubbornly.

"Yo Archer, you a'ight?" Someone says.

"I'm fiiiine. Go away, I'm talking to Dar....cy..." Archer tries to say.

"Archer, just tell me where you are and I'll come get you." I say, somewhat annoyed.

"But then you'll know who I am..." Archer whines and I hear the guy from before groan.

"Hey, whoever you are, Archer's over at-"

"SSSHHHH!!!!" Archer suddenly shouts and I roll my eyes.

"Archer?" I ask, trying a different method.

"Huh?" He asks.

"If you let me bring you home, you can have anything and I mean anythingyou want from me." I say in as much of a persuasive voice as I can.

"...Really?" He asks.

"Yes, really. I will swim across the Pacific Ocean if you ask." I say.

"Promise not to look at me?" Archer asks.

"I... promise." I say, hesitantly. What? I am curious.

"Pinky swear?" Archer asks. Oh my freaking goodness.

"Pink fücking to hell and back swear." I say and Archer laughs.

"I love your jokes..." He says groggily.

"Archer, tell me where you are... please?" I plead and I hear Archer moaning.

"Cielo..." Archer says and I hear a thud.

"Come on Arch!" The same guy from before shouts in the background before I hear the phone being picked up.

"Hey, Darcy, right? I'll be waiting for you to pick up Arch at the entrance. God knows how this man drinks- probably shouldn't have invited him here on a bad night." The unknown man says and I bite my bottom lip.

"A bad night?" I asked and the man sighs.

"Never mind that. I can talk about it later. Just please, come fetch this drunk fella as soon as you can." He says.

"Alright. I'll be there asap." I say.

As I hang up and speed to my bathroom, I realize something.

I might just meet him today.

I might just see him.

I will finally see him.

...Woo.

# Chapter 16

With my hair flowing in wild curls from my bun from earlier, my pajamas all crinkled, and a certainly annoyed stranger calling me, I finally made it to Cielo inside the luxury minivan. Wesley already seemed to understand what was going on and I was so glad that he looked like he never slept. Seriously. This guy needs a major raise.

"Thanks Wes. I'll be right back." I say and Wesley nods as I make my way out the door.

There's a long line but I pay no mind to that as I spot two guys sitting on the edge of the sidewalk.

"Archer?!" I call out and one them look up.

He pats the other guy's back as he motions for me to come over.

"Archer's right over here!" He yells and I make my way past the judgemental stares of the people in line. It's not like I was even going to go in, like please.

"How is he?" I asked, noticing that "Archer" was slumped on the side with a hoodie on.

"He's good. Told me to buy him a face mask, shades, and a hoodie though." The guy says and I roll my eyes. "The name's Jaime."

I nod as I shake his hand. Jaime was dark skinned and had his hair in a buzz cut. He had a kind smile and wore a pair of ripped jeans, a grey shirt, and a pair of, well, classic Jordans. My knowledge of Jordans was minimal-but when you grow up in a shoe-obsessed high school population, they were hard to miss.

"Darcy." I say as I give him a smile. "Has Archer said anything about me?" I asked.

"Only that you're his bachelorette. Gotta say though, Nate didn't think the guy would even make it through the night."

"Nate?" I ask, ignoring the whole bachelorette comment.

"He's the one who brought him out in the first place. Nate's his best friend, he's got a wife and kid downtown and Archer's the kid's godfather. They were supposed to be celebrating something- but something bad went down." Jaime says and I nod.

"Well, I hope it isn't anything too serious." I sigh. "Thanks for taking care of him."

"Yeah, well, not like you have much choice. That guy's a terrible drunk. Hell, I don't even know why we try to bring him to these things." Jaime says and I giggle.

"Thanks Jaime." I say and he shrugs.

"No problem. Tell him when he gets up tomorrow that he deserves the hangover, guy needs to learn some sort of control!" Jaime says with a wide smile.

"Got it. I will properly scold him from head to damned toe." I say and Jaime nods.

"A'ight then, I'm gonna go run back in and get myself hammered. I'll see ya around Darcy!" He says and I grin as he scurries back inside, giving me one last wave before disappearing inside.

"Archer?" I call out as I sit down beside him.

Jaime wasn't kidding. Archer had a pair of dark shades on, a surgical mask, and a hoodie. He was completely hiding his face from me.

"...Go away." He says and I roll my eyes.

"If I go away, I'm never talking to you again." I threaten and I'm about to stand up when I feel him hold my wrist. I smirk triumphantly. "Up we go then." I say and I try to pull him but he doesn't budge.

"...Do you like Lawrence?" Archer asks and I give him a look- but then I see that he's not even looking at me. He's looking out at the open road and I sigh.

"Can I answer you later?" I asked. "I can't lift you home, Archer."

I hear him sigh and all of a sudden, the minivan is already brought near us and I hear Wesley get out.

"I'll bring him inside Ms. Darcy." Wesley says and I nod as I slide the door open and plop into an individual seat.

Wesley then slings Archer's arm around his own. Archer grumbles a series of slurred words before he's left on the other seat. I bite my bottom lip as the door closes and Wesley re-enters the car.

"Is everything okay, Ms. Bleu?" Wesley asks me, I nod.

"Y-yeah. Everything's fine." I say, stuttering a bit. I was a bit nervous.

My heart was practically leaping out of my chest. Here he was. My mystery phone buddy- well, romantically inclined phone buddy. But a phone buddy nonetheless.

"Should I drive us to Sir Archer's home or yours?" Wesley asks and I sigh.

"Mine. I don't think he'd be comfortable with me snooping around his home." I say with a shrug and Wesley nods curtly before pulling out of the way.

Wesley is seriously my freaking savior. He carried Archer soundlessly up to the penthouse and well... uh, into my room. Wesley told me it was okay, considering that the other guest room was taken up by my mom. But then again, I'm pretty sure there's more than one guest room. I think Wesley's setting me up- but he insisted, and Wesley was the one carrying Archer up to the penthouse in the first place. Who was I to complain?

I sighed as I thanked Wesley and climbed back up to my room. Archer had already been laid on the bed, his shoes were on the floor and he was slightly snoring. Cute. I think to myself before shaking my head. Stop creeping on him Darce. I think to myself before I lie down on the opposite side and yawn.

I checked the time. It was only 3:30 in the morning. Ugh.

I seriously need my sleep.

I sighed to myself.

I'm sure he wouldn't mind if I slept beside him.

I probably should've known better.

The first thing that I thought of when I got up was one word- hot. Not the 'that guy is hot' kind of hot either. More like the 'why is it so fücking hot in here' kind of hot. I opened my eyes and almost had a heart attack.

Archer's arms were wrapped around my shoulders and my head, bringing my face close to his chest. My legs were intertwined with his and I was so close I could feel his breath through the face mask. Awkward... I think to myself.

I glanced up at him.

The mask was slightly moved and I could make out the faint lines of his lips. His shades were bent upwards and I could see his long lashes- well one set- the other eye was still hidden. Ugh. Why couldn't he just meet me like a normal person? I think to myself.

"Darcy?" I hear someone at the door call. Oh crap.

That was my mother.

Oh.... CRAP!

I decide not to answer.

Please mom... do not open that door! I think to myself. I should have locked it! Ugh!

"I think she's still asleep." Lawrence's voice says and I sigh in relief.

"Oh, well, I guess I can just leave her a note. I have a meeting with my friend like... soon." My mom says and I hear Lawrence say something but I can't comprehend what it is.

I sigh before trying to disentangle myself from Mr. Stranger here. Tried.

"...Don't go..." Archer's voice, low and gruff from the morning, says. I smirk.

"Only if you take off those glasses." I say and I hear Archer chuckle lowly.

"Can you stay in bed for longer?" He asks and I grin.

"Do you want me to?" I ask and he nods in response.

"I have a terrible hangover, babe." He says and I giggle lightly.

"Ew, babe." I say rolling my eyes. "You, sir, would lose against me in a drinking contest." I say tapping my pointer finger against his chest.

He chuckles again and I feel the notion vibrate at my fingertip.

"I heard your tolerance lasted you 10 drinks and more." He says and although I can't really see his face, I know he's smirking.

"Uh huh." I say and Archer uses his free hand to trail his fingers across my cheek and down to my jawline. I gulp nervously, not knowing what else to do.

"Do you really want to know who I am?" He asks and I nod slowly.

I watch as he slowly reaches for his ears and he unlatches one elastic from his ear. I bite my bottom lip and Archer slowly reaches for the other one. I feel my heart thump against my chest in absolute excitement.

This is it.

This is freaking it-

"GET YOUR ÄSS UP!" A familiarly annoying voice yells as my unlocked and defenseless door is slammed open.

I immediately throw all the covers onto Archer. I don't even know how I did that in so quickly. But my duvet, blankets, and just about everything, were thrown on top of Archer so that I had one side of my bed covered in sheets.

"If you were up the entire time, you should have just gotten up." Keaton says, folding his arms over his chest.

"Do you have a good reason to even be in here? Get out." I hiss.

"I'm trying to get you up because you just missed your mom."

"Get. Out." I snap again, not listening to him. Keaton rolls his eyes and runs a hand through his hair.

"...Fine." He growls but I send him the hardest glare and I watch as he tenses up before leaving with a door slammed locked.

I sigh in relief before removing the covers from Archer.

"Sorry about that." I say and Archer, I think, grins through his mask.

"Nice cover." He says and I roll my eyes.

"You know what, I'm gonna go to the bathroom for a bit, you go... do your stranger things for a bit." I say, winking at him. Archer chuckles before I scurry off into the bathroom to do my girly things.

Day 2 at least would be better... right? I decide to take a quick shower to scrub myself off. I get out and run a towel through my hair as I walk out in a fluffy navy blue robe and well- an extra pair of undies for my less than convenient situation.

"I should come here more often." Archer says in a low voice and I jump in surprise as I see him standing shirtless with his back against my closet door.

I stared at him for what seemed like hours. This guy was lean but not overly-so. I wasn't really into the whole 8-pack overly muscle-y look. But Archer had muscle and a six pack that wasn't too pronounced. And well... the V of his...

I'm going to shut up now.

I cleared my throat before I trailed my eyes up to his face and I frowned.

"Okay, this would probably be a lot hotter if you weren't wearing shades and a mask." I say, folding my arms over my chest in an attempt to calm my pounding heart.

"Speaking of which, I believe this is the most I've ever shown you." He says as he reaches out and tucks one of my wet strands of hair behind my ear.

I feel the heat spread out from there and I know my face has probably turned tomato red.

"Archer..." I say in a hushed tone. Archer reaches for my hands and makes me drop the towel on the floor.

He places them on his ears where the latches of his stupid mask are.

"Go for it." He says and I can feel how shaky his grip is on me.

He's nervous? Hell I'm freaking nervous. I think to myself as I bite my bottom lip. I hook my pointer fingers through the thin elastic that stuck to the back of his ears.

"You sure?" I asked and I watch as Archer swallows and nods stiffly.

"...Yeah." He says and I take a deep breath as I slowly unhook the mask.

Once I unlatch both of them, I move slowly to remove them, not because I want a dramatic moment. But because he was so tense that I felt that he wouldn't want me to just take it out and stare. Once I got the mask off, I dropped it on the floor and he took my right hand and placed it on the tip of his glasses.

"This is a lot more nerve-wracking than I thought it would be." Archer says with a nervous laugh. I nod and give him an encouraging smile.

"You let me see your face and we can go on a date. Considering Keaton's date was absolute shit- well it ended-"

"I know." Archer says, silencing me by tilting my chin up to my face. "And I remember you saying you'd do anything if I let you take me home." He says with a smirk that I can now perfectly see.

I try not to stare. I really do. But when I last actually saw him, the lights were dimmed and I was too busy dancing to really think about his face... Then again, I still had the photo on my phone. But seeing him on a screen and seeing him in real life really had a completely different effect.

"Okay, I did say that, but I didn't think you'd remember." I say, rolling my eyes. "But I'd never say that unless I wanted to and besides, I got you to let me do this." I say as I slowly move to pull the dark glasses from his face.

His eyes capture my gaze again. Those green eyes that are tinged with a pretty golden yellow. I don't think I stare at anything other than those eyes for the next 5 seconds...

Then my eyes trail down and I end up... well... gawking.

"Darcy, I swear if you don't stop staring, I may or may not do something that I'm not sure you'll love." I arch a brow.

"Now I want to keep staring, but I think you need to clean up- I have a big old shirt somewhere in my old luggage bag and also, I need to change if we're going on a little date, babe." I say with a smile. I wanted to lighten the mood

Because to be honest. I would die staring at this little... piece of sugar, spice and everything goddamn nice.

"Well, babe, I'm sure I had a few clothes for me tucked away in the back of the third drawer to the right of that door." Archer says with a wink.

"...You have clothes in my closet?" I asked. Archer grins and I think I'm about to have a stroke. This guy is going to kill me... I think to myself.

"I was going to take it home, but I was working on getting everything organized, I don't trust the 'help' really well, and I didn't want anyone working through that particularly interesting drawer. I placed them in the back corner and I slept for a bit. I'm sor-"

"You're rambling and it's adorable." I say with a smile and Archer blinks at me before returning my smile. He reaches out to my cheek and tips my face up to plant a soft kiss on my cheek.

My face heats up and he chuckles.

"I've wanted to do that for a long time." He says and it was my turn to nervously swallow a non-existent lump in my throat. Before I can say anything, he smiles and enters the bathroom.

"...Well... damn..." I mutter to myself before disappearing into my closet and closing the door.

My heart was pounding. What is this man doing to me? I thought to myself. If I thought my petty crush on Lawrence was bad, this was worse. But what I found myself wondering the most was why. Why today? Why was he showing me his face all of a sudden?

Because technically you still don't know him for who he is. My snarky subconscious tells me at the back of my mind.

That, of course, was undoubtedly true. I mean, we texted and all, but let's be honest. I didn't really know him.

I sighed to myself. Overthinking makes me sad and depressed and makes me question life's very existence.

I walked over to my closet and dressed in a bright outfit that would make me happy and quirky. I had had my eye on a pair of bright äss heels and I decided today was the day I'd rock them. I pulled on a pair of somewhat distressed pale blue high waisted jeans, a neon yellow cropped blouse, a loose and brightly pink and purple feather patterned kimono cardigan, and a few black and gold accessories- not forgetting my bracelet of course.

I grab a small boxed bag and place a pair of shades and other things in before I decided that I better give Archer his stuff before he walks out naked... That was tempting, but not a good idea. Especially not for my poor heart.

I opened the "third drawer to the right of the door" and gawked at it. How had I not noticed this? In that drawer was big white box. And I knew by the brand on that box that there was a dress in that. A very expensive kind of dress worn only a few times in someone's life. On the side of that box was a neatly folded navy blue button down, a pair of white jeans, and um... well... Calvin Klein boxers that I discreetly snuck between the shirt and the jeans.

I bite my bottom lip, grab Archer's clothes, and close the drawer. I can not bring that up yet.

I open the door and sigh in relief when I see that Archer hasn't left the bathroom yet. I place the clothes on the floor, sweeping my towel and all the other things up to tidy my room. Then I rush back into the closet and put on some mascara and a pretty natural looking pink lipstick. I pull my hair into a neat low bun, spritz on some perfume and smile in approval at my appearance.

I feel a pair of arms wrap around my waist. Since my skin is bare, I feel tingles run up my back and I tense.

"Ready?" He asks and I nod as I stare at us in the reflection.

Archer's got his head resting on top of mine and I frown.

"Ugh, don't rub your tall-ness in." I say before sticking my tongue out and Archer laughs and I can feel his chest vibrate against my head. Archer's hair is a wet mess of long strands and I turn around so I face him.

"Did you look at it?" Archer asks, I blank at that before I realize he's talking about the large box.

"I didn't yet... It's... Well..." I trail off and Archer shakes his head and offers me a wide smile before bringing me closer to him.

I'm pushed against his chest and I can hear how fast his heart is beating and the action makes me a red hot mess.

"Don't worry, I'll wait for it to be right time." Archer says. "Besides, I have trouble picking rings in the first place- and no, you don't have to wear that gown- I didn't choose it, hell I haven't even seen it- but my cousin and my sister did."

"Holly and Jen?" I asked and Archer nods against my head. I look up at him and that was honestly a bad choice.

I was literally mere centimeters away from his (gorgeous) face. I look at his eyes and his gaze strikes me in a deep and thoughtful way.

"...I was hoping for a better scenario but..." Archer says and I stare at him blankly before one of his arms leave my waist and he tilts my face upwards and our lips brush for mere seconds. "This works." He whispers against my lips.

I mentally have a blank before I feel my entire body warm up at the realization at what Archer had just done. Seconds pass and Archer begins to try to talk.

"...Did you not like the ki-" Archer starts but I pull him down again and I sigh in contentment as our lips meet.

This was the third kiss in my entire life. So don't expect any amazing make-out sessions. Our kisses were short and sweet, eyes were closed, and fluttery feelings roamed around my belly, and Archer didn't mind that. He grinned as he placed soft kisses against my lips and I giggled at how ridiculous we were being.

"Okay, we've got to stop before my heart leaps out of my chest and we spend our date in the hospital." I say and Archer places one final kiss to my lips before smiling at me.

His smile is freaking contagious, I'll tell you that.

He looked so happy, he could levitate.

"Good idea." He says and I smile as he places his hand around my waist and leads me out the door.

The fluttery feeling in my stomach made me feel like fainting and I could swear my face was as hot as a volcano.

"...Y-you look happy." I stutter, mentally cursing myself.

"I am." Archer says contently. "You kissed me back." He says with what I would describe as a stupid smile on his face.

It's the type of smile someone that's extremely proud puts on and they can't help it. As in the type of smile that could last absolutely forever and when people ask you why you're smiling, you just end up in a daze.

"Rub it in, will you." I say, playfully elbowing him.

"I will. You. Kissed. Me. Back." Archer says, making sure to enunciate every word. I roll my eyes and giggle before he walks us down the steps.

When we reach the bottom of the steps, Archer still has a smile plastered onto his face that I almost want to smack him for. But he starts laughing and I smile at how pleased he looks just as he lifts my body up and spins me around until we end up by the large glass windows and he plants a soft kiss on my lips that I return with as much sweetness as I can. This time, it's Archer who sighs happily against my lips and I giggle as I feel his grin.

My stomach growls and so does Archer's and we both pause before laughing at each other.

"Let's go eat something other than each other's lips." Archer says and I laugh.

"Buvette?" I asked and Archer shakes his head.

"Let's try something more familiar. You up for Chili's?" Archer asks and I nod excitedly, my stomach growling already at the thought of a classic burger.

"Let's go!" I say excitedly and Archer nods as we make our way out of the apartment.

# Chapter 17

"Archer Klein Carter, give me back my shoes!" I shout as I run after him.

Archer had brought us to the fairly empty beach and I took off my shoes because hell, what type of stupid woman would run around the beach with stiletto heels on? We had been running around the place and we decided to dip our feet in and Archer had decided that it'd be funny if he suggested we go to the car when the sun was beating down on hot burning sand.

"If my feet blister, I will kill you." I say and he chuckles.

"No problem."

Archer says as he walks over to me and in one swift movement, I'm slung over his shoulder.

"Archer!!!" I scream. "Let. Me. Down!" I squeal and Archer laughs as he walks over to the pavement.

"Never." He says and I roll my eyes as I try to squirm around but his grip around my waist is too strong for me to break from.

"You are such a kid." I say and Archer chuckles as he slowly places me down and I stand on his shoes. I look up at him and he brushes his lips against mine.

"Better?" Archer asks and I feel my face burn up. Archer smiles as he lifts me again and has me sit on one of the wide stone railings.

He places my shoes on the ledge, takes one and slowly puts them on my feet.

"I am perfectly able to put my own shoes on, dad." I tease, Archer smiles to himself but continues to work on my shoes until both of them are on.

"If you get tired, tell me. Wouldn't want you to fall all over the place now would we?" Archer asks and I smirk at him before he presses a kiss on my forehead and I practically jump off the ledge.

"Where are we off to next?" I asked as I intertwined my fingers in Archer's.

"Actually, I want to show you the office I work in." Archer says as he stops and lifts my hand up to his lips. I giggle as he kisses it and roll my eyes.

"Don't tell me you're ditching me for work, Mr. A." I say and Archer chuckles.

"I'm not ditching you for anything Darcy. I want to show you where I have panic attacks and nervous breakdowns about your responses to my messages."

"Uh huh." I say with a smile. "Let's go then."

"This place is huge." I say, gawking.

What kind of guy needs one fourth of an entire top floor for his office? I mean, what the hell are you going to do in that space?

Archer's office was ridiculous. I mean that in the nicest way possible. He has a flat screen that's currently flashing beautiful pictures of sunsets, sunrises, and other scenic photos. His desk is propped up in the corner and the glass walls give me a giddy feeling. A large section of the floor is covered by an expensive looking black carpet. The ceiling is way too tall for a normal office and... hold up. Why does someone need a pool table in an office?

I look over at it and bite my bottom lip. Talk about intimidating. I think to myself.

Did I mention how it even felt to have Archer with his hand around my waist as we went in? Let's just say the whole "who the hell is this" stares were brought onto a whole other level. I swear. The people in the office obviously tried to be civil about it and had their best behaviour on, granted, Archer was of obvious high status, but I mean, had Archer not been there, they looked like they were ready to pounce and tear me to shreds. Let's not even get started on the women.

"Like it?" Archer asks just as he leaves my side and goes to his neat black and white modernist desk.

"Uh huh." I say plainly. "Why is there a pool table?" I asked.

"Don't ask me. I have another sister named Carly, she's an interior designer, she told me it would look good. Granted, I've never used the thing, and I'm terrible at pool."

"That makes two of us." I comment as I walk around.

There are abstract paintings placed in pitch black frames. They're all arranged at different heights to create a really clean modern look. I loved this office- except for the pool table. Can't get over that.

"What exactly do you do?" I asked. "I mean, you do have a large äss office." I say Archer grins as I watch him sit on his desk chair and type up a few things on his large computer. This place just speaks large in excessive size and expense.

"I do various things, like buying companies, expanding the company, etcetera. Not much to tell really." He says.

"Not much to tell?" I gawk. "Yeah, yeah, sure." I say sarcastically and Archer smiles.

"Come here." He says and I walk over to him.

He pulls me onto his lap and I'm all of a sudden sitting horizontally across him. The crook of my knees lie in his arms and my upper body rests on his chest.

"This. Doesn't make me different from anyone else." He says to me and I nod as I snuggle into his chest.

"You're lucky I'm tiny, otherwise, you might wanna get a bigger chair." I joke and Archer smiles before kissing my cheek.

"Or maybe give you a chair of your own." He says. "I like having you around me."

"I like having you around me too." I admit and Archer's dimples pop again- well- they've been there since this morning and let's just say I'm trying not to swoon.

Archer places a hand at the small of my back and adjust us so that I'm straddling him. The chair creaks and I giggle as it moves back and reclines.

"We are going to fall." I say and Archer shakes his head. He reaches for the back of my head and soon enough my hair falls in messy curls around my face.

"I like it better when you let it down." He says and I feel my face heat up.

"...I liked it better when you couldn't see my face. This embarrasses the absolute hell out of me." I blurt and Archer brings me down so that my face is in the crook of his neck and I feel him breathe in.

"You smell of the ocean Ms. Bleu." He says and I giggle.

"So do you." I say, drawing little circles on his shoulder blade. "Say..." I begin as I slightly push against him so that we're facing each other again.

"Whatever happened to, 'I don't wanna get you involved in my life of blah blah blah'?" I ask, referring to one of the first letters that he'd given me. He reaches for my face and runs a hand down my jaw again.

"I still don't. I have hesitations. Don't even tell me that you didn't feel uncomfortable on the way here. I was testing waters and you know how the people in this building reacted." He says and I nod, appreciating that he was at least, aware that I was being belittled by his 'co-workers' or whoever they were.

"They won't give you an easy time, that's for sure, and you can just imagine how much crap they're spouting on out there. You're in university, you have priorities that shouldn't be destroyed just because of some people that don't like you. Granted, there's always some ässhole like that no matter where you go. But I want you to live your life the way you want it." He says.

"What makes you think I won't be able to?" I ask.

"I'm not saying that. I'm saying that I want you to live a normal college life- because let's face it, I feel like an old man, and technically I am and I'm only in this position because my own old man decided to give me a chance. I'm only 24, Darce. These people are ready to pounce at me no matter what."

Wait.

What?

"24?!" I exclaim and Archer rolls his eyes.

"Uh huh."

"But. Well. You. Office. Uh." I say, not able to comprehend things.

"I didn't get here the way most people do, Darce."

"You do realize the age gap between us is 6 years, right?" I asked.

"Technically 5, not that it matters now, does it?" He asks and I see a flicker of uncertainty cross his eyes.

"By a couple years older, I thought Holly meant ages 19-22." I say- ruining what may have been a serious moment.

"Does that bother you? My age?" Archer asks and I shake my head.

"No, but it sure makes you look even more intimidating than I thought you were. Hell, is our relationship even legal?" I asked and Archer's face suddenly... twitches.

"...Relationship?" He asks with a smile.

Oh boy.

There it is again. The smile.

"Did I say that? I meant to say 'thing'. You know the type of 'thing' you don't really know what to call, I mean I get that-"

"Darcy." Archer calls and I look into his eyes. Damn it. Those things need to stop luring me in with their fancy colors.

"...What?" I asked. Archer smiles at me and this time, he reaches for the back of my neck and brings my face down so that we're only centimeters apart.

"Tell me, what is our relationship, exactly?" Archer asks, a mischievous and proud grin plastered on his face. Damn it. Stupid brain, stupid mouth, stupid words.

"I dunno." I squeak.

"Darcy..." Archer whines as he runs a hand through my hair.

I am dangerously close to this man. He might as well squish my face against his.

"Archer..." I whine back and Archer smirks.

His hand suddenly brings me down and I brace myself for a soft peck. My heart races against my chest again and the butterflies practically bounce around my stomach-

"Archer Klein Carter, you open this door right now!" A female voice that I absolutely don't recognize shouts behind the wide dark wooden double doors of Archer's office. I blush furiously as I stumble to get off Archer but he holds me against him.

"It's my mother." Archer says with a disappointed huff.

"...What?" I ask, dazed, Archer smirks as he pulls me down quickly and plants a chaste kiss on my lips.

"Looks like you're about to meet my family, babe." He says, chuckling as he watches me bite my bottom lip.

"Kill me now." I mutter and he laughs this time. I sigh and run a hand through my hair before standing up.

Archer walks over to me and wraps his hand around my waist from behind.

"She loves you already, you do know that right?" He asks.

"How?"

"Holly and Jen don't exactly have closed mouths when it comes to mom. She's a bit on the happy-go-lucky side of things." He says and I nod as Archer turns me around and places one soft kiss against my forehead.

He takes my hand in his and walks over to the door. My heart is frantic, and I swear, one of these days, Archer is going to give me a goddamned heart attack. It's like my body has a mind of its own. Archer gives me one last encouraging smile before he opens the door. I barely even have the time to compose myself when the door swings open...

And voila.

There stood a woman who was fairly short, my height if I wasn't wearing heels. Her hair was a pale brown but had slight silver streaks in it. She had a really short haircut that had been styled to look almost like Julie Andrews in the Princess Diaries.

Scratch that.

She was practically her. I mean, her outfit was the same, a smooth cream creaseless blazer over a plain white blouse and a matching skirt. Her face was natural, wrinkles showing her age on her face. At first, she doesn't notice me, and she frowns at Archer. But as she's about to speak, she glances at me and her eyes widen.

"Oh my goodness. Is this her?" She asks, in a happy and excited voice.

"Yes, mom." Archer says with a sigh, rolling his eyes.

"Archer, dear, don't roll your eyes at me. You know how much I hate it when you do that." She says and I giggle as he gets scolded.

"Hi..." I trail off, not knowing what to call her.

"Gabbie. Please, don't call me anything other than that. That or mom." Gabbie says happily. I giggle and nod as she takes my hand in hers. "My goodness, Archer, you really shouldn't keep things from your mother. Especially not when you decide to run off and bring her to the office."

"It was a spontaneous event mom." Archer says as his mom and I walk over to large lounge-like area of the room.

Gabbie and I sit on the smooth cream couch and she grins as she gazes at me.

"So tell me my dear, how is my Archer doing on the... well, you know." She asks and I bite my bottom lip as I watch Archer pretend to go back to work.

I move closer to Gabbie and whisper in her ear.

"I have zero complaints." I say and Gabbie giggles as she looks over at her son.

Sh"You know I can hear the both of you." Archer says loudly.

"Oh hush over there, you need to go to work while I enjoy this fine young lady's company. I believe you've occupied her enough." She says and I give Archer a smile. Gabbie turns back to me and takes my hand, squeezing it slightly. "Archer, darling, could you be a wonderful son and get me my handbag from... what's her name... The receptionist, was it, Beverly? I can't even remember." Gabbie says.

"Sarah. I'll have her bring it over."

"Nope. I want you to get it you lazy bastard." Gabbie says in such a funny tone that I can't help but laugh.

Archer gives me a warning look but I can't help the giggles that escape my mouth.

"Fine." He says with a groan as he gets up, he walks over to me and kisses my cheek before giving his mom a soft glare. "Don't embarrass me. Please." Archer says and Gabbie grins.

"Oh I'm not sure if I can't, Archer, you did have a pretty funny child-hood." She says and Archer runs a frustrated hand through his hair before leaving the room.

"Now then, where were we?" Gabbie asks. "Oh, yes. Tell me darling, how is the... experience?" I pause and think for a moment.

"Oh. That experience. Hmm... I find it, well, okay I guess."

"I understand my husband told you all about it."

"Yeah. 'Uncle Gerald', right?" I asked and Gabbie giggles. "He told me all about it, it's weird, and uh, they don't seem to know that I know. But so far, I'm pretty certain on which one I'm not picking."

"It doesn't take a genius to figure out, Darcy." Gabbie says. "I mean, granted, my sons are both wonderful, I mean, they are my children. But Keaton's known to be very... well... how do I put this. My son has very inappropriate tastes."

"Mmhmm." I murmur.

"Is my son treating you well, though? This son I mean." Gabbie asks and I look around before looking at Gabbie. I nod shyly and she laughs as she places a hand on my shoulder.

"Please, darling, I may be wrong, but you two look terribly smitten with each other. And I mean that in a very good way."

"I'm just unsure... I've never actually had a relationship before and I have no idea what I feel and what I do." I admit, embarrassed.

"To be honest, I didn't know if I loved Gerald either. I was rather con-vinced that he was only after the money I could offer." She says with a shrug. "But, in time, I'm sure, you'll figure it out. And besides, I'll always be here to help a fellow candidate out." Gabbie says with an encouraging smile.

"This is just so weird." I admit and she smiles.

"Trust me. It could be worse. I remember hearing stories of roofs covered in nothing but flowers because he wanted the candidate so bad." She says.

"What if the candidate is a guy?" I asked.

"It's happened before, trust me, nothing has been funnier. Unfortunately, most of the time, the only people who want to participate are the men of the company- not to mention, there are more of them than there are us in this place." Gabbie says.

"Huh." I say simply just as the doors to Archer's office swing open and he walks in with a plain white structured bag that has a signature Burberry scarf wrapped around the handle.

"Here's your bag." Archer says grumpily and Gabbie chuckles as she takes it and Archer comes to my side. He sits beside me and circles his left arm around my waist.

"The two of you and your youth make me envious." Gabbie says with a smile. "We should all have dinner some time... Next week Friday seems to be free for me." She says.

I look at Archer and he gives me a nod.

"Sounds good to us." I say.

"I'll make sure to keep it free." He says.

Gabbie nods as she stands up. We follow suit until we reach the door.

"Well, I'm gonna go ahead and talk to your father. Lord knows what he's up to these days." Gabbie says and Archer and I nod in unison as we kiss her cheeks.

As we hug each other for a wonderful first meeting, she whispers into my ear.

"If my sons give you any trouble, give me a call." I giggle and Archer arches his brow at me just as his mother leaves.

I close the door to his office and turn to face Archer. He's immediately in front of me and rests his head on top of mine.

"I'm not a pillow." I huff and Archer laughs as he wraps his arms around my waist. How the hell is this guy so tall?! He takes a deep breath before lifting his head and looking at me.

"Hungry yet?" He asks and I shake my head.

"Not really. But you look like you're starving." I say with a shrug and he kisses my forehead.

"We can have lunch at one of the family restaurants. I need to make a surprise inspection anyways."

"Big shot." I mumble.

"What?"

"Nothing!" I say with a big smile.

I moan in delight at the taste of the steak we... well Archer, was having.

"Good right?" Archer asks.

"Mmhmm..." I say and Archer laughs.

"You should've ordered one." He says and I roll my eyes.

"Do you remember how much food I ate at Chili's? I could die of food right now. Not that that would be a terrible way to go." I say with a shrug.

"But you're only having a-"

"Strawberry smoothie. Yup." I complete for him as I take a big sip.

"You're not on a diet are you?" He asks me and I roll my eyes.

"Me? On a diet?" I laugh and Archer grins at me.

Archer had us sitting together on the same side of a rounded booth. Speaking of which, he did that this morning too. He always had me by his side rather than across him. The restaurant that he was talking about happened to sit at the 15th floor of Carter-Pavel hotel and it was pretty sleek and fancy. There were rounded booths, pretty buffet sets, and a decent amount of posh people chatting about.

"You really like sitting together, don't you?" I muse aloud and Archer smiles.

"It keeps you close to me." Archer says, unembarrassed.

"I'm not going anywhere." I say.

"Doesn't mean I can't keep my eye on you." He says, pausing. "I can't have anyone else sweeping you away." I feel my cheeks heat up and I poke him playfully on his chest.

"Chill. Out." I say, pouting and he laughs as he intertwines our hands under the table. Ugh. I can just imagine what Clara and Martin would say if they were-

"Darcy!"

Oh.

Well then.

I look up at the source of the voice and spot Clara. I'm sooooo gonna get it from her.

"Y-yeah?" I stutter, clearing my throat as Archer quietly chuckles beside me. I try to untangle my fingers and Archer simply grips onto them- not tight so that I squeal in pain- but tight so that I can't let go.

"Thank golly gracious that you're-" Clara begins and then she pauses. "Oh... My... Gosh... Are you Darcy's boyfriend!?" She practically screams and I feel my cheeks burn up to the point that I think I could have boiled water on my face.

Archer laughs freely just as Clara sits across us. I legit want to disappear.

Archer squeezes my hand and rubs circles on the back of it with his thumb.

"Really, Clara?" I ask and she giggles.

"Oh come on, you know you had it coming." She teases. "So, Mr. I-don't-really-know-you, are you or are you not Darcy Darling Baby Bleu's boyfriend?" Where the hell did that name come from? I wonder.

"Darling Baby Bleu?" Archer muses.

"Please. Don't. Say. That." I whine.

"I think I just found your new nickname on my phone." Archer says happily and I sigh before running a hand through my now loose hair.

"Really Clara?" I manage to whine and she giggles at my misery. Great, now I know how it feels when I make fun of Martin.

"Come on guys. Tell. Me." Clara says with obvious excitement in her eyes.

I bite my bottom lip and look up at Archer. He smirks down at me and I look down at our fingers.

"...y...eah..." I mumble silently and Archer arches a brow.

"Hm?" He utters.

"Yeah, Darce, what did you say?" Clara asks.

"...ye...ah..." I say in an almost whisper and Clara, who's obviously enjoying this, giggles to the point of no return.

"Just say it, cutie pie!" Clara squeals as a waiter places a glass of water at her side.

But are we? I mean, he hasn't even asked me that. And besides, technically I'm in this whole Bachelorette fiasco... Who the hell knows if he-

"Darcy Bleu." Archer calls and I look up at him again and he grins as he brings our intertwined fingers up to his lips. "Will you do me the honor of becoming my girlfriend?"

That's it.

That's so freaking it.

My freaking face is at 1000 degrees.

Oh my god.

That is so it.

I'm so done.

"...W-w-what?" I stutter and Archer smiles at me and further takes my hand.

He presses a soft kiss against each and every knuckle and I bite my bottom lip nervously.

"You know what I said." He says as he looks away and I suddenly notice how red he is.

Clara's squealing is completely out of control.

"Oh my gosh, it's like watching a freaking sitcom!" She giggles and I burn in embarrassment.

"Ye-"

"Clara, next time you call for us, make sure you do it thirty minutes ahead of time. Erik and I were watching-" Martin begins but he stops when he notices Clara's deathly glare.

"What?" Martin asks as Erik pops up behind him.

"You interrupted a seriously adorable moment!" Clara exclaimed.

"Excuse me?" Martin asks- and that's when he sees me.

Archer and I are looking away from each other now. My face is probably the shade of a tomato and my heart won't stop beating against my damned chest.

"Oh shït." Martin curses.

"You really need to read the mood a bit." Erik says with a sigh.

"For... real..." Clara moans just as Archer tightens his grip on my hand under the table. "She was about to freaking say yes and you just had to whine about me calling you! Ugh!" Clara says, practically voicing my frustrations.

"Say yes to what?"

"To being his girlfriend!" Clara shouts.

And I mean.

Shouts.

Everything was damned quiet in the restaurant now and I could feel the freaking stares.

And then... it began.

One clap.

Another one.

A cheer.

A whistle...

Archer clenches his hand around mine and before I know it, he's moved so fast that I'm literally inches away from his face.

Clara squeals again and I feel my face burn up.

"Archer..." I whisper and Archer stares straight into my eyes.

"Darcy..." He mirrors.

"Ugh you two are so fücking cheesy. Just kiss already." Martin says, rolling his eyes. I hear a large "thwack" and assume Clara's hit him because Martin's all of a sudden groaning about pain.

Archer smirks as he closes the gap between us-

And that.

Is the exact moment that my body decides to save the excitement...

For later.

Because guess who just fainted for the second time in her entire life?

# Chapter 18

I groaned as I opened my eyes. I was in my room and was still wearing the same clothes from yesterday. On the pillow next to me is a note that I gingerly pick up and read.

Went out to buy us breakfast- if I'm not back by the time you wake up go downstairs ;)

-Mr. A

I smirked at the little note before putting it down and making my way to the bathroom. I took a quick shower and pulled on a pretty ombre pink to red skirt matched with a simple black lace cropped top. I padded my way barefoot downstairs, pulling my hair into a side braid.

"Looks like Ms. Faint-a-Lot is up." Lawrence says with a smile as he sips his cup of coffee.

"Archer told you." I mutter and he nods.

"Of course he did."

"Yeah, yeah, shut up." I say as I make my way to the fridge and pull out a bottle of water.

"You going somewhere?" Lawrence asks and I shrug.

"Not really, just felt like wearing a fancy little skirt, that's all." I say just as I drink from the bottle. Lawrence checks the time on his watch.

"Okay... I gotta go catch my lecture in 10 minutes. I'll see you later." Lawrence says and I barely have time to react as Lawrence practically teleports to the door and disappears.

"See ya." I mumble before skipping over to the living room and lying down on the couch. I turn on the TV and listen mindlessly to the news before I hear the door to the apartment open.

I sit up quickly and grin as I spot Archer walking in with a large paper bag of what I'm guessing is food. Archer sets it down on the dining table and he hasn't noticed me yet, so I quietly pad my way towards him before snaking my arms around his stomach. I could practically feel how strong his build was through the sleek black dress shirt he'd worn. He was wearing grey jeans and he turned, causing me to let go of him. I smiled as he looked down at me.

"Good morning." I greeted, he smiled and gave me a quick peck on the lips before brushing a few strands of hair out of my face.

"Morning." He says with a smile before wrapping his arms around my waist. "Sleep well?" Archer asks and I nod my head.

"I fainted." I say making Archer chuckle, the sound resonating in his chest. He pulls me closer to him and leans against the dining table.

"I know." He says before tilting my chin up. I stare into the hazel orbs that stare straight back at me before I hear my stomach grumble.

I flush in embarrassment and Archer laughs.

"Food. Now." I say before kissing Archer quickly and looking through the paper bag.

I unloaded the bag and placed two neat boxes of food on the table, Archer placed spoons and forks whilst I plopped down onto a chair.

"What's on the menu?" I asked and Archer grinned as he sat beside me.

"Two sets of English Breakfast with your favourite coffee." Archer answers and I smirk. "I have work later today so I wanted to know if you had anything planned as well."

"Not really. But I think I might ask Clara and Martin out. I do need a few other people to talk to other than you, Holly, and Lawrence." I say and Archer pouts at me.

"Needing space already?"

"Oh shut up." I say rolling my eyes, Archer chuckles as we spend the rest of breakfast talking about our plans for the day and decided that we meet up tonight for dinner.

Afterwards, Archer left for work and I texted Martin and Clara to meet up in our usual café. I pulled on some studded flats, a few pieces of rose gold jewelry, and a neat handbag that was a similar nude color. I pulled on a pair of fancy looking headphones and blasted Charlie Puth's "Marvin Gaye" before making my way downstairs. As usual, Wes was already waiting for me by the lobby, so I told him where I needed to go and off we went.

"Love the outfit, girl. You are looking fiiine." Clara compliments when I spot her by the windows of the café.

"Thanks Clara." I say with a smirk. "Where's Martin at?" I asked and Clara sighs.

"Him and his bae ditched us for a cutesy date over at Central Park." Clara says with a smile and I nod as I take my seat. "B.T.W. I'm still waiting for an answer of whether or not you and Archer are dating." She adds and I chuckle.

"We're dating. It's not anything official yet." I explain and Clara pouts at me.

"But he adores you. Look at Martin, he hasn't known the guy for a month and they're already getting it on." I arch a brow and Clara giggles. "Gay guys for. the. win." Clara says and I roll my eyes.

"Hey hashtag 'gay is okay'." I say with a wink and we giggle at each other. "So what have you been up to?" I ask.

"Oh nothing, the usual, trying to get guys to notice lil old me when both my friends have cuties of their own." She says.

"Clara, you don't have to try. Just look in a mirror for god's sake. You look hot." I point out, and she was.

Clara had been gradually letting her purple dip-dyed hair climb higher until it made up half of her hair. Her hair had suddenly become a mesmerising ombre that went from pitch black to softly blended pink and purple waves. Today she had worn a pair of tall black wedges with a sleek all white playsuit and I know that there were guys eyeing her in this café.

"Yeah, yeah. No wonder no guy has ever come up to me." She says sulkily and I smirk as I eye the surrounding area.

"How about..." I trail off... "Ooh! Okay, guy sitting by himself over at the corner." I whisper and Clara sneakily turns her head to look.

The guy looked like a lonely type. But he had cropped ash blonde hair and he looked so frustrated with what he was reading- which was a book of some sort. I turned to look at Clara and she scrutinised the guy from afar.

"That guy, really?" Clara asked and I rolled my eyes.

"Why not?" I asked.

"Because he looks like he might just kill me with a look." She tells me and I sigh.

"Why don't we talk him up a bit- I think he's reading..."

"Darce... he's reading Twilight." Clara says with a sigh.

"Well... that doesn't mean anything! He looks like that book is giving him hell." I point out and Clara groans. "Okay. You know what, you need some confidence in that tiny body of yours."

"Hey I am not that tiny." She argues and I roll my eyes.

"But you're not confident either." I argue back and she takes a deep breath.

"If I do get to talk to him, you're winging me." She says with a pointed look in her face. I nod my head submissively.

"Yes ma'am. Now go!" I say hurrying her to stand up.

With a shaky breath, Clara gets up and makes her way towards the guy. I watch as she strikes a conversation with him and I grin when Clara manages to let her nerves go and let her cute and bubbly self go. I quickly call for a waiter and order a latte whilst I brought out my phone.

I went through my messages and sent a quick reply to Holly who had texted me if I had any plans for the weekend. As I did so, a familiar looking face started walking over to me. I squinted my eyes before realising who it was.

It was Xavier. The lawyer.

He smiled at me before stopping by my table.

"Hello, Ms. Bleu. It's been a while." Xavier greets and I roll my eyes.

"The last time I saw you, I was still angry over the engagement fiasco. But that was my fault." I admit and Xavier smiles.

"I'm glad to know you're understanding." Xavier says. "May I?" He asks, motioning to the other chair across me. I nod my head, glancing in Clara's direction and smiling when I see the two new "friends" have begun talking enthusiastically over what I suspect is the Twilight novel.

"I wanted to see how you were doing, Ms. Bleu." Xavier says and I look over at him.

"I'm doing fine, and call me Darcy. I'm only 18- barely old enough to really handle myself." I mutter and Xavier grins.

"I heard that you and Mr. A have now developed a relationship." Xavier says and I nod.

"Something like that. How long have you been working with their family on this?" I asked.

"This is my first time. They change their lawyers for this case quite often. It's amusing, though." He tells me. "I am slightly concerned over the documents Mr. Archer sent me." I arch a brow.

"Documents?" I asked.

"Oh, no worries. They're documents about the nature of the agreement. I wasn't sure why he'd asked for them at first. But then I thought that perhaps you had already made your decision. It was only by chance that I was able to catch you." Xavier says while looking for something in a sleek black briefcase, classic lawyer. "I wanted to run these requested documents by you before I gave them to Mr. Archer." Xavier explained as he pulled out a few sheets of paper.

I took them from Xavier and skimmed through them...

It was documentation of my financial situation, my scholarship letter, and...

"Why is Archer requesting for my mother and father's finance records?" I asked.

"He said he wanted to make sure that everything was going smoothly. I'm afraid I cannot elaborate without-"

"Without making him look like he's investigating me for swindling." I interrupt with a sigh. "When did he ask for these?" I asked.

"Yesterday, Ms. Ble- I mean Darcy."

"Yesterday? Does his dad know?" Xavier shook his head.

"I'm afraid Mr. Carter himself hasn't told me anything. Which is why I hesitated and wanted to talk to him today as well. Afterwards I was going to talk to you- but it seems we have crossed paths." Xavier says and I swallow a lump in my throat.

"I need to know something, does Archer have access to see all my transactions?" I asked and Xavier gave me a solemn look.

"I'm not the one to answer that."

"So there is possibility... Of course there would be." I say, leaning back into my chair. The waiter suddenly comes by and smiles as he places my latte on the table, I thank him silently before looking over at Xavier.

"Do you want anything?" I asked him and he nodded. The waiter took notice and stopped in front of Xavier, taking his order before leaving us alone.

"I am... very sorry for ambushing you with this. I'm certain my first impression was not a good one. But I was doing my job." Xavier said and I nodded.

"Never mind that. I want to know about Archer's concerns. I understand why it looks like I might be swindling money... but- trust goes both ways." I say, half muttering my words. "I'm sorry Xavier. But do you think you could do me a favor?" I asked and then it was Xavier's turn to arch his brow.

I left Xavier a few hours later. I'd already given Clara a sign that told her I needed to be alone and talk. So she gave it her all and looked like she enjoyed the guy I'd totally set her up with. I smirked to myself as I walked home. I didn't mind walking down the city. I missed it in fact.

I actually missed normal living. It didn't even matter that I lived in such an expensive apartment or that I had every designer piece of clothing at my disposal. So if Archer was investigating me over something like swindling- then he can go right ahead. But he could at least be up front about it. I sighed as I blasted some OneRepublic into my ears and made my way into the apartment building.

Once I got to the apartment, I went straight to my room and looked for the luggage bag I'd brought from home. Then, I shoved my legs into my old comfy varsity shorts and a knitted sweater that had gone all fuzzy from all the use. I shed my face of every layer of makeup I'd put on and then I made my way downstairs to chill by the TV. As I was about to begin my cheer-up anime marathon, my phone buzzed.

I picked it up as I began to watch Ao Haru Ride.

"Who and why?" I asked plainly, since I didn't bother to see who called.

"Darcy? Where are you? I thought we were having dinner together?" Archer asks, his voice sounding concerned.

"Oh. About that, I feel a little bit sick- so why don't we just meet up tomorrow?" I asked.

"How about I head over there and see how you're doing? Then we can cuddle up and watch a movie together." He suggests.

"...Okay." I say, not knowing how to reject him.

"I'll be there in an hour. Love you." He says before hanging up. I sigh to myself.

Just as the anime finally begins, the door to the apartment swings open and I see Lawrence lugging in a large box.

"The hell is that?" I ask and Lawrence grins at me.

"Package from Daisy." He says with a lazy grin.

"Damn... that's one hell of a package." I say and Lawrence chuckles.

"A little help here?" Lawrence asks and I roll my eyes as I get up to help him push it in. I groan as we manage to bring it in far enough so that the door can close.

"What the hell did she send you? A dead elephant?"

"Care package." Lawrence says and I smirk.

"How sweet of her. You should give your darling sister a call." I say, not knowing if Lawrence would pick up on the sister comment or not.

"Yeah, she is a great sis-" Lawrence begins but then he looks over at me, his eyes wide. "Oh shit."

"Yeah 'oh shit'." I repeat, rolling my eyes.

"Who told you?" He asks and I smirk before making my way back onto the couch. Lawrence follows me as we sit on the couch.

"Keaton's been hinting at it non-stop, Lars." I say as I press play, letting the first scene of the anime roll by.

"That little shi- Oh, by the way, how is you and the Arch?" Lawrence asks, changing the subject. I sigh.

"Fine. Okay. Good..." I trail off before realizing that Archer was actually on his damned way. "Oh god. Lars. Emergency. Is your room locked?" I asked him quickly and Lawrence gives me a weird look.

"Uh, no? I trust you enough not to lock that thing, why?" Lawrence asks and I give myself a mental fist pump.

"Okay. Archer's gonna be here in about 5 minutes." I explain. "I have a little bit of a problem with him at the moment- but he doesn't know that. So like..."

I quickly grab the remote and turn off the TV.

"Tell him I'm not here and I'll go hide out in your room because I don't want him to find me. Okay?" I ask quickly.

"...O...kay?" Lawrence says, unsure.

"Great. Thanks Lars. I owe you one- actually- you know what- consider the Daisy thing forgotten. I'm gonna go sprint up to your room right now because I have a feeling-" My phone buzzes and I groan. "He's here. Okay. Oh gosh. Please Lars, for the love of God. Do not tell him I'm here. Tell him... that Martin and- actually no. Tell him I accidentally forgot something back at the uh..."

"Darce. Chill, I got you. But... you owe me one- even with the Daisy thing." Lawrence says and I nod my head. A knock hits the door and I bite back a scream. I kiss Lawrence's cheek and hug him tight.

"You are such a bro." I whisper before quickly and quietly padding my way upstairs.

I take one last look at Lawrence who smiles at me and gives me a thumbs up as I disappear into the third floor. I hear the door open and Archer's slightly muffled voice before I sneak my way into Lawrence's room- a room right beside mine.

The lights are off when I walk in and I sigh in relief as I close the door as silently as possible. I flip the dim yellow lights on and  I smirk at the room before me. It was slightly different from mine. The walls were painted a deep navy blue and the floor was clean and polished dark wood. He has no TV on his walls, instead, the entire two sides are pure glass that make me envy his spectacular view. His bed is a king-sized plain black bed with two pillows and an unfolded messy black comforter.

His floors are clean but his desk is cluttered with papers. On the left walls are two doors that are adjacent to each other. I know that they're the closet and the bathroom. I sit down on Lawrence's bed and lie down, the bed stank of mint- which I'm guessing was Lawrence's favorite. I roll over in the bed and sigh as I pull out my phone.

Hey, where are you? Lars told me that your friends asked you for a sleep-over. Why didn't you tell me? Archer texted. I roll my eyes at Lawrence's excuse.

Sorry, I set Clara up with someone and she was too excited for it- I'll tell you all about it :) But Clara's buggin me right now so, good night okay? :) <3

I don't wait for his reply, knowing that it'll just make the weight on my shoulders feel heavier than they already are. I sigh as I twist and turn on the bed.

Damn it, Darcy. He's the one who's questioning you. Stop feeling bad! I think to myself. I groan as I decide to get comfy on the bed.

I hear footsteps going up and I feel my heart burst against my chest.

"Archer what the hell?!" Lawrence's only slightly muted voice shouts from outside the door. I stand up and quietly creep my way to the door as well.

"What the hell did you tell her?!" Archer shouts back and I feel a strange twist in my chest.

"I didn't tell her anything! Jesus, Arch, she's with Clara!" Lawrence yells.

"Stop lying to me!" Archer yells.

"You need to calm down. She's not here right now." Lawrence says in exasperation.

"I am calm!"

"You are not!" Lawrence says and I hear a loud thud against the wall right next to the door. I bite my bottom lip to stop any noise from coming out.

"Listen here you piece of crap! I don't know what the hell you did but you have no right to puppy guard Darcy, got it? We're all in the same goddamned boat and I'll be damned if you think you can keep her to yourself by pretending you give a damn!" Lawrence says angrily.

"... Get off of me." Archer says and I hear the sounds of what seems like Archer brushing his shoulders off. "Tell her I'll see her tomorrow." I hear Lawrence grunt before the sound of footsteps begin to disappear.

The doorknob is twisted open and Lawrence walks in and slams the door shut. I shudder and he looks over at me.

"Sorry. I wanted him to hear that." He says rubbing the back of his head.

I feel something wet travel down my face and Lawrence's eyes widen.

"Oh crap. Darcy, are you okay?" He asks and man... do I hate the words 'are you okay'.

"Oh god. It's not stopping is it?" I ask and my eyes well up and Lawrence reaches out for me. I surrender to the crying- not knowing what exactly made me cry.

The fact that I was right about Archer's distrust.

Or the fact that my past was repeating itself in the worst way possible.

# Chapter 19

My mom used to tell me that you should never hate your own blood. She reminded me that every time my dad asked me if my mom had taken my allowance from me, if she'd taken the money I got for Christmas, or whenever my dad asked me if my mom had bought me anything expensive.

I hated that.

Calculating how much someone spent over how much you loved them. Putting money before family. Cash before blood. God... did I hate that life.

I hated that he never wanted me to leave. Hated that my own dad didn't support me when I tried to apply for scholarships.

Sure he was proud I got a full scholarship to Pavelton. But the path to getting there was not easy.

Taking the SATs only once sucks. Especially when you were no higher than the average. My 1830 was just high enough for a select few of my chosen universities. A second test was not possible. Sports competitions were hard to pay for, uniform prices were an issue, and then there was the issue at home.

I hate the idea of counting money. I hate the idea of money being the basis of trust and this whole engagement thing is going to bring out the worst in me...

After the tears kept on pouring Lawrence had carried me into my room and set me down.

"I'll go get you some water downstairs, okay?" Lawrence asks and I nod my head as I wipe my stupid tears with the sleeves of my sweater. I groan as I cuddle straight into my bed and wrap the covers around me.

A few minutes later, Lawrence walks in and sets a glass down by my bedside table.

"You okay?" He asks and I shrug.

"I don't know." I manage to say and Lawrence sighs.

"Listen... I don't know what happened with Archer but... whatever it is, I got your back." He says reassuringly and I nod my head.

"Thanks Lars. You up for a little weird anime marathon with me? Just so that I get these tears gone from my face?" I ask and Lawrence grins.

"Why the hell not? Want pancakes?" I roll my eyes.

"That is legit the only thing you're amazing at cooking. And no. I do not want pancakes. I want friendship and anime." I say and Lawrence smirks.

"Deal."

My stomach is rumbling. I groan as I turn in the bed. Damn it. I really don't wanna get out of bed. I'm in that really comfortable position where you just don't wanna move. Like ever. I continue to twist and turn in the bed until I feel something odd.

It's something extremely warm... My eyes snap open and for a brief moment, I thought of kicking whatever it was off the bed. But then I realized that it was just Lawrence. I sighed to myself and crept out of my bed as quietly as I could. Lawrence was deep asleep and cuddling a pillow to himself. I smirked as made my way to my closet. As I reached for the drawers, I stopped myself.

Shaking my head at the longing I felt to open those drawers, I looked around for my long-untouched luggage bag. I found it hidden in a corner and I sighed to myself as I opened it up. I grabbed a pair of old jeans that still smelled fairly decent, underwear, a white top with some text on it (that I can't be bothered to read), and then a pair of my old favorite Sperry loafers, before making my way into the bathroom for a quick shower. Once I was done getting ready, I pulled the makeup from my luggage bag and smirked.

If there was anything I ever really spent on, it was makeup. Not that I was that much amazing at it.

I did a fairly simple look, adding just the tiniest tinge of eyeshadow before applying my mascara and slipping out of the closet. I hear a yawning voice and I smirk as I grab my damp towel.

I walk over to my bed and smack Lawrence with it, earning a large groan from him.

"What the hell man!" Lawrence shouts and I laugh.

"Morning!" I greet happily. Lawrence pauses, removes the towel and sighs.

"You seem chirpy." He says and I shrug.

"Life is way too short to think on things too much. So you know what? We're going to have a fun day and we are going to go do everything that a fun day in New York City entails!" I announce.

Lawrence rolls his eyes at me as he sits down, cuddling one of my pillows.

"Wow... a little more excitement would be nice, friend." I say, rolling my own eyes. When Lawrence doesn't get up, I grab the pillow from him and smack his head with it.

"We are going to go out, have breakfast, probably call Martin and Clara, and then we are going to go have fun! No phones allowed!" I proclaim.

"Yeah, sure. Wait 'til you know who catches you." Lawrence says and I pout.

"Well he isn't going to catch me, unless you tell him where we're going." I point out.

"And where exactly are we going?"

"Hell." I say sarcastically. "Seriously though. Let's. Go."

Lawrence sighs, rubs the back of his head, and then stands up.

"Fine. But you owe me." He says and I nod my head excitedly.

"Now go get ready! I'm gonna go down and fix breakfast, text my friends, and all that wonderful stuff." I say and I watch as Lawrence lazily walks out the door.

I grab my phone and one of my old messenger bags from my luggage bag. I fill it up with my usual stuff, my phone - now turned off - a few little girly things, and a little camera. Afterwards, I made my way downstairs and fixed up a quick meal. I toasted some bread with butter, pulled out a bunch of frozen berries, some yogurt, and then I took out the nutella.

Lawrence came down a few minutes later dressed in a loose white long sleeve shirt that had three black lines straight across his chest. He paired it with a pair of loose pale blue jeans and a pair of classic cream sneakers.

"I get dressed and I don't get pancakes. What type of cruel world is this?" Lawrence says, I laugh and throw a blueberry at him which hits the corner of his mouth, he catches it with his hand and  pops it into his mouth anyways.

"Whatever, just eat so we can go." I whine and Lawrence nods his head.

"Yes ma'am." He says.

Lawrence and I met up with Clara and Martin at a nearby mall. Clara and Martin asked me what happened and when I told them I didn't want to talk about it, they took the hint. We took a whirl around the mall going from shop to shop for mindless window-shopping until we made a go for the arcade, karaoke, etcetera etcetera.

"So what is the deal, baby girl?" Martin asks while the three of us wait for Lawrence who're redeeming our points for a handful of marbles.

"Relationship problems. The big kind." I say with a shrug.

"Oh. Did Archer do something?" He asks, I nod my head and rest my back against the railing.

"He doesn't trust me- well, I guess it's early on but... it's an issue." I try to explain.

"Sounds like a pretty big trust issue." Clara comments.

"Yup. It's a money issue too." I say with a sigh.

"Money issue?" Martin asks.

"Yup. Archer's got a position in a company and he's basically investigating me and my financial background. I might as well be accused of being a gold-digger or a social-climber."

"Have you talked to him?" Clara asks, looking worried.

"Haven't. Can't put the words in order yet." I say, staring at my feet. "Am I being a little too sensitive? I mean maybe he was just making sure my family's doing okay... right?" I ask, looking at my two friends, but their faces tell me that they're thinking what I'm thinking.

"Look, whatever happens baby girl, we're here." Martin says reassuringly as he places an arm around me. I smirk.

"Thanks babe." I say teasingly as I nudge him with my shoulder, he fakes a flinch and makes a face at me, which I return.

The three of us share a little bear hug in front of the arcade and I pull my camera out.

"Let's take one lil photo before Lars comes back." I say and Martin and Clara squeeze beside me as we take a quick wacky photo.

"Gee, thanks guys, I totally did not just purchase marbles for us to have fun bonding time." Lawrence interrupts.

We all roll our eyes and laugh before taking another photo.

The next few hours are spent trying to throw marbles into poor un-knowing peoples' bags and hoodies.

We're a little crazy group of friends.

It's about 8 pm when we all decide to get rid of each other and go home. Clara and Martin all gave me bear hugs whilst Lawrence continued to whine about not having pancakes. That dude is obsessed. Lars and I walked on home and we paused to take a longer route that would let us see the bay.

"So, did today help you forget your problems?" Lawrence asks me and I nod.

"For a brief moment yeah. I'll have to talk to Archer sometime." I say with a sigh. "Man, I hate drama."

"Talk about it." Lawrence says with a chuckle. I look out over the bay and savor the salty smell of the air from the sea.

"You seem pretty easy-going for this type of thing." I blurt aloud.

"What type of thing?" He asks.

"Oh come on Lars, the obvious thing... the competition thing." I say as I turn away from the dim view of Liberty Island that's just about to light up.

"Well, let's just say I'm fine with the way things are. I don't have an older sibling to compare myself to and my family is as laid back as can be." Lawrence says casually.

"Good for you." I say with a sigh.

"What are your plans?" Lawrence asks. "Not that you have an obligation to tell me or anything like that..."

"I don't know. Graduate. Take a brief break. Go back for Law School. Get a job." I enumerate. "To be honest... I don't know. I've always wanted to do something with my life that meant something. Being a lawyer seemed exciting- a real big achievement. But then again I don't know anymore if that's something I really want or just something I felt was going to make everyone happy and proud."

"Well. What do you really want to do? More than anything else?" Lawrence asks.

I pause for a moment to think about it. Then, I laugh.

"What's funny?" Lawrence asks me and I look at him with a soft smile on my face.

"Makeup. I want to be the one behind the scenes on TV sets and runways, putting makeup on models, celebrities... It sounds pretty fücking stupid." I say, embarrassed. But Lawrence shakes his head at me before standing real close beside me.

"It is not stupid. And you can get there." Lawrence encourages. I smile before leaning over the smooth stone railing, listening to the soft water.

"It's stupid." I say, shaking my head. "It's not something realistic."

"Now who's saying that? You or someone holding you back?"

"More like society. I have zero connections, Lars." I say.

"You have me- you have Jen, take advantage of it." He points out.

"No thanks. I don't wanna get Archer's family involved."

"Then don't. But I can help out. Actually. You know what, Daisy has a college homecoming this coming  Friday. Why don't you help her and her friends out? She'll love it."

"I'm sure that won't be awkward. Seeing as you pretended she was your girlfriend. How twisted did that even seem to her?" I asked.

"Well, she's into theater so... she said sure, she'll just pretend that I was totally not her brother. Also... that meant I had to pay for her trip here- including all of her shopping expenses. Which puts my budget for the month at an all-time low."

"Huh. You know what? I'll do it. I don't think there's anything on, next Friday anyways." I say with a shrug. "But you'll take me there and wait for me, right?" I asked.

"Sure thing. I'll hold your tools and stuff." Lawrence says happily. I grin and nudge him with my side. "Now let's get our âsses back home before we freeze to death. Winter is coming."

"Did you just go all Game of Thrones on me?" I asked before having a laugh. "Damn, well then, lead the way Jon Snow." I say happily.

"I think I'm more of a Khal Drogo." I scoff at his comment.

"Oh hell no, you look like a stick compared to him." I say.

"Ouch, Cersei, calm down."

"Oh my God, SHAME!" I shout as I smack Lawrence playfully on the back as we walk home.

Lawrence and I are laughing by the time he opens the door to the apartment.

"Lawrence, shut the hell up, I can't freaking breathe!" I say as I break into another fit of laughter.

"Oh please you're the one that pulled the-"

"Glad to see you two are getting along." A familiar voice says.

The smile on my face is instantly wiped off and Lawrence immediately steps in front of me.

"What are you doing here?" Lawrence hisses.

"What, I can't visit my girlfriend?" Archer asks and I flinch at the harshness of his tone.

"Archer, she needs a break." Lawrence responds.

"And I need to hear that from her not you." Archer says coldly and I feel my heart thud against my chest.

"Lawrence." I say, Lawrence looks over at me and I give him an encouraging look. "I'll be with you in just a bit. I'll scream for help if I need it." I say jokingly.

Lawrence nods but his face remains serious as he turns to face Archer.

"You lay a goddamn hand on her and I swear you can shove your goddamned company up your âss." Lawrence threatens before he makes his way upstairs.

I take a deep breath as I walk my way towards Archer, who's beens standing by the kitchen for God-knows how long.

"Darcy." Archer says in a soft voice. But I watch myself... I can't be this trusting forever.

"Archer." I say coldly.

"What happened yesterday?" Archer asks and I scoff.

"What happened yesterday? I met Xavier, that's what happened." I say.

"So? What does that have to do with anything?"

"Really Archer? My parents' financial backgrounds? Are you fücking with me right now?" I ask.

"You can't blame me for looking it up. You're going to inherit my family's company."

"Yeah and I didn't know that when I signed up for it." I defend.

"Well now you do know and you tell me how I'm supposed to know if I can trust you'll keep the company."

"Keep the company? I don't give a damn about your company, Archer!" I yell and he scoffs.

"Yeah, because while you wear your fancy clothes and live in this fancy apartment, you don't know that the company is funding all of it." Archer says.

"...Are you shïtting me right now?" I hiss. "This is exactly what I did not come here for. You want your money? You can take it the hell back." I say before marching up the stairs.

"Where the hell do you think you're going?" Archer shouts as he starts to follow me.

"To pack my things. If this goddamn apartment is so fücking important to you then you can go shove your budget up your-"

"And where the hell are you gonna go? You have nothing."

"And you have a pole shoved up your äss! Mr. A, Klein, whoever the hell you are... I want nothing to do with you and your stupid mind games." I say as I make my way to my- no- the room I've been sleeping in. I walk in and slam the door, locking it behind me before grabbing my old luggage bag and shoving my things in there.

I grab my other things from around the room and message Wes to come up to bring my things down. I don't care anymore. This is the last time I'll ask something of Wes- should Archer even try to use a driver against me.

I message Lawrence as well, telling him that I need a place to stay. He quickly responds, telling me that he'd wait at the parking lot asap. It's not even a few seconds later that I hear Lawrence's door slam open and him stomping heavily away. I grab my things and wait for a few moments.

I will myself not to cry. Remind myself that I'll be fine. If Archer says another word, my eyes will threaten to leak.

When you watch someone become weak and crumble down crying and you think why can't she be any stronger it's easy to think that you can be strong. It's harder to do. I could yell words and pretend to be strong. But the tears will fall down because everything in me aches. Archer strung me along since Day 1.

I believed he genuinely wanted to know me.

Am I that stupid?

Of course he wanted money. Just like dad wanted money.

I shook my head and mustered up the rest of my courage. I heard a soft knock at the door.

"Ms. Bleu? Are you okay?" Wes asks and before I can even hear Archer say a word, I open the door, hand Wes my old luggage bag, and I pull on my old backpack that I came to New York with.

The bracelet that Archer had given me had dangled on my wrist. I quickly unfastened it and gripped it tightly as I nodded at Wes. We both made our way down to the first floor and Archer's quick to move to the door.

"Out of my goddamned way." I hiss.

"Where will you go?" He asks coldly.

"Why do you care?!"

"Because you're-"

"I'm your goddamned money bank. Right? Well, rest-assured, I'll be fine. You can go bring this back to wherever you found it. Make sure to get your money back- wouldn't want you to lose any money cause of me, right?" I retort as I shove the bracelet in his chest. I open the door, grab my keys and throw it at Archer as well.

"Huh, was this how you tossed your dad away?" Archer asks.

And I snap.

"You know what? You're a little manipulative ásshole that knows nothing outside of money. You're just like him and if you wanna know him so badly, why don't you talk to him? You two might just get along fine." I hiss before stalking off to the elevators.

Wes walks in and I stab the buttons with my thumb.

Archer is not going to bring me back.

He can't.

# Chapter 20

"Are you sure you'll be okay, Ms. Bleu?" Wes asks me as he places my luggage into the trunk of Lawrence's white BMW.

"Yeah, I'll be fine Wes. Thanks for everything." I say with a smile, he gives me a concerned look, but I do my best to not pay attention to it. "I'll see you around." I say and Wes nods as we close the trunk and I get into the passenger's seat.

Lawrence talks briefly with Wes before he slides in as well.

"Anywhere in particular that you wanna go?" Lawrence asks.

"I'll message Martin and Clara to see if I can crash in either of their houses." I say with a sigh as Lawrence begins to drive.

I wave goodbye to Wes quickly before fishing out my phone.

"You could live in my old apartment, just a suggestion." Lawrence says. "It's not much- since it's a work in progress.

"Old apartment?" I asked, curiously.

"Before I went to enter the competition, I had this idea of having a little tiny studio apartment down by Central Park. So I rented one and still rent it. It's far from the university so I can't live there. Daisy's got her own apartment- she said mine was too small..." Lawrence says with a sigh.

"Well, can't blame her for wanting space. Not that I'm picky about things. I don't mind small apartments at all." I say and Lawrence nods.

"Then let's go over there so you can check it out."

The drive there is spent talking about random things that distract me. Lawrence didn't even try to bring what happened up, which I'm grateful for. Lawrence parks by the sidewalk, grabs my luggage and leads me into a cozy little building. It's got a pretty okay mini-lobby that has a security guard on stand-by.

"Hey Shan, this is Darcy Bleu, I think I might have her stay over in my apartment so keep her face in mind." Shan smiles brightly at me, her skin's a gorgeous dark brown hue, and her hair is pulled into a smooth bun.

"Sure thing. I got two keys for you, honey." She says as she reaches into her desk and pulls out two keys that are placed into a single key-ring. "Glad to know I won't have to keep on checking the place for any bugs now." I chuckle at her comment and Lawrence rolls his eyes as he takes the keys from her.

"Thanks Shan." Lawrence says and she rolls her eyes as well before smiling at me.

Lawrence leads the way as we climb up two flights of stairs in order to get to the door just by them. He unlocks the door, throws the keys into a little black bowl, and smiles as he flips the lights on. The apartment isn't big, it's a small cozy place with grey tones and sweet white floors. The design is modern and simple, grey being the major color. The closet is directly to the left of the door and is fairly small but good enough. It's inserted into the wall to save space. There's a door to the right that I'm guessing is the bathroom, and as soon as you pass the tiny hallway the mini-kitchen is there in a corner.

In front of it is a small dining set for two people, a cozy living room with a flat screen, and one area that's been platformed and partitioned off makes the bedroom with a little desk area. A large window that shows a quaint view of Central Park sits right in the middle of the "bedroom" and there's a tiny window by the kitchen as well.

"Not too shabby for a tiny apartment, Lars." I compliment.

"Thanks. It's meant to be extremely cozy and space-saving." He say with a smile.

"I think I'll do just fine here." I say and Lawrence grins.

"Great. Um, you can tell where everything is- it should all be working fine- and if you want to change the sheets and stuff, go ahead. Um... I paid for everything this month so you should be fine..."

"I'll go get a job somewhere and help out with the payment." I say with a shrug.

"Oh, well you don't really have to. I stash cash away for this place every month- it's all good."

"But I can't just live here without paying somehow."

"Okay, fine. I'll drop by ever so often, and when I do, you have to cook me food- so food's all on you." Lawrence says and I nod my head.

"Sounds good!" I say excitedly.

"Right. Then I'll leave you right here so that I can go back and sort things out with Archer. Hit me up if you need anything- I'll give you Daisy's details for the thing we talked about." Lawrence said with a wink. I nodded my head.

"Thanks Lars." I say, he smiles before walking over to me and giving me a huge bear hug.

"You'll be fine." He says and I nod my head into his chest.

"I hope so." I say just as I push lightly against him. He grins at me and I return it.

"...Well. I better go then! See ya!" Lawrence said quickly, before practically making a run for the door. He stumbles a bit, making me giggle as he leaves.

Once he was gone I immediately set about cleaning my stuff and changing into a pair of comfy shorts and a baggy T-shirt. I shut the lights and made my way over to the bed with my phone and camera in my hands. I switched my phone back on and grabbed my camera to look over the photos we took today. I hadn't brought my camera out in ages- not that it was an amazing camera or anything- but I wasn't normally the type to photograph things.

I smirked at the photos of us fooling around at the mall. Clara, Martin and Lawrence were amazing friends. They made sure I didn't even have time to think about my problems- and for a while, it didn't seem like I had any. I sighed to myself. Autumn was here and back where I'm from, the seasons only moved from wet to dry. Snow was something I'd never really experienced. As I started to daydream in Lawrence's surprisingly clean bed, my phone buzzed.

I looked over at the Caller ID and rolled my eyes.

"Hello?" I asked as I answered the call.

"Hey, how's the place goin'?" Lawrence asks.

"Good. You don't have to check up on me you know. You left like 10 minutes ago, I think I can handle myself." I say.

"Oh puh-lease." Lawrence says in a girly tone and I giggle. I lay down on the bed and sigh.

"You back home?" I asked.

"Yup, Archer's long gone though. Probably looking for you."

"Not that I really care." I say. "I'm probably lucky that I found out soon enough- before I- you know."

"Yeah..." Lawrence said awkwardly.

"Okay, let's get off that topic. Do you have any good movie recommendations?" I asked.

"You are obsessed with movies."

"And anime. Don't forget anime." I add.

"Try watching 'The Wedding Ringer'." Lawrence says and I smirk.

"Watched it." I say in a bored tone.

"Trainwreck?"

"Ha. That, I definitely wanna see." I say with a wide grin. "Shall we both play it together?" I ask.

"Sure, I've got it on my laptop so we can Skype and share screens for the movie."

"Sounds like a plan- what's the wifi password?"

"...Don't laugh." Lawrence

"I won't." I say, wondering what the hell it is.

"It's CaptainLarsofMars. Capital C, L, and M. No spaces."

"...Wow." I comment as I stand up, pressing my phone to my ear, and grabbing my bag to take my laptop. "Who the hell thought of that password?" I asked as I took my laptop and carried it to the bed.

"I just thought it was cool and unpredictable since I didn't really like Mars- but it rhymed." He reasons.

"Aye, aye, Captain Lars." I say.

"Shut up." Lawrence says with a laugh.

"Yes Cap'n." I say in my best 'pirate' accent.

"You're never going to stop, are you?" Lawrence asks and I laugh.

"Me, stop? Never, captain."

"Whatever, just log in on Skype already."

"Sure thing, Captain Lars." I say with a smirk on my face.

"...I'm... so... sleepy..." I trail off in a groggy voice.

"Want pancakes?" Lawrence asks and I roll my eyes.

"No... I want to go to bed... Damn it." I say.

"But don't you wanna see the sunrise?"

"No... Not if I'm sacrificing precious sleep time." I reply.

"Well, you should. The sunrise is beautiful where you're at." Lawrence tells me, I'm still surprised at how alive this guy is... considering it was a little past 6 am.

"Well too bad I'm sleepy then."

"Come on... Okay, I got an idea. Tell me a story." Lawrence says giddily.

I pull the duvet over me and sigh.

"What kind of story?"

"I don't know, a random one. The first one that comes to your mind." I pause.

"Hm... Well... when I was in third grade, my parents and a few friends decided to go to the beach. The thing was, the waves were so strong that they could have easily carried me away... I remember walking with my father, grasping his hand so tightly as he led me into the water. Man... I was so scared. I held onto him like my life depended on it. We got about 5 meters in, the water was already chest-deep for me...

And this huge wave pulls in and just devours me. I probably tumbled around the water for a good ten seconds. Guess my grip must've slipped." I add.

"You lived, though. So that's good." Lawrence comments.

"...Yeah. I lived." I say in a sad tone. "...I miss home, Lars... I miss home so damn much..."

"I know you do." Lawrence responds.

"I just wish I still had one, you know? Sucks to say it when I'm supposed to be a grown-up, independent, eighteen-year-old... But it really sucks to not have a mom and dad to come home to." I ramble. "It sucks..."

"...Sit by the window, will you?" Lawrence says, and I sigh as I look at my screen, only to find his camera turned off. I roll my eyes and lift my laptop, moving towards the window and sitting by the ledge.

"I'm here." I say, setting the laptop down on the ledge as well, before looking outside.

"Okay, now we wait..." Lawrence says.

I waited in silence as I looked at the sky. A slow purple haze seeped in, and from where I was, I had just enough room to see the orange hue of the sun touch the trees and buildings. I couldn't quite see the sun- granted, I was only on the second floor- but the view of the sunrise in the city looked absolutely wonderful.

"Wow." I muttered under my breath.

"You seeing what I'm seeing?" Lawrence asks.

"Oh yeah..." I say in awe.

"Then you might as well look down." He says and I arch a brow.

"Say what?" I ask, breaking the moment.

"Look down." He repeats, I roll my eyes and sigh.

"Kay." I say as I peek through the window, in the slightly dark and purple light, stood Lawrence in a thick black hoodie, carrying what looked like a picnic basket. "The hell are you doing there?" I asked, hoping the mic on my laptop could hear me.

"You sounded like you needed a pick-me-up."

"No, I sounded like I needed some sleep." I say pointedly as I glare at him through the window.

"But we have a picnic to do..." Lawrence says, puffs of mist coming out from his mouth, and I roll my eyes.

"Lars, I will, without a doubt, fall asleep." I point out.

"And I will, without a doubt, die of over-eating." Lawrence says.

"Oh shut it. Get your áss up here." I say.

"But what about the picnic?" Lawrence asks with a pout.

"Sleep now, picnic later. Now get up here before you freeze your nose off."

"It's not that cold."

"Oh my God, Lars. Just shut up and get in here." I say and Lawrence grins before nodding.

"As you wish." He says happily, before disappearing.

"Idiot." I mutter.

"I'm still on the call!!!" He shouts.

"How is your internet so good?!" I shout back.

"Captain Lars never tells his secrets." Lawrence announces.

"Oh Christ, help me."

"Don't you mean Captain?"

"Shut it, Lars."

# Chapter 21

A couple of hours later, at around 11, I dressed up, for the first time, in Autumn clothes. Which was basically a comfy old black sweater, some black jeans, a pair of black leather boots, and my favorite cat-eared black bonnet. I put some mascara on my lashes and placed some pink lip balm on my lips before deciding to head out with Lawrence with just some money and my phone in my pockets.

"I re-heated the food- but I ended up downing the three cans of Arizona and the fruit cups while waiting- so we should probably hit the supermarket for a re-fill." Lawrence says as he rubs the back of his head. I roll my eyes.

"Do you have a thermos around here?" I asked and Lawrence nods as he opens one of the cupboards and brings out a silver and somewhat large thermos. I smirk and heat some water with the electric kettle. "Coffee packets?" I asked.

"None. Those are just nasty." Lawrence says and I sigh.

"Fine, we need to buy hot chocolate packets then."

"Hallelujah!" Lawrence says with a wide grin.

"Since this is food, this one's on me, okay?"

"Yeah, yeah."

"And we are not going to go buy more pancake mix."

"But-"

"Lawrence, shut up."

"Okay, Lawrence, I am not buying three boxes of poptarts... or any for that matter." I say as I push the cart.

"But poptarts are awesome." He whines.

"Yeah, but I want real food, Lars. Plus, we're not going shopping for the apartment, we're shopping for our little picnic."

"But we might as well shop for the apartment." Lawrence says and I sigh.

"No." I say and Lawrence pouts as I ignore his pleas.

We leave the supermarket and head back to Central Park with our paper bags of food and the picnic basket.

"So... have you figured out what you were going to do yet?" Lawrence asks as we set up our little picnic.

"Nope. I'm still waiting on something. I have a few ideas, but none that are sure yet. I was thinking of taking a break... Not that I have the cash for it yet anyways."

"Well you're still financially backed by the company, you could do it if you really wanted to."

"Thanks, but no thanks. I'd rather not look like I just decided to go on a spree... Especially with all the money crap." I say as I pop a french fry into my mouth.

"Oh come on. You are rightfully given fifty thousand dollars for a vacation trip. Plus, the scholarship answers for most prices for any university in the world. All you need to do is re-apply and get going." Lawrence explains. I nod my head in response.

"I'll think about it Lars... Thanks." I say with a smile as I nudge him with my elbow. He nudges me back and we spend the rest of our time talking about other things.

Once we're done, Lawrence tells me that he has a lecture, gives me the details on Daisy's homecoming thing, and leaves as soon as he brought me to my apartment. I laughed when he stumbled a few times before he even got out the door. His fault for putting a big rug in the apartment.

2 days later,  I pulled open my laptop and sat on the couch. I decided to be productive and do any assignments I hadn't done yet. Truth be told, I was usually the procrastinator... but work tends to help me get my mind off of things.

Just as I had finished my last assignment, my phone began to ring to my new default tone, the chorus of "Stitches" by Shawn Mendes.

I looked at the Caller ID and sighed. There was no way I was answering him. It'd already been days since we last talked and he thinks he can get me with a call? No fücking way.

I put my phone underneath a pillow and groaned as I stood up and stretched my arms out. I made my way to the refrigerator and groaned when I realized I hadn't bought anything for dinner... Guess I should have bought stuff earlier today. I closed the refrigerator, grabbed my phone (begrudgingly...), pulled on a thick jacket, and grabbed some cash before getting out and locking the apartment.

"Heading out?" Shan asks as I pass the little lobby area and I smile at her.

"Yeah, need to get some dinner. You want anything?" I ask her, she shakes her head.

"Nah, had dinner a while ago, it's a bit late already isn't it?" She asks me.

"Yeah, I sorta buried myself in work. Anyways, my stomach is killing me, I'll see you later, Shan." I say and she nods her head with a wide smile as I leave. I take a quick walk to Whole Foods Market.

I mindlessly go through aisles and pick up a few things. I grab some coffee packets, corned beef and potatoes for breakfast, 2 cartons of water, and some lasagna from the hot food area. I walk out of Whole Foods and sigh as I check the time. It was already past 8:30... My stomach grumbled and I decided to make my way to Central Park for a late night mini picnic for me. As I walk along the sidewalk... I get a strange feeling, as if I was being followed. I immediately feel my heart thud against my chest as I walk faster and faster. When I make it to Central Park, I ditch the idea of eating there and decide to just try to get to the apartment building.

As I continue walking, I notice a car slowly drive behind me. I sigh and quickly make my way towards a place with more people. Once I do, I turn around and look at the vehicle. A familiar looking minivan. I curse under my breath and stop walking. I make my way towards it and knock hard on the door.

It immediately slides open to reveal none other than Archer Carter's face.

"What the hell do you want from me?" I hiss.

"I want to talk to you." He says in a soft voice.

"You want to talk? Why didn't you get out of the van and call out? You know, like normal people do?" I ask with a harsh tone.

"You wouldn't have listened." He says and I sigh.

"Yeah. I wouldn't have and I still shouldn't." I say. "Hey, Wes. Next time, honk a horn will you?" I greet, Wes nods and I see that he's smiling. I look back at Archer, expecting a conversation and whose green eyes I can't see in the dark.

What I do see is how much of a mess he looks. His hair is all over the place, his clothes are rumpled, and he looks like he's stressed to hell... Not that I should care. After he still remains silent, I sigh to myself.

"Well. This sure was a nice talk. Now if you excuse me, I'm gonna go eat dinner." I say but before I can even leave, Archer grabs my arm and pulls me into the van.

"...Sorry." He says, his face is inches away from mine and with the slight light, I see that his eyes reflect the fatigue in them. "We can have dinner together..." He trails off.

"Actually... could we have dinner together?" He asks in a weak voice.

"Archer, we can't do this." I say but he shakes his head and I feel his hands grip my jacket tighter so that I don't leave. I shake my head and sigh. "Dinner. Just once." I say before pulling his hands away from me, I turn, close the door, and sit down in the spare chair I always sat in.

"Hey Wes, get us to the nearest restaurant, I'm starving." I say, Wes nods his head at me through the rearview mirror and I sigh as I rest my head against my elbow.

I look out at the city through the windows of the minivan. What the hell am I even doing here...

Wes drops us off at a hotel called Excelsior and I roll my eyes. Did he have to bring us to a hotel?

"Pick us up when I call." Archer says as he finally leaves the van. He runs a hand through his hair and I sigh as I make my way in, not bothering to wait for him.

Once we finally get to the restaurant, Archer quickly orders for me and we sit in silence. The place is unusually empty and I mentally groaned when I noticed that Archer was staring right at me.

"So... what did you want to talk about?" I asked and Archer blinks before he finally speaks.

"I'm sorry... the things I said... weren't supposed to come out that way." Archer said and I arched a brow.

"The things you said?" I asked in an incredulous tone. "I... You know what. I don't even want to talk about it. I'm here to listen, eat, and leave." I say with finality. The waiter comes in with our food and drinks and I sigh as I patiently eat the mouthwateringly delicious paella.

Archer, however, doesn't touch his food.

"You look like you're doing well." He says, I nod my head and swallow my food, wiping my mouth before speaking.

"I'm coping well. I can only live on what funds I'm given if I maintain my GPA." I point out.

"I know." Archer says.

"Great. Glad to hear it." I say as I eat once more.

"Will you ever forgive me?" Archer asks and I sigh.

"I don't know." I answer straight out. "Archer... let's set things straight... I have things under lock and key and I almost gave you the key that would've destroyed me and you've already started to rattle that lock. And unlike some girls- the way I deal with that isn't by crying."

"I noticed." Archer said, popping a slight smile.

"...Are you... going to eat?" I asked, concerned.

"...No."

"When was the last time you ate?" I asked.

"This morning."

"What did you eat?"

"Toast." I shook my head.

"Eat, Archer. I may not be in a... relationship with you anymore but I don't want anyone starving themselves."

"I'm not hungry."

"Yeah, well, I'm not staying if you don't eat." I say with a sigh. Archer stares at me and then at his plate, before he picks up his fork and gets a bit of his paella to eat.

He swallows it and I notice how tense he is.

"You look like you've been thinking about something big." I comment.

"It's nothing." He quickly says and I arch a brow.

"Of course. Nevermind that I asked." I said.

"...Will you come to dinner at my family's house?" He asks suddenly.

"...What?"

"There's a dinner... at the house on Friday. Grace, my mom, really liked you and she wanted you to be there. It's a small family event. Just a little dinner and then you can leave." He says quickly, as if he's afraid I'd say no.

"...Archer, I have something on Friday." I say, remembering my makeup scheduled with Daisy.

"You can come at 7, 8 even. Just... please." Archer pleads and I sigh.

"I'll think about it." I say and Archer sighs.

"I messed up big time, didn't I?" He mutters and I decide not to respond.

He eats a bit more before he leaves a few bills on the table. I take that as our cue to leave and we make our way out of the hotel.

"Do you mind if we take a walk?" Archer asks and I shake my head.

"Around Central Park." I suggest and he nods as we walk towards the park's direction.

We make it to the park and I sigh as we enter. The air I breath creates slight puffs and I rub my cold nose. The two of us walk side by side in silence, not even daring to touch each other as we pass the benches.

"Where would you go if you left?" Archer asked. "And I mean that as in where would you study." He adds, I shrug.

"Europe? Japan? Somewhere I can start over... again." I say as I look up at the cloudy night sky.

"Where in Europe?"

"Germany, probably. There's a lot of cool history there." I say, hoping this slightly-awkward conversation works its way out.

"Yeah." Archer says and I bite my bottom lip.

A cold breeze blows and I shiver. Archer immediately turns to me, places his arms around me, capturing me in an embrace. The warmth of his arms relax me and I can't help but inhale the scent of his perfume. I tense when I realize what I'm doing.

"...Archer. We can't do this." I say. "We're not-"

"Please." He says in a quiet and solemn tone and I look up at him and see his eyes filled with a piteous type of sadness.

"Archer, I-"

"Screw it." Archer says and he tilts my chin up and comes down to my face. He's literally a centimeter away when he stares deep into my eyes, searching for approval.

His eyes reveal a sad emotion coming from them. It's something that I can't discern... But what I do know... is that Archer is causing my heart to take leaps of faith and it's killing me that I feel this way. It's killing me that the feelings I've been ignoring are coming out. I let out a shaky breath and I feel Archer's grip on me lose its strength.

"You're right." I say. "Screw it." I mutter just as I reach for the back of his head and pull him down to me.

Our lips crash into each other. The warmth we share warms my every being. I feel relaxed and normal. I don't feel like I have a weight that I'm trying to hide. It's cheesy and loving and... it just feels right to have him. To have the Archer that tried to get to know me, the one that left cheesy notes around... the one that I... am confused with. Lost with.

Our kisses deepen and we pull apart for air. Archer is still only centimeters away from my face... and I know we'll talk about our issues later. But right now, Archer needs someone, and although our problems aren't over... the one he looked for was me... and the feeling my heart gets when I realize that scares me. It scares me that I can't turn these feelings off.

Archer holds me and I'm reeling. Until he tilts my face up to stare into his eyes again and I see that he's begging me and that he's trying not to lose his cool. And it's all it takes for me to give him a chance.

Because I've never had someone affect me like this.

And... I've never felt the urge to comfort someone this bad before... And for the first time, someone is desperate to have me, no, to need me.

# Chapter 22

Archer's apartment is a mess. There's broken pieces of glass on the floor, papers litter the place, and there are glasses with foul smelling liquor everywhere.

"Archer, what happened?" I ask, worried.

"It's... I don't want to talk about it yet... Sorry." He says in a weak voice as he runs a hand through his hair.

"...Okay." I say as I make my way past the trashed floor. "Is your bedroom clean?" I asked.

"It... should be. I haven't been in there unless it was to change." He says and I sigh.

"You don't even look like you've had a clean shower. Come." I say as I take his arm and lead him up the stairs to his room.

His room is clean and the bed looks so creaseless that I worry about where he's been and what's caused it.

"Shower. Now." I scold and Archer chuckles softly.

"I don't really feel like it-"

"Shut up and shower," I say. "Otherwise, I'm going to go home. I am not spending the night here with you like this."

"You're spending the night?" He asks.

"It's 11, Archer. Why did I even come here if I was just going to go home?" I asked rhetorically. "Now go shower. I'm gonna go steal a shirt from you for the night." I say and Archer nods.

"Okay." He says and I sigh as I watch him make his way to the bathroom. I quietly make my way to his walk-in closet and pull open a drawer to grab a shirt.

I slip into a plain white shirt, glad that I decided to wear leggings today. I folded my clothes and set them aside, just as I was going to leave, I noticed that Archer's phone was somehow set up on a tripod by the counter along with my bracelet... I arched a brow. I quickly went by the door to listen in on the shower. It was still running and I immediately closed the door to the closet and sighed in relief when I realized that Archer's phone... doesn't have a passcode.

I check on his camera roll and find a long video- and I mean long. It's around an hour long.

I press play and put it on full volume.

Archer is standing in front of a mirror and sighing.

"Okay, okay... Shít. Umm... okay." He says nervously before clearing his throat and looking at the mirror.

"Hey... Darcy... I am so... sorry for... crap. That sounds bad." Archer runs a hand through his hair before shaking his head and starting over.

"Darcy. I called you because I wanted to say that I was sorry for trying to... Damn it." He says, before putting both his hands on the edge of the counter.

"I'm sorry. I didn't mean to come across as an ässhole. I was just trying to get some... transparency.... Crap. Seriously Arch? Transparency?" He hisses at himself.

I watch as Archer frustratedly looks around on the counter. He picks up the bracelet and groans.

"Damn it. I got this. Come on..." He mutters to himself.

"Hey Darce... I am so sorry about what I did. I didn't mean any of it. I didn't mean to look like I didn't trust you. That... wasn't how it was supposed to come out... I... I said things that I didn't want to because I was angry. You were avoiding me like the plague and... shit... I... I thought I was right. I thought that you were one of those people I warned you about. The type that used people for... advantages.

I am so sorry that I had you investigated. I'm... not even sure what brought it on. I think it's the fact that Keaton and I have been talking. It's nothing for you to really worry about- it's just that, he's my brother, and I have to listen to him too. I didn't mean for it to... affect me so far. I talked to Keaton after you called in about staying over at Clara's. He... I know I can't blame him but... we just started to put all our doubts together... and then all of a sudden I was drinking. And all of a sudden, I had the urge to confront you about it but... you weren't home and you were with Lawrence. And I thought that you were... that you were gonna use me...

I... I can't explain it very well. I just... sometimes I can feel myself sink into this terrible feeling. I hate that I'm doing this and yet I can't help doubting people- and... it's not just you. I doubt Lawrence, I doubt my friends... damn I doubt everyone. Money changes things, you know? Anyways... I should stop... rambling. I doubt you'll ever even-"

The door swings open and I jump.

"Jesus Christ, Archer, knock!" I scream. I also turn a shade of red... Archer is wearing a single towel around his waist. Boys.

"It's my house. Why do I have to knock?" He says with a chuckle before his eyes widen. "...Is... that... my... phone?" He asks.

"Uh... no?" I say, in a stupid attempt to save my soul. "I totally was not watching this practice vid you were filming." I mutter in a string of words.

"Give it back, Darcy." He says as a warning. I see a mischievous look pass his eyes as well as a hint of red tinge his cheeks.

"Smooth talking there, Mr. A. Love the whole stuttering thing." I tease and Archer immediately lunges for me. I dodge him and squeal as I run around a large counter. "Archer, get dressed!" I scream.

"Not until you give that back." He warns and I roll my eyes. He is on the other side of the counter and the door is right behind me, I glance at it and Archer narrows his eyes at me. "Don't. Even. Think. About. It." He says and I stick my tongue out at him as I run for the door.

I'm barely even a foot out when I'm grabbed and I fall down onto the floor, phone in hand, and... Archer pinning my arms down in nothing but a towel.

"Phone. Now. Darce." He says and I roll my eyes.

"Get off of me you oaf."

"Phone."

"Uh, why don't you just grab it?" I ask. "Kind of underneath superman here." I say, trying not to look anywhere other than Archer's face. He smirks.

"I like us like this." He says as he puts his face closer to mine.

"I like you clothed, thank you very much." I say and he smirks.

"I hope that changes."

"Oh shut the fùck up." I say as I squirm underneath him. "Get off me, this floor is cold." I whine.

"I like my view." He says and I roll my eyes.

"This is not how I like mine." I say and Archer rolls his eyes.

"Hm." He hums before lowering himself down onto me. His face ends up right at the crook of my neck and I shiver when I feel his breath there.

I gasp when I feel his lips there.

"Archer what the-"

"Sshhh..." Archer says as he places a finger on my lips and very quickly kisses his way up from my neck to my jaw. "I'm sorry..." He whispers.

"I get it. I sort of watched the video." I say, rolling my eyes, and he smirks but continues to kiss his way around my face until he finally gets to my lips.

"Guessing we'll talk later?" He asks and I sigh.

"You know we're talking later." I say and he smirks as he swoops down to capture my lips with his. He immediately pulls away and I groan as I push against his chest.

"Up we go." I mutter and Archer chuckles as gets off of me. I sit up and Archer holds his hand out. "What?" I ask. He arches a brow and I groan.

"Fiiiine." I whine as I hand the phone over to him.

"Great. I'll delete that video and we can talk after I get dressed." He says and I pout by nod my head as we both get up and he disappears into his closet.

I sigh as I make my way over to the bed and sit down. A thousand scenarios run through my head. As well as a thousand questions. For example, what the hell happened to his apartment? My phone buzzes in my pocket and I quickly grab it. It was a message from Xavier- a long one at that. I read through it quickly and sighed... Not exactly what I was going for... but close enough. I thought to myself.

"Alright. Let's talk." Archer's voice says, pulling me out of my thoughts. I nod my head as he sits beside me.

"Okay, let's start with my question. Why did you have Xavier investigate me and my financial records?" I asked. Archer sighed and ran a hand through his damp hair.

"I just wanted to make sure you were who you said you were... I told you that I had issues. The world I live in is hard, and I wanted to make sure that you weren't someone who would use me." Archer explains, I take a deep breath. It's not really hard to understand, he'd already told me this before- in the form of 'I don't wanna meet you yet because my world sucks' notes from back when he labeled himself Mr. A.

"Okay... I'm trying to be open-minded here." I say with a sigh. "It's a bit hard for me to deal with trust issues Archer. You're not the only one with them." I explain.

"I get that- and I'm sorry if I ruined your trust. I didn't mean to come off that way. I just- You know what? Here." He says as he stands up and pulls out the drawer of the bedside table closest to him. He takes out a manila envelope sealed in thick plastic and hands it to me. "This, is a compilation of all the data I asked for... I... I haven't opened them. They're sealed shut. I... I didn't want to upset you anymore than I already have." He says, carefully selecting his words.

I look at the sealed plastic and play with the corners. I sighed to myself as I tore the plastic open. The manila envelope was still sealed as well, and I slipped my long fingernails through a gap and tore it open as well.

"You don't have to-" Archer begins, but I stop him with my hand on his.

"We have to," I say, "If we want to put this behind us, I want to make sure everything is crystal clear between us. No more trust issues on this- on money, myself, my family, no more. Okay, Archer? Any problem you have with me, you talk to me about." I say, a harsh edge in my tone of voice.

"Okay." He says simply, nodding as he replies.

The first document was my mother's background and family finances.

"My mother has nothing to really worry about. She has one last payment to make before her debt to the bank is paid. She's getting re-married soon, she's happy, and I know her new husband, Gavin, will make her happy too." I say with a shrug, Archer smiles.

"I'm sure he will." He comments and I nod.

The next one was a quick file on me.

"Well, this is easy. I'm an all-around student that's got above-average grades-ish and loves being a busy-body. I have interests in the make-up business- although I have hopes in law. I have a bit of an issue with my dad- but we're... okay- since I barely talk to him." I say, slowly decreasing the tone of my voice, Archer nods and I swallow a dry lump in my throat as I move on to the next document.

I sigh and I feel Archer move closer to me.

"Okay... so... this here is my dad." I say as I flip to my dad's resume photo. He was a chubby man with a kind smile.

"I could tell you all about the paper things like his salary and stuff. But I'll tell you why I'm not... close to him." I say and Archer looks at me and I give him a sad smile. "In fifth grade, mom found out he was having an affair... with a guy. That was when the fights began. It got better after but... that was the first time he actually tried to hit me- and I had no idea why he wanted to either. It didn't happen again.

My mom confronted him that same year and it sort of died down... It popped back up late in 6th grade and I almost cried when they started shouting at each other at home too. All of a sudden... dad was no longer making enough money to really 'provide'. We were only lucky the school paid for most of our bills- other than bank bills of course. My mom found out he was having another affair again... She cried just about every night. I remember both of them being missing sometimes." I say sadly, pausing to stop the water that had started to well up in my eyes. Archer pats my back and rubs it in slow motions, calming me down.

"Again... my mom confronted him. They fought- they stopped, and all of a sudden, while I was away, I came back to a quiet household. The whole thing had died down again- but there was no turning back. Mom slept in my room with me and dad was alone. The money problems never stopped. He started blaming my mom for broken objects, missing items, and eventually started backstabbing her.

But my mom and I held through it. At the beginning of 9th grade, my dad became distant. To the point that he only talked to us to give us commands- like clean the house, cook dinner, set the table... Then he would put comments. 'You're too fúcking lazy', 'Why can't you be useful and work?'... All that stuff." I say, gulping down the other lump forming in my throat.

"Well... to just put this short... my dad slowly but surely destroyed my mom's reputation with his family. Then he tried to destroy her reputation with me. My dad was... and... is still a money-obsessed guy. He has what he wants now... he makes a living for himself, spends all his money on himself... all that stuff. I never want to go back to him- and I don't mean that lightly. I can't ever really just look at him as a loving father- I just remember that he is capable of so much... pain. Pain for his family for something a small as money." I say with a sigh.

"So... that's that." I conclude and Archer sighs as he wraps an arm around my shoulders and pulls me close.

"I'm sorry." Archer says as he reaches for my hands... which are shaking. I let out a weak laugh.

"You know? Those words have never even left my dad's mouth unless it was sarcastic..." I say as the tears well up in my eyes again. "And it's stupid and annoying and fills me with so much anger that I feel it eat me up sometimes. My time here in New York has helped me change that- I barely ever had the time to let my anger consume me. But to be put in a situation where I can't be trusted just brings it all back." I say as I lean into Archer.

"I'm really sorry, Darcy." He says as he hugs me now, kissing the top of my head. I let him say soft apologies mixed in with reassuring words, it was something that I had needed ever since I was a kid, just to have someone be strong for me.

Because to be honest, no one can hold the whole world up by themsel ves... And my world has collapsed so many times that I'm too tired to put it all back together. So I left pieces behind, my father, the memories, the pain...

But I guess it was about time I sucked it up and put it back together.

Archer stays by me and comforts me for what seemed like hours but was only really an hour or so. After that, Archer kneels in front of me and stares right into my eyes.

"I promise, to never do something that betrays your trust again, okay? I'm not perfect, but I'll sure as hell try to avoid hurting you again, okay?" He says and I nod my head.

"I promise the same... So... I need to tell you what I made Xavier do." I say and Archer's eyes widen in surprise but he nods anyways. "When I saw him and he told me about what you were gonna do... I told him to talk with Gerald about a few things... I put my own holds on my contract by reducing certain benefits- so I rendered most of the credit cards and cash void until I made my decision... I wanted all of the cards void... but, your dad is a hard one to argue with- Xavier's updated me via text- about it and I was going to sign it tomorrow..."

"You don't have to do that." Archer says and I shake my head.

"I want to do it. I don't need the cash, Archer." I say as I hold my hands out to cup his face. "It's cheesy, I know. But all I want is who you are, I could care less if I got cash or not." I say with a shrug.

"I'm just hoping you feel the same way." I add and Archer smirks at me.

"Of course I do." He says with a smile as he kisses the inside of my left palm.

"Huh, then, Mr. A... I want you to tell me why the hell your apartment looks like it's been trashed." I say and Archer sighs.

"Can we talk about it in the morning? It's almost 1..." He whines and I roll my eyes.

"No way, I spilled my beans, you spill yours." I demand.

"Okay, okay... I have... extreme breakdowns sometimes. I thought I was over it- but I was just thinking  about how much I'd fùcked up and... one moment I was sitting down and the next thing I knew, the room was spinning, my hands we shaking, and I was throwing things and breaking things out of frustration..." Archer says.

"Archer..."

"I know. It's a problem..." He says as he lets go of my hands to run a hand through his hair. "I'm visiting my psychiatrist tomorrow... Haven't seen that guy in a while." He says and I pull him to me so that his face is right in front of me.

"I'm sorry as well." I say and before he even opens his mouth to protest, I place a feather-light kiss on his lips.

"Tease." Archer says and I roll my eyes as he lowers me down onto the bed, kissing my lips and my neck several times before rolling to my left side.

"Are we okay now?" I asked, feeling my eyelids start to fall down.

"Yeah. We're okay- I'll make sure we're never not okay." Archer says and I give a weak laugh.

"Ha ha... Sure... thing..." I say as I drift off to sleep with Archer's arms around me and my arms around him.

# Chapter 23

I feel warm and cozy as I snuggle up to the source of heat with me. It's a calming feeling that strangely smells like... lavender body wash... I open my eyes and find myself staring right at Archer's chest. He's breathing softly and I look up to study his face. He has a peaceful look, like it's the first time he's rested in days, and I smile. He has his arms wound around me and I'm surprised that they haven't gone numb- or maybe they have and I'm just not moving.

I sigh contently to myself. No more fighting with this one... hopefully. I add in my head. I carefully attempt to untangle my arms from his but I find that he only holds me still. I huff in frustration.

"Archer... I need to make breakfast." I whine quietly as I poke his face. His face crinkles at the action and I giggle, causing him to pull me even further into his embrace.

He leans his head into the crook of my neck and I feel his breath. He takes a deep breath and sighs as he leaves me in that position.

"Archer..." I whine.

"10... more... minutes..." He says groggily. I roll my eyes and spot the clock on his bedside table. It was 9 in the morning.

"Don't you have work?" I asked.

"Day... off..." He replies.

"Archer, you're already awake if you can respond." I point out and he only snuggles into me more, making my body heat up.

"Not... ready..."

"Archer come on, I'm really hungry." I say, and I was, my stomach was going to grumble soon. But Archer ignores me and simply nuzzles my neck even more, breathing in my scent.

I look at his neck and press a soft kiss in the crook of his neck, then I work my way up to his jawline until he's shifted so that his face is right in front of me. When I kiss his chin, I laugh when his eyes open and he gives me a frustrated look. I kiss the other side of his jaw and stop at his chin, never touching his lips and I feel his arms pull me even closer to him. I laugh and I kiss the tip of his nose and watch as he frowns and makes a frustrated grunt. He pulls me so that I'm now on top of him and I sit down, his eyes are now wide open and I smirk as I put my hands on his chest and kiss the gap between his nose and lips.

"Quit teasing me, woman." He says and I giggle.

"We need breakfast." I say as I teasingly kiss the tip of his nose again, he places a hand at my back and at my neck as he brings me down to his face and I roll my eyes. "We gotta get up babe."

"Boy did I miss you calling me that... even if you hate it." Archer says with a smile. I laugh and kiss the corners of his mouth. "Damn it."

"Breakfast in 10." I say. "I'll borrow a shirt." I say and he nods as I kiss his lips quickly and immediately hop off of him, rushing to the bathroom- but before I can leave, Archer grabs my arm, pulls me down to him, and gives me a long sweet kiss, morning breath and all.

"I missed you." He says after and I blush as I nod my head.

"Me too." I admit and he smiles before nudging me away.

"Go get dressed and stuff. I'll be up in a bit." He says and I nod as I make my way to the bathroom.

I decide to take a quick shower, taking in the smell of lavender bodywash that Archer seems to love using. Afterwards, I wrap a towel around myself and wipe the mirror with a little towel and examine my face.

My roots have grown, showing deep brown hair through my lighter, borderline blonde highlights. I quickly make my way into the closet and shriek when I bump into Archer.

"Christ!" I mutter under my breath, Archer chuckles. He's already changed into a pair of denim jeans and a grey sweater.

Archer holds out a set of clothes.

"When Holly came over when you first stayed the night, she left all of these things for you." He says and I nod gratefully.

"Thanks." I say as Archer kisses my lips quickly.

"I'll see you downstairs, okay? Gotta make a call for a housekeeper or two."

"Get on it then." I say as I kiss him again. He smiles goofily and I roll my eyes as he leaves me alone in the closet.

I quickly get ready, dressing myself in the suede brown leggings, fit-and-flare cream dress, and beige suede ankle boots. Then I pulled on the big bright red coat and grab a couple of red-tinged jewelry before quickly working on my makeup, adding a bit of care, in case we went somewhere. I hadn't gotten this 'dolled up' for a normal day in what seems like ages.

I get out of the closet feeling adorable as I finished brushing my teeth with the spare toothbrush in Archer's bathroom.

I walk out of the bathroom and make my way downstairs, greeted by Archer trying to clean up the apartment.

"No housekeeper?" I asked and Archer turns around and smiles at me.

"I got two, but I didn't want them to think I had a 'panic attack' or anything." He says in a joking tone, I roll my eyes and wrap my arms around him.

"Breakfast?" I asked and he nods.

"Let's go." He says as he kisses my forehead. He throws some stuff into a trashcan and grabs a black coat from the coat hangers before we head off.

"Move in with me." Archer says as we walked along the beach.

"...What?" I asked, unsure if I heard him correctly.

"Don't... make me say it again." Archer says nervously and I look into his eyes. He places his arms around my back and pulls me to him

"You sure you want a roomie like me? I'm pretty crap at the whole roomie thing." I say as a joke and Archer grins.

"Yeah. I want you. I want you to be with me all the time... I want to know that you won't disappear... not that I'm saying you will! Just-"

"I get it, Arch," I say with a smile. We were facing each other and I reached for his hands. "I'll move in with you." I add with a smile. Archer's eyes widen in surprise and his smile makes his dimples pop.

"Seriously?!" He shouts happily.

"Yeah." I say and I watch as Archer shouts in joy towards the cold ocean and he runs back to me with a large smile on his face.

"Oh god, I have wanted to ask that for so goddamn long!" He says and he grabs me by my waist and I suddenly feel myself being lifted off the ground. I shriek in surprise but as Archer spins me around, my shrieks turn into giggles.

"Wait, quick question, though." He says and I arch a brow as he puts me back down.

"What?" I ask.

"We're sleeping in the same bed, right? Cause beds are expensive and I don't wanna have to get another one ordered just cause-"

"Yeah, yeah, shut up." I say as I roll my eyes at his sarcasm. I reach up to him and pull his face down to my level. "I really really love you." I whisper and Archer grins as he pulls us even closer together until the tips of our noses are touching.

"I love you too." He says as he kisses the tip of my nose. I giggle before Archer finally swoops in and plants a soft kiss on my lips.

A few days later...

"Okay, okay, Darcy, I need your opinion, blue dress or deep red?" Daisy's friend, Melissa, asks me. I roll my eyes as I finish Daisy's eyeliner.

"I made your eyes more bronze because I thought you were wearing blue." I say and Melissa sighs.

"But the red is just calling out to me." Melissa whines and I sigh.

"Daisy, talk some sense into her, for me, will you?" I ask as I put the eyeliner away and grab a brush to blend some eyeshadow with, Daisy giggles in response before speaking.

"Melissa, red is probably gonna be worn everywhere." Daisy points out. "The blue dress will be so much more you." I watch as Melissa still looks unsure but then spots Daisy's other friend, Savannah, who I'd already finished as well.

"OMG, Savannah come here!" Melissa screams and Daisy and I roll our eyes as we watch Melissa drag poor Savannah into the room, who sends us a look that screamed 'help me'.

"She can never makeup her mind." Daisy says with a sigh.

"Tell me about it, a while ago, she wouldn't shut up about me picking the right blush. Thank God she shut up when I used the same shade as her lip." I say with a sigh.

"We sound like such girls." Daisy says with a giggle.

"Not that it's a bad thing." I add before finishing Daisy's look off with a quick setting spray. "Alright, and you are done." I say, proud of my work.

Daisy looked adorable and natural, her lashes were fuller from the individuals I put on, her eyes were slightly smokey, and her nude lip color made her look adorable. She grinned at me.

"Wow." She said as she looked at herself.

"Uh huh." I say with approval. "Told you I got you."

"I love it." She says and I watch as she takes an even closer look at herself. "This is so awesome. Thank you so much, Darce!" Daisy squeals as she hugs me, carefully avoiding touching my face with hers. For good reason, too.

"Well, you are absolutely freaking welcome." I say as she lets go.

"Okay, I'm gonna go pull on my dress and then we all need to take a picture before you get your butt towards Archer's house for dinner." Daisy says and I nod as she disappears into her room.

I begin to pack up my things just as Archer calls me. I instantly pick up.

"You done?" Archer asks and I nod.

"Yup, I'm done. This isn't a very formal dinner is it? Because I'm still in my black sweater, black leggings, and black Nikes." I point out as I tuck my phone between my shoulder and ear.

"I've got a dress delivery on coming." He says and I laugh.

"Well, unless that dress is coming in 5 minutes, I'm not wearing it." I say as I finish putting everything into my makeup bag.

"That can be arranged." Archer says and just as he finishes speaking, someone rings the doorbell and I roll my eyes.

"Yeah, well, if you told me you were coming..." I trail off and Archer chuckles.

"What would be the fun in that?" He asks and I roll my eyes before putting the phone away from my mouth to shout at the girls.

"Hey guys! Archer's here to pick me up- so if you want a picture, we gotta get it done asap!" I shout as I make my way to the door. I grin when I open it to find Archer with a large shopping bag filled with what I suspect is what I'm supposed to wear tonight.

"Delivery for Ms. Darcy Bleu?" Archer asks, he's dressed in an all-black outfit consisting of a crisp black button down polo, a pair of black slacks, and matte black leather shoes. I snort.

"Hey Daisy! Can this delivery man that looks like he's a part of the mafia, come in?" I ask and I watch as Daisy pops her head in and laughs.

"What the hell? Archer you look like you need to have a drink to calm your damn ti-"

"Daisy, where are my earrings?" Melissa's voice shouts and Daisy rolls her eyes.

"Come on in." Daisy mutters before going back into her room. "It's on Sav's desk!" Daisy shouts later.

I look at Archer and he smirks at me.

"I think you should go as is, babe. We match real well." Archer says as he wiggles his eyebrows. I giggle at his words.

"Brow wiggling is both weird and hilarious." I mutter before Archer steps in and hands me the bag.

"I agree. How was your little makeup-thingy-majiggy?" Archer asks and I smirk as he shuts the door and we make our way inside.

Daisy's apartment was fairly big, considering it was being shared between three girls. It had red brick walls and a homey feel to it. There was an area with a large ceiling, but the rooms were only on the first floor and most of the place was currently covered with a bunch of other makeup that they'd wanted me to try on them.

"It was fun. Tiring, but fun." I say with a smile as Archer walks up to me and kisses my cheek.

"Get changed, I can't wait to see how the stuff looks on you." He says with a smile and I kiss his cheek as well before smiling.

"Okay, then. I'll be right back." I say as I disappear into the bathroom right by the hall.

I quickly get undressed and sigh as I look at myself. I'd only put on a bit of mascara and some deep plum lip liner earlier so with a bit of a touch up, I should be good for a dinner. I looked through the bag and rolled my eyes. Inside it was a black long-sleeved dress and a large all white coat to keep me warm. I slipped the black long sleeved turtleneck dress on and look contently as it wraps around my body like a glove. I put on the jewelry, which included some gold and black earrings and a pretty statement necklace, while I moved the bracelet that Archer gave me along my arm. I shoved my feet into the cute booties with a chunky heel and a cute gold buckle design on it before I fixed my makeup a bit and spritzed on the perfume that Archer brought.

Afterwards, I put all of my worn clothes into the bag and I walked out, grabbing my favorite handbag and my phone.

"Gorgeous." Archer says as he walks over to me and kisses me full on the lips. I giggle and kiss his chin afterwards.

"Thanks. You're not so bad yourself." I say as I nudge him with my elbow.

"Okay, okay, we're ready for a photo-op with the budding makeup artist now!" Melissa shouts and I roll my eyes.

"Do you mind?" I ask as I hand him my phone. Archer chuckles.

"Give me that." He says and he takes it. I giggle when the girls all come out and I'm glad that Archer brought me a pair of heels, because otherwise, I would have completely shrunk in comparison to these girls. I'm seriously thankful that Savannah wore the same size heels I did, we aren't too tall, just cutesy enough.

The three of us gather around each other and pose for a few pictures. I laugh when Melissa's earring gets caught in her hair and we easily take it out. After a couple more selfies with them, we finally get going.

"Alright, I gotta run girls. You guys enjoy!" I say as I make my way to the door with my bags.

"Yup. Bye Darce!!!" The girls shout just as Archer and I leave.

As soon as we're alone, Archer wraps an arm around my hip and takes the large shopping bag from me. I lean into him as we make our way down to the lobby to meet with Wes, who greets me with a large smile.

"Good evening." He greets and I laugh.

"So formal. Thanks Wes." I say with a giggle as Archer hands him the bag with a courteous nod.

We both head inside and Wes quickly places the bag into the back before getting back into the sleek silver BMW. Archer runs his fingers over my knuckles in the car and I sigh contently against him.

"You know, you could make a career out of makeup artistry... and I would totally support that." He says as I lean my head on his shoulder.

"I know. But I do want my Bachelor's degree in English first. I'll try to do it part-time." I say with a shrug.

"Do what you want for yourself, babe." He says and I laugh.

"Damn. That pet name is going to stick isn't it?"

"It's already stuck." Archer says with a shrug and I smile at him. Archer takes the moment to kiss me quickly on the lips and I giggle.

As it turns out, Archer's family 'estate' is a large yet homey place. I mean... I find it pretty cool that it's designed in such an old-style family home way, just enlarged. There's no pretentious entrance and to be honest it's quite modest. The bigger thing really was the estate itself, which seemed to make up the entire area we were in. But there were other people living around as well, and Archer told me that they liked to keep their maids and drivers close by so they had houses built for them. The place was an hour drive away but it was beautiful and country-side like.

Archer helped me out of the car as we walked on the brick road going to the house, which had a front yard covered with all types of bushes and flowers that were neatly taken care of and trimmed. A series of trees are the only things that really "gated" their estate and Archer told me that his parents wanted them to live a modest life, so that was why their home wasn't a grand palace or anything.

When the little white door was opened, I was greeted by Grace who wore a long white blouse over a pair of flowy black pants.

"Oh my gosh, I didn't think you two would make it for a second." Grace greeted as she kissed my cheeks, I giggled as Archer came in and his mother kissed his cheeks too.

I smiled at the scene before me. The hall way was fairly large, but it felt warm and very cozy. It just seemed like the perfect storybook home. I laughed when I saw Gerald, Archer's dad, in the dining room just by the hall, fumble about with a jar he couldn't open.

"Long time no see, Gerald." I say as soon as I got my coat off of me. Gerald looks up from his jar with a wide smile.

He wore a matching outfit to Grace's by wearing a white polo shirt over some black slacks. He chuckled.

"Long time no see." He says as he offers me a big bear hug before letting go. "I think I'm getting old. Look at this jar, it's not opening no matter what I do to it."

"May I?" I ask and he hands it to me.

"Knock yourself out." I grin before I use the table cloth to quickly unscrew the lid and hand it over to Gerald.

"There ya go." Gerald gives me a bewildered look before he laughs it off.

"Thanks." He says and just as Gerald turns around, a pair of arms snake their way around my waist. I instantly recognize the scent of Archer's new favorite vanilla scent and lean into him.

"You hungry?" I nodded my head and turned to face him.

"Super." I say and he laughs as he kisses my forehead.

"Okay, okay. Well, we can go set the table... It's tradition, since this is the day mom and dad got engaged- not married though."

"Are you trying to tell me something Mr. A?" I asked and Archer's eyes widened.

"No no no no... I swear, I didn't mean to imply that-" Archer began but I shushed him by putting a finger on his lips.

"Don't get too defensive over it." I say with a smile as I kiss the corner of his mouth. "We have a hell of a lot of time together anyways." I add and he laughs.

"Exactly." He says with a reassuring smile.

The two of us quickly work to set the table and once that's done, Grace comes out with a pot of food while Gerald follows behind her with a tray of baked potatoes. I laugh as Grace scolds her husband for not putting some sort of sauce on the table and I smile even further when I realize that Grace and Gerald have been working on dinner for us by themselves.

"Sorry about the messy organization." Gerald says as he sits down, Archer and I sit across from each other and smile. "We wanted to cook for each other, since that's what we did when I proposed."

"Took him long enough. Did you know he waited until I finished my Master's Degree in France? He visited every month for that time but 8 years, Darcy. I had to wait 8 very very long years. Please, Archer, be a darling and propose to her sooner." Archer flushes a red color and I laugh at their conversation.

The rest of our dinner passes in peace and Archer decides that we should take a long walk out in the garden area where he says they have a similar Cinderella styled swing... I laughed when I asked him if he watched the movie and he only blamed Holly for it.

Speaking of Holly... Where has that girl been? I mean I haven't seen her in what feels like aaaaages.

"You okay?" Archer asks me as we walk hand-in-hand down the cutest little cobblestone path.

"Yeah, just thinking about Holly and how I haven't seen her in like, forever." I say with a shrug and Archer grins at me.

"She's been busy working lately, I heard she established a new café business- so she's getting into that." Archer tells me and I nod my head just as he pushes a tiny little gate covered in flowers and ivy. "This way milady." He says and I laugh at him.

"Thank you, kind sir." I say in a posh accent and Archer laughs as we make our way into the little green garden covered with a variety of flowers that make the air full of a sweet floral scent.

"Wow." I gawk.

"Pretty, right?" Archer comments and I nod my head enthusiastically as I spot two large trees with a beautiful wooden swinging bench underneath the center.

"Straight out of a movie." I say as we walk over. Archer and I sit on the wooden bench and swing it slowly back forth as I lean into him.

"God, I love you so much." Archer says as he fiddles with my hair. I laugh as I look up at him.

"I love you too." I say as we intertwine our hands and we smile at each other like idiots before we laugh it off.

After all the drama and the mystery, I finally know who my beloved stranger is.

"You know, if you want to... They converted my room into a home theater." Archer says and I arch a brow.

"Horror movie night. That's it. Last one in is an idiot." I scream as I make a run for the house.

"Hey!" Archer yells and just as I make it to the gate, I find myself on the ground with Archer on top of me.

"We seem to get into these situations often, Mr. A." I say with a giggle.

"Hm... I do love it when we're together like this, Ms. Bleu." He replies and with a laugh he presses a soft kiss on my nose and does what I do.

He kisses every crease and corner of my face but not my lips. I make a noise out if frustration before reaching out to wrap my arms around his neck. I pull him down to me and laugh as he kisses my neck.

"Mr. A, our movie awaits us." I say in a dramatic voice and Archer grins.

"Ms. Bleu, please. Be patient." He says and I roll my eyes as I pull him down for a long and deep kiss that leaves both of us breathless. "Or not." He adds afterwards.

I laugh at him as I pull him back down and give him a quick kiss before he rolls us over.

"Okay, this is getting a little ridiculous." I say and Archer laughs.

"I like ridiculous." He says and I snort.

"Dork."

"Geek."

"...Why would you say geek?" I ask. "It doesn't-"

"SSshhhhh." Archer says as he puta a finger on my lips. "You're ruining the moment." I roll my eyes and sigh.

"Movie. Now." I say and he laughs.

"Alright babe." He says and I snort once more.

"Yeah babe."

"Laters babe."

"Oh you did not just go Christian Grey on me." I say.

"Grey says 'Laters baby' not 'babe', okay?" I gawk at him before smiling.

"Looks like someone's had a taste of Fifty." I say and Archer blushes in embarrassment. "Oh god. I know what we're watching." I say excitedly even as we're still on the ground, me straddling his hips and him being the goofball that is messing with me, pulls me close to him.

"Darcy... No." Archer warns and I pout.

"But it's going to be soooo funny!" I say and Archer rolls his eyes.

"It's gonna be weird! What if my parents walk in?!"

"They won't walk in. It's not like we're actually watching pòrn." I whine.

"It practically is!" He retorts and I laugh.

"Wuss."

"Am not."

"Are too."

"Am not!"

"Jesus we sound like children!" I say before I kiss him one more time. "Fine. We won't watch it. We'll watch something ridiculous like... Train-wreck."

"Agreed. Thanks." He says as he kisses me.

"You're welcome." I say flipping my hair before I kiss him once more. "I love you." I say and Archer grins.

"I love you too babe."

"Ugh...." I whine and we laugh at each other as we get up and finally go for a good movie night.

# Chapter 24

"So I heard you and Archer are currently going strong." Lawrence says just as I place the tray filled with our cups of coffee and Lars' cheesecake.

"We talked, about the depressing things and all that. Sorry about abruptly leaving your apartment." I say as I take a seat. We were currently in the usual coffee shop where Clara, Martin, and I hung out.

"It's all good. I heard you and Daisy had a great time, glad you got started on the whole little makeup dream thing." Lawrence tells me and I grin.

"Yeah, that was fun." I say with a laugh and Lawrence smirks at me.

"I'm happy for you, I really am." Lawrence says.

"Thank you, Lars. You've seriously done so much for me." I say just as my phone buzzes.

"I'm guessing that's Archer." Lawrence says as he picks up his fork and slices his cake, I roll my eyes and answer my phone.

"Hello." I greet.

"Did you guys say you wanted red velvet or chocolate truffle?" Archer asks and I smirk.

"Lawrence told me red velvet, I wanted chocolate. Where are you?" I ask and Archer makes a huffing sound.

"In the elevator. Tell Lawrence his red velvet stuff is so generic." Archer says and I roll my eyes as I look at Lawrence who's watching me with a wide smile on his face.

"Archer wants to tell you that your order of red velvet cupcakes are so generic." I say and Lawrence laughs.

"They're better than your ugly salted caramel ones." He says, just loud enough for my phone to pick up his voice.

"Excuse me? Ugly? None of my mom's cupcakes are ugly." Archer says and I laugh.

"Of course not, how long are you gonna take getting up here?" I ask and Archer sighs.

"One minute?"

"Lame." I mutter and I watch the entrance to the cafe. Lawrence does the same and we laugh when we spot Archer with a small white rectangular box run in.

Archer was dressed in a sleek grey suit, he came from work and he had his hair combed neatly to the side. He spots us and quickly makes his way to our table.

"I hate you guys." Archer whines as he places the box on the table.

"It was a much needed cupcake run." Lawrence says as he immediately grabs the box and opens it up, bringing out the three ginormous "cup" cakes, all of which were the size of two fists.

"Your mom needs to learn that cupcakes are supposed to be cup sized." I say and Archer laughs.

"She likes to make sure her customers get more than what they pay for. Besides, I was gonna make her give us some normal sized ones, but when she heard it was for us- she went all out." Archer says and Lawrence laughs as he already digs into his generic cupcake.

1 year later

I watch the pretty view from the windows and sigh. I was doing a paper for History and there was nothing I wanted more than to relax... But Archer was still at work and here I was, waiting around in the apartment.

I was wearing a pair of thick cream leggings and one of Archer's big grey sweaters over a loose black singlet with my feet wrapped up in cute little fluffy socks.

Today had been fairly busy, Clara and Martin took me around for some early Christmas shopping and we went into just about every store open. I honestly don't know how I could get through so many shops in one day. I only picked up a few things considering I needed to get my mom and Gavin- my now weird-enough-to-say step dad, a present. He's cool though. Lawrence has pretty much been the same- we hang every now and then, although recently he's been into this girl named Flora- funny thing, we bumped into her on our way to Daisy's performance and we all watched it together. Suffice to say, Flora and I have been talking too and man, they both have it hard for each other. Keaton is apparently out partying in the UK or something, Archer tells me sometimes but I honestly don't really care, we've had a few words but we really like to dodge each other like bullets.

As I finish up my paper, I hear my phone ring and answer it, seeing as it was Archer.

"You okay?" Archer asks and I smirk as I save my work.

"Yeah, why wouldn't I be?" I ask and he chuckles.

"I was wondering if you wanted to join me in a little night trip, like around the bay- even if it's late, and all that stuff."

"All that stuff? Really?" I joke. "Of course. I'll pull on some shoes."

"Okay, I'll fetch you in the lobby in 10 minutes."

I hang up on him and shove my phone into the tiny and thankfully stretchy pockets of my leggings before I shoved my feet into a pair of white Timberlands. I pulled on my favorite cat-eared beanie as well- which I always kept by the door with a white scarf since autumn is way too cold and winter was fast approaching.

I locked the door behind me and sighed as I made my way down to the lobby. Once I got there, I walked to the automatic doors and smirked when I saw Archer standing in front of his Range Rover, hands tucked into a thick black coat that matched with his black suit. I grinned and walked over to him, greeting him with a quick kiss.

"You look like a spy." I comment and he chuckles.

"I've been told that since I pulled the coat on. That bad?" He asks and I shake my head before he opens the door to the passenger's seat. I make my way in and Archer runs over to the opposite side before pulling into the main road.

"So... what's on the itinerary?" I ask.

"How long has it been since you've legit partied your âss off?" Archer asks me and I smirk.

"High school. I'm not legal here so, there's that. Plus, you know I've been busy."

"Right... And who said we were drinking tonight?" Archer asks and I roll my eyes before he drives off.

We end up in a busy looking club downtown and I don't even get to read what it's called when Archer practically drags me into the place. Archer doesn't waste any time and when we cut the line, Archer only gives a slight nod before the bouncer lets us in. The fact that I just walked in wearing a large sweater, a pair of leggings, and some Timberlands. Archer leads me onto the already crowd-filled dance floor- "The Hills" was playing and I roll my eyes as Archer tries and  fails to get me to spin into his arms. I laugh at him and I squeeze up against him as the crowd grows.

The music is pretty damn loud, but we continue to dance our sober âsses off. After about three songs, Archer and I are sweating like pigs and I've gotten the sweater wrapped around my hips as I lose myself to the song. Archer's arms protectively hang around my hips as we move along to the song. I have my back to him as I shake my hips up and down the floor and laugh when I spin to see him as he pulls me close. I wrap my arms around his neck, pulling him down as he places a soft kiss against my lips. "I Took A Pill In Ibiza" starts to play and I smirk as Archer turns it into a fun dance mixing in a few jumps and grinding in. He nuzzles my neck in a soft moment and hugs me close to him and I hug him too. But the height difference lands me smack into his chest instead of his neck so I let him do as he pleases as I turn my head away. His hands land on the small of my back where my little singlet has started to lift, our hands our warm and sweaty and when he pulls back and looks into my eyes, I swear I melt.

His heated gaze makes my cheeks heat up, so when he took my hand and brought us back out of the club, I sighed in relief when the cold air hit my skin. Archer gripped my hand tightly and kissed my fingertips one by one before he smiled at me and led me wordlessly back into the car. He held my hand the entire time as he drove off into the dark road. The car's clock dictated that it was already 1 in the morning, and I watched as Archer smiled to himself. I turned on the radio and we listened to some old mellow beats.

"Where are we off to next?" I ask as I sigh in content when the heating finally kicks in full swing and warms up my body.

"Driving along the Bay area- and walking along later." Archer says as he brings my hand to his mouth and kisses my fingers once more.

"I probably should have brought more warm clothes." I mutter and Archer chuckles, squeezing my hand.

"You'll be fine. Trust me." Archer says and I look at him.

"I do." I say as I squeeze his hand back and kiss his cheek quickly before settling back down.

After discussing it thoroughly, we go through a, thankfully, open Starbucks drive-through and grab two hot Christmas drinks before we drove off. Archer parked close by and we got out, Starbucks in hand, we walked along sipping and chatting along the way.

"Have you tried calling your dad at all?" Archer asked as we found a bench to sit on. I shook my head.

"I haven't had... the time. Or the courage. I know he'd be more than happy to talk to me. I know he'd love it if I invited him over... I'm his only girl after all... But he brings back memories that are hard to push away." I say with a sigh, Archer nods and puts an arm around me, bringing me some comfort with his warmth.

"You'll have to call him some time." Archer says and I snuggle into him.

"I know." I say with a shrug.

I watch as Archer clears his throat and I feel him tense up. I arch a brow and look at him.

"Anything wrong?" I ask and he looks at me, swallows a lump in his throat, and then shakes his head.

"Nothing." He says and I arch a brow, before turning from him.

"What is it?" I ask and he smiles at me reassuringly.

"It's nothing, I swear." He says and I narrow my eyes at him.

"Are you absolutely positively sure?" I ask and Archer nods his head.

"I'm sure. Sorry." He says and I sigh before kissing his cheek.

"Let's get back to the house... the cold is killing me." I say and Archer nods.

"Okay, let me just throw out our cups and s-stuff." Archer says and he stutters for a bit- probably because of the cold. I nod my head and watch as Archer grabs our two cups with one hand shoves his other hand into his coat's pocket.

He pauses for a bit before he throws the cups into the bin and walks over to me with a brief look of hesitance in his eyes. It disappears quickly and soon enough we've already driven home. Archer had gone to his little office to grab a few things while I changed into one of Archer's shirts, my favorite sleeping outfit for the past few weeks. Once I'd changed, I decided to check on Archer and I smirked when I found his door unlocked. I walked in and sighed when I realized that he went into the bathroom inside his office. Why he even had a bathroom in there... I don't know.

I sighed as I looked at his desk and looked at the pictures he placed under the glass display. We had a few together and a lot with his family. There's one from when Archer and I went to my mother's wedding and we dressed up all fancy for the photo-booth. As I looked along his desk I noticed a cute wooden box that I'd never seen before. I arched a brow and picked it up, it looked sleek and pretty. I rattled it for a bit and heard the sound of something slightly loose wriggle through. Curiosity, getting the better of me, I began to slide the box open-

"Darcy!" Archer shouts from the bathroom door and he runs over to me, snatching the box away.

"What?" I ask, looking at the box and pouting. "What's in the box?" I ask, folding my arms over my chest.

"Nothing. It's- It's-... It's for my mom's Christmas gift."

"Yeah right." I say rolling my eyes. "If it is, you would've let me see it." I whine.

"I can't. It's a secret." Archer says quickly and I shake my head.

"Liar." I hiss and Archer sighs.

"Darcy..." He whines as I turn on my heel and I feel his arms wrap around me. The box resting in his hand that is resting on my left arm.

I immediately grab it and sprint to the corner. Archer's eyes are wide as I slide the box open and stare at its contents.

Or content.

I look at it with wide eyes.

Inside the box was a simple engagement ring, a silver band with a single diamond topping it off. I look at it stare between Archer's shocked face and the ring.

"Um." I muttered.

"Damn it." Archer cursed under his breath as he ran a hand through his hair. He was blushing and I continued to stare at him as he made his way over to me.

I hadn't even noticed that I was gawking at him with my mouth wide open until he reached over and lifted my lower jaw up to a close. I stared into his eyes, in shock, and he took the box from me.

"Darcy Bleu, you, I swear, are the most important person to the world to me. And yes, I know it's only been a year and a few mont-"

"2 months." I interrupt, blushing in embarrassment for doing so. Archer chuckles and looks into my eyes again before he takes the box gently from my hand and begins to bend on one knee.

"Yeah, a year and 2 months, since we first 'met' through letters, e-mails, phone calls, and all that stuff. I cannot be any happier. And, I just want to know, that with this ring, you'll have your hold on me and I on you. That you accept me and believe I can be yours. With this ring... I have wanted to ask you... and trust me this speech was not easy to think of within the last few seconds- but trust me... trust me enough when I ask you,

Will you marry me?" Archer asks as he presents the ring to me. I feel water build up in my eyes as I nod my head.

"Oh goddamn it Archer..." I curse before wrapping my arms around his head and he chuckles and breathes into my neck.

I'm a swirl of butterflies and rainbows. My mind probably thinks this is all just a dream. But this is real. He's real.

I smile as we pull apart and laugh at each other.

"I was gonna do it at the bench- but I lost the moment." Archer admits and I laugh. He smiles before we face each other, both on our knees in his office as lifts my left hand and slides the ring onto my ring finger.

It was simple, understated, and full of promise.

"I hoped you didn't mind..." Archer adds and I look at him oddly before he pulls out his phone. "I called your dad a few days ago about it. If you don't want to talk to him about this, it's fine. But I want you to do it, because he really does care about you, Darce." Archer says and I sigh.

"Tomorrow." I say and Archer sighs but I hold onto his hands. "I won't put it off, trust me." I say as I kiss the corner of his mouth. He smiles as I kiss the other corner and squeeze his hands.

"I just want to enjoy this moment, together. Okay?" I ask and Archer nods his head as he kisses me, my hair tangled up in his fingers as we both deepen the kiss.

Archer pulls me up off the floor, our lips still connected as he presses me against the wall. He trails his fingers down my back and I press one hand onto his chest as the other travels to his hair as well. His lips leave mine and his eyes are filled with an intense gaze that leaves me breathless as he lowers his head to the crook of my neck. He kisses me around before nipping at my skin, my breath hitches and I place my arms over his shoulders as he works his way down before his hands make it to my hips.

"I love you." He whispers into my neck as he brings himself up again and kisses my lips quickly.

"I love you." I say softly and he smiles, taking my fingers and kissing them one by one, before stopping at the ring and smiling even wider.

He laughs and wraps his arms around me before swinging me around, causing me to turn into a mess of giggles.

"This reminds me of our first kiss." I comment when he sets me down, his arms still around my waist.

"It's the same feeling." He admits as he embraces me again and I laugh as he lifts my body and carries me off, bridal style, into the bedroom. "God, I love you." He says and I laugh again.

"We sound like cheeseballs."

"You're a cheeseball." Archer counters and I roll my eyes.

"Bug off." I mutter before he sets me down on the bed and he kisses me again before he pulls the sheets and wraps me with them and then bringing me into his arms. "I can't move like this, babe." I say and Archer smirks as he lies down and takes the top duvet to wrap both of us in.

"You're not moving at all tomorrow." He says.

"I have class."

"It's a holiday- you got engaged." He says and I roll my eyes.

"But-"

"No 'but's."

"Archeerrrrrrr." I whine and he rolls his  eyes before kissing me on the forehead.

"Sleep."

"No."

"Darcyyyyy." He whines and I frown at him before sticking my tongue out. I feel the silver band in my finger and sigh before moving my upper body to kiss his forehead too.

"Fine. Good night." I say and Archer smiles.

"Good morning." He answers back, I roll my eyes at him before I finally free my left hand to admire the ring. Archer watches me before snuggling up to me and allowing me to rest on the crook of his neck.

I couldn't wait for tomorrow. Because even if I called him... Even if I had a lot to go through- I had this guy, right here. My stranger. Mr. A. I had someone else to lean on now.

And I couldn't be happier.

# Chapter 25

I sigh as I look at myself in the mirror. I looked at my face, my hair, and examined every spot and detail.

Flawless.

Right?

I squinted my eyes. I decided not to wear glasses but damn, I am blind as a bat. I just couldn't wear contacts.

"Hey, you ready?" Holly's muffled voice asks from the other side of the doors.

I was in the dressing room and I was worried. About what, I had no idea.

"Just a few more minutes!" I shout and I hear whispers outside my door. I fumbled with the bracelet around my wrist and sighed.

"Game time, Darce. Game time." I tell myself. I stepped away from the mirror and sighed to myself.

I gripped the bouquet of white and pale blue hued carnations in my right hand as I use my left hand to put the veil back over my face. I breathed out a shaky breath and sighed once more.

No worries... It's your day, Darce. You've gone way too far to ditch.

I release a shaky breath. I was totally perfect. Right?

My dress was what was in the box that Archer and Holly got me in the apartment- and it had been sent to customs by request of both my mom and dad. It was simple, a soft white lace bodice that was corseted and gradually intertwined with layers of white and carefully placed tulle.

Beneath all the white and if I lifted the tulle, the bottom of the dress was made of a soft blue tulle to add volume. The tail of my dress wasn't too long, but that was where a bit of the pretty blue almost teal colored tulle was. It had a low back and a pretty sweetheart neckline. I had one tiny diamond necklace on that Grace allowed me to borrow- traditions of course being that I had to have a Something Borrowed and all that type of stuff. My dad had given me a pair of dainty diamond studs that were small enough to match the necklace without over doing the jewelry.

Speaking of my dad.

He was right behind those doors, waiting to escort me to Archer.

To be honest, things were still a bit icy between us and the rift was easy to feel. But he was my dad and we were okay... His boyfriend was in there as well, that part still makes me feel uneasy, but I needed to let go of my grudges and Archer had helped me get used to that.

My mom was in there too, she'd already married Gavin and they were in the front row. Camera at the ready, I only know this because of a quick practice run we had.

The wedding venue was not that big. I didn't want something too ginormous. So we picked a pretty little ballroom in a more "empty" area in New York. Not that it stopped Holly- or Martin- or Clara to send about 200 invites out to Archer and I's family. Thankfully the venue was just big enough to have them all present. The plain veil I had on was what I had requested, nothing fancy, just a simple and light veil that flowed with my movements- and somewhat followed the form of my dress.

I sighed once more before Wes walked out from another entrance and smiled.

"It's time." He says and I groan.

"Okay, okay. Thanks Wes." I say and he chuckles.

"You will be fine."

"Thanks for the encouragement." I say with a kind smile. He nods before going in front of me.

Wes opens the doors and I take a deep breath.

Here we go.

The familiar tune of Yiruma's "Love Me", starts to play, and I smile as I see the guests stand up. Archer's wide grin at the end of the aisle makes me smile wider. My dad comes by my side, he's pretty and he links his arms around mine as I carry my bouquet and we wordlessly walk towards Archer. I smile at Clara, Martin, Lawrence, and Holly who are all together. Clara is taking pictures and Martin is with Erik, smiling at us and threatening to cry.

Lawrence is with Flora and she's grinning widely as I pass, I wink at her and she giggles. I spot Grace and Gerald at the very front, Grace is already crying and I smile at her. My dad squeezes my arm and use one of my hands to squeeze him back. My mom and my step-dad Gavin are up as well and she's crying too, I feel a bit of water in my eyes but I fight it back as I make my way up to Archer.

Once I'm there, my dad kisses my cheek briefly before I step away from him and make my way to Archer.

There was no grand parade of people. No large array of flower girls. My bridesmaids were seated in the front row along with Archer's groomsmen. The wedding was like a total blur. Our words were set in stone and to steal the show, I had Wes' daughter who had soft black hair, and who was wearing a pale blue dress, walk the aisle with the rings. We all giggled as she slowly made her way towards us and handed the rings over.

We all laughed when she waited behind us and Archer and I realized she wanted us to kiss her cheeks. Wes was laughing hard in the background as Archer and I kissed his daughter's cheeks.

Archer took my hand in his and smiled as he lifted the veil away from my face. I smiled brightly at him as he took hand, the words were all a blur and the crowd faded away once he looked into my eyes and slid my ring on. I followed his words and smiled as I slid his ring onto his finger and we both looked at each other, laughing a bit, before we came close and shared a soft kiss that sealed us together.

# Epilogue

Lawrence's POV

"Lawrence why the hell do you always get the time wrong?!" Archer asks me as we rush off towards the theater, we were making a sprint across the parking lot. Darcy and Archer were kind enough to join me- but I totally got the time wrong... by 30 minutes.

Kind of sucks.

"I'm sorry, okay?!" I shout as we make a run for it.

"We run through the halls going to the library for a shortcut!" Darcy yells and I raise my eyebrows as we run into the university.

"How do you know that?" I ask and Darcy laughs.

"Erik's brother Maurice studies here!" She shouts back and I shake my head.

"Of course." I mutter under my breath.

Darcy takes a sharp left, followed by Archer and before I know it, I turn at the left and I feel a hard wall hit me. Well... a soft cushiony wall that is.

My hands land in front of me on cold asphalt and I groan as I get up.

"Ow..." A female voice says and I immediately look down in front of me. There, on the ground, was a girl whose beautiful pastel pink hair immediately captures my attention.

She groaned as she rubbed her head and I immediately extended a hand to her.

"I'm so so so sorry! I wasn't looking where I was going and I'm late to my sister's performance and there's like a rush and my friends took a turn and-" I began blabbering but the girl simply smiled at me as she took my hand and pulled herself up.

"It's fine." She says and when I look up into her eyes, I'm stunned by a striking pair of silver eyes. She smiles kindly at me before wiping the dirt off of herself. "I wasn't looking where I was going either... Actually, you said you were going to a performance? I was looking for the theater but the whole place is a maze and I can't figure out where to go."

"You should come with us." Darcy's voice says and I look at Darcy with a weird look. She winks at me and the girl turns her head to look at her.

"Darcy Bleu?" The girl asks and Darcy smiles.

"That's me. Probably heard about me from-"

"Your work during Fashion Week? I mean, I know it's all about the models and the clothes but, I stared at the behind the scenes makeup looks for days!" She says. "Oh, my name is Flora. Flora Devoncourt." She says and Darcy grins.

"Well you know who I am, this guy here behind me is Archer, my fiancé. And the guy who bumped into you is Lawrence Peters." Darcy tells her and Flora turns around and smiles widely at me before extending her hand.

"Nice to meet you." She greets and I grin widely as I shake her hand.

We stare at each other for a few moments before Archer clears his throat.

"You guys think we can get a move on? I'm sure the prelude began like 10 minutes ago." Archer says and I watch as Darcy elbows him hard in the stomach and he suppresses a groan. Flora laughs before smiling at me.

"Shall we?" She asks and I nod.

"We shall." I respond before we both make a run, following a smirking Darcy to the theater.

Gee, thanks Darcy.

Once we arrive at the theater and we're led to our seats. Darcy, purposefully, makes me sit away from her and Archer while I sit beside Flora, who Darcy also purposefully put as a barrier between me and our friends. Flora is absolutely oblivious as Darcy constantly pointed things about Daisy and well... me.

My phone buzzes as the first act begins and I roll my eyes. It was a message from Daisy.

Who's the girl beside you? ;) I like her hair. Before I can reply, Flora leans over to me and points at the stage.

"See that girl in the red dress? That's my friend, Corinne, she's..." Flora's voice sort of fades as I catch a whiff of her floral perfume.

Oh this is gonna be a long freaking night for me isn't it? I think to myself.